Books by Spider Robinson

SPIDER ROBINSON
THE
CALLAHAN
TOUCH

ACE BOOKS, NEW YORK

Portions of this novel appeared, in substantially different form, in *Analog* magazine, as "The Immediate Family" and "The End of the Painbow."

The filksong "Callahan's Place" is excerpted by permission of its author, Jordin Kare; its lyrics have been altered by Spider Robinson with Mr. Kare's gracious consent. All other song lyrics in this novel are by Spider Robinson (© 1992).

This Ace Book contains the complete text of
the original hardcover edition.

THE CALLAHAN TOUCH

An Ace Book / published by arrangement with
the author

PRINTING HISTORY
Ace hardcover edition / October 1993
Ace paperback edition / January 1995

All rights reserved.
Copyright © 1993 by Spider Robinson.
Cover art by James Warhola.
This book may not be reproduced in whole or in part,
by mimeograph or any other means, without permission.
For information address: The Berkley Publishing Group,
200 Madison Avenue, New York, New York 10016.

ISBN: 0-441-00133-5

ACE®
Ace Books are published by The Berkley Publishing Group,
200 Madison Avenue, New York, New York 10016.
ACE and the "A" design
are trademarks belonging to Charter Communications, Inc.

PRINTED IN THE UNITED STATES OF AMERICA

10 9 8 7 6 5 4 3 2 1

THIS BOOK IS FOR SOLACE,
AND FOR JOHN VARLEY

The Immediate Family

Opposites make good companions sometimes.

The reason Irish coffee is the perfect beverage is that the stimulant and the depressant play tug of war with your consciousness, thereby stretching and exercising it. Isometric intoxication, opposed tensions producing calm at the center, in the eye of the metabolic hurricane. You end up an alert drunk. I suppose speedballs—the cocaine-heroin combination that killed John Belushi—must be a similar phenomenon, on a more vivid and lethal level. Fear and lust is another good, heady mixture of opposites . . . as many have learned in war zones or hostage situations.

But if you can get hope and pride and serious fear all going at the same time, balanced in roughly equal portions, let me tell you, then you've really got something *powerful*.

You can turn your head around with a mixture like that, end up spinning like a top and paralyzed, exhausted and insomniac, starving and nauseous, running a fine cold sweat. Like a car in neutral, with the accelerator to the floor. It's exhilarating, in a queasy kind of way.

I'm embarrassed to admit I binged on it for days before I realized that was what I was doing, and then another day before I made up my mind to kick. Finally I admitted to myself that I was being selfish, that other people's hopes—and cash—were involved in this too. They'd been waiting a long time already. Besides, in a *three*-way tug of war, the chances of one side suddenly letting go with a loud snap are doubled.

Hell, I'd already *jumped.* It was time to open my eyes and see where I was going to land . . .

So one fine day in May of 1988, I picked up the phone and made the call.

"Hello there, son," he said when they finally tracked him down. "I was just thinking about you. Been too long. What's the good word?" His voice was strong and clear despite the lousy connection. As always.

"I think I'm ready," I said.

Short pause. "Say that again. Like you believe it, this time."

I cleared my throat. "Well, I don't know if *I'll* ever be ready. But I think *it's* ready. I truly do, Sam. As ready as it's ever gonna be."

"Why, that's fine! Uh . . . want me to come over and take a look? Before you—"

"Thanks. But no. I'll take it all in one dose. Put the word out for me, okay? I open Friday at nine. Just the immediate family."

"Friday, huh? Appropriate date. We'll all be there. I'm looking forward to it. It's been awful too damn long. Good luck—wups, Code Blue, got to go!" The line was dead.

Friday was two days away. Time for one last binge of conflicting emotions before the balloon went up . . .

THE CALLAHAN TOUCH

• • •

The thing is, I had accomplished a miracle—and I knew in my heart it wasn't good enough.

After two years of careful planning and hard work, I had produced something excellent. I believed that, and I guess I should have been proud. Oh hell, I guess I was proud. But I was trying to match something long-gone that, in its own backassward way, had been perfect. And it seemed to me, in those last couple of days, that the distance on the scale between lousy and excellent is *nothing* compared to the distance between excellent and perfect.

There was nothing I could do about it. Perfection exceeded my grasp. I didn't have the tools. Nonetheless, I spent those last days like a frustrated cat, trying to bite myself on the small of the back.

My staff was the first to arrive that Friday night, pulling in at about eight, but he didn't count. He'd already seen the place, under oath of secrecy, because I'd needed his help in finishing it. (If you can't trust a guy with *his* background to keep a vow, who can you trust?) But I was glad to see him, and gladder when he was dressed for work.

It was the sheer familiarity of the sight of him in that getup, I think. So much about this place was different from the old one, and he was a thread of continuity that I appreciated. Some of those differences had been driving me crazy.

Getting ready to open took us a combined total of maybe five minutes. I'd been there all afternoon—and we'd been essentially ready for a week. Then he had the grace to not only suggest a game of darts, but fail to notice how badly I was playing. It took him some doing; at one point I actually threw one shank-first. It bounced halfway back to me. Terrific omen, for those who believe in such.

3

At ten minutes to nine, I left him in command and went out into the big foyer, letting the swinging door close behind me. Its breeze started all the empty coat hangers whispering. I felt the need to wait out there, to talk to the whole crew, at least for a few minutes, before I brought them inside and showed them the place.

At nine precisely, the outer door burst open and Doc Webster, Long-Drink McGonnigle, Fast Eddie Costigan, Noah Gonzalez, Tommy Janssen, Margie Shorter, Marty Matthias and his new wife Dave, all three Masers, Ralph von Wau Wau, Willard and Maureen Hooker, Isham Latimer and *his* new wife Tanya, Bill Gerrity, Jordin and Mary Kay Kare, and both of the Cheerful Charlies all came crowding into the foyer at once. Don't tell me that's physically impossible; I'm telling you what I saw.

My head *pulsed* like a giant heart, and my heart spun like a little head. A couple of fairly bad years began to melt away . . .

Δ   Δ   Δ

They advanced on me like a lynch mob, baying and whooping, arms outstretched, and then we all hugged each other. Don't tell me that's physically impossible; I'm telling you what we did. The coat hangers became Zen bells. The more physically demonstrative of us pummeled the rest of us and each other, hard enough to raise bruises, and all of us grinned until the tears flowed. Somewhere in there it occurred to me that the foyer now held every single soul who had been present on the first night I ever had a drink in Callahan's Place—with the two exceptions of Callahan himself, and of course Tom Flannery (it was the twelfth anniversary of Tom's death that night). We stopped hugging when our arms stopped working.

There was a moment of warm silence. Then the combined pressure of them tried to back me into the bar, and I stood my ground.

"Hold it a second, folks," I said, smiling ruefully. "There's something I want to get straight before we go in, okay?"

"It's your place, Jake," Doc Webster said.

"That's the first thing to get straight," I said. "It's not. It's *our* place. I know I hogged all the fun of putting it together, but that's because a design committee is a contradiction in terms, and I had some strong opinions. And . . . well, I wanted to surprise you all. But if there's anything you really don't like, we can change it."

"You're saying you want us to complain?" Long-Drink asked.

"I tink we c'u'd handle dat," Fast Eddie said helpfully.

"I hate the Jacuzzi," the Doc said promptly, and Ralph bit him on the ankle just as promptly. In fact, the dog may have started to bite before the Doc had started to wisecrack. They know each other.

"Come on, let's see de jernt," Eddie said.

"One more thing," I said. "Before I show you all what Mary's Place *is,* I want to talk for a second about what it is *not."* I could see that they all knew more or less where I was going, but I said it anyway. "This is not Callahan's Place. This is Mary's Place. It will never be Callahan's Place. No place will ever be that place again, and certainly no place we build. Even if Mike should ever come back from the future and open another bar, it wouldn't be Callahan's Place, and he wouldn't call it that if he did. We can all have some fun here—but if we try and make this be Callahan's Place, it will all go sour on us."

"Hell, we know that," Long-Drink said indignantly.

"Relax, Jake," Tommy Janssen said. "Nobody expected you to work miracles."

"We're not fools," Susie Maser said. Then she glanced at her husband Slippery Joe and co-wife Suzy. "Wait a minute, maybe I take your point. We *are* fools."

"Look," I pressed on, "I don't mean that the layout is different or the setup is different. I don't even mean just that Mike is gone. He'll be *less* gone in this building than anywhere else, I think, because he'll be in our collective memories, and maybe if we're lucky a little bit of Callahan magic will linger on.

"*But a lot of it won't.* Some of the specific 'magic,' if that's what you want to call it, that made Callahan's Place work is simply not available to us anymore."

Rooba rooba rooba. The Doc's foghorn baritone rose over the rest. "What are you saying, Jake?"

"For one thing, I'm talking about whatever kind of magic it was that watched over that Place like a door-checker. The Invisible Protective Shield—a selectively permeable shield. You all know damn well what I mean. Did anybody ever wander into Callahan's who didn't belong there? And did anybody who needed to go there bad enough ever fail to find it?"

That stopped them. "I don't know about that last part," the Doc said. "There *were* suicides on Long Island during those years. And I can remember one or two jokers that came in who didn't belong there. But as Susie said a minute ago, I take your point. Those few jokers didn't stay. In all those years, '48 to '86, we never seemed to get normal bar traffic. No bikers, or predators, or jerks looking to get stupid, or goons looking for someone drunk enough to screw even them—"

"Hell, no *drunks,*" Long-Drink said, looking thunderstruck. "Not one."

"No grabasses," Margie said.

"No brawlers," Tommy supplied. "No jackrollers."

Fast Eddie summed it up. "No pains in de ass."

"Was that magic?" the Doc asked. "Or some kind of advanced technology we don't savvy yet? Like Mickey Finn's 'magic' raincoat?"

"What's the difference?" I told him. "We haven't got it—and so this is going to be a different kind of joint. It doesn't matter what it was. For all I know, it was just a sustained run of incredibly good l—"

SCREECH!

I had been peripherally aware of rapidly growing automotive sounds from the world outside, but before I could finish my sentence we all heard the nerve-jangling shriek of brake shoes doing their very best (a sound I happen to find even more disturbing than most people do), *much* too close to the door. We all froze, expecting a vehicle to come crashing in and kill us all. Just as the noise reached its crescendo and died away, there was a violent, expensive-sounding *clang! crump!,* and then a single knock at the door.

Silence . . .

There was a harsh emphatic *crack!* sound. *Behind* me, in the bar. And then a heavy, dull *thop!* from the same place, followed by a gasp, and a faint, hard-to-identify sound that made me think of a gerbil, curling.

Fast Eddie happened to be closest to the outside door. He opened it experimentally, and it was a good thing it opened inward. The front grille of a Studebaker filled the doorway, faint tendrils of steam curling out of it. The rest of a Studebaker was attached in the usual manner. The only unusual thing about it was the pair of rumpled frayed blue jeans on the hood.

"Hi, guys," Shorty Steinitz's voice came hollowly from the passenger compartment. "Sorry I'm late. Did I kill him?"

One mystery solved. Shorty is the worst driver alive. But how had he managed to punch someone through that door and through all of us and into the bar, without any of us noticing it happen?

I turned and pushed open the swinging door, just as tentatively as Eddie had opened the outside door.

A stranger was sitting at my bar, in one of the tall armchairs I use instead of barstools. Kindling lay in the sawdust at his feet, and there appeared to be either more sawdust or heavy dandruff on his hairy head. He was just finishing a big gulp of beer. Tom Hauptman, my assistant bartender, was gaping at him. This seemed understandable, for the stranger had no pants on.

He caught my eye, looked me up and down briefly, and pursed his lips as if preparing to sneer. "Evening, stringbean," he said. He gestured toward the fireplace. "Mind if I warm myself at your fire?"

"Na dean fochmoid fàinn," I heard myself say, and wondered what the hell that meant. It sounded a little like Gaelic—and I don't speak Gaelic.

"What choice have I got?" he replied.

He was short and hairy. His eyes and nose and lips and the upper slopes of his cheeks were the only parts of his head that were not covered with tight curls of brown hair. As far as I could see, they did not share that distinction with any other part of his body except his fingernails. He made me think of hobbits. Surly hobbits. He wore a brown leather jacket, a long scarf, a black turtleneck, basketball shoes, and white jockey shorts. There were a motorcycle helmet and a pair of leather gloves on the bar beside him.

"How did you get in there?" I asked, as calmly as I could, aware of people gawping over my shoulder.

He looked at me as if I had asked a very stupid question, and pointed silently upward.

Like Callahan's Place before it, Mary's Place had an access hatch to the roof. Or rather, it *had* had. I hadn't rigged up a ladder to it yet, because it was awkwardly placed, almost directly over the bar. Now there was no longer a hatch there— just a yawning hole where the hatch had been. The hatch cover was the kindling around the stranger's feet.

"You broke in from the roof?" I said.

He grimaced. "Not voluntarily," he assured me. "I could have done without the last eight feet or so of that little journey. But I didn't get a vote. This is good beer." He made the last part sound like a grudging admission.

"Rickard's Red," I said, seeing the color. "From Canada."

"No," he said, frowning as though I'd called an automatic a revolver, or spelled "adrenalin" with an *e* on the end. "From Ontario. Americans always make that mistake."

Shorty came bustling up behind me. "Is he alive?" he asked.

"Are you alive?" I asked the stranger.

"No, I'm on tape," he said disgustedly, and gulped more beer.

"Honest to God, Mister," Shorty said, trying to push past me, "I never saw you. Be honest, I wasn't looking—it just never occurred to me anybody could be on my tail at that speed—"

"I was in your slipstream, Andretti, saving gas; are you familiar with the concept or shall I do a lecture on elementary aerodynamics? Even a rocket scientist like you will concede that there's not much point in *doing* that unless the guy is going at a hell of a clip, now is there?"

"Well, I never seen ya," Shorty said uncertainly.

"That's because you weren't *looking,*" the stranger explained.

"One of you want to tell me what happened?" I asked. To my pleased surprise I heard my voice come out the way Mike Callahan would have said it in my place. A quiet, polite request for information, with the explicitly mortal threat all in the undertones.

The stranger looked up at the ceiling again. No, at the sky. Apparently God signaled him to get it over with. He sighed. "I was following that maniac at a—"

" 'Idiot,' " Long-Drink interrupted. "If they're in front of you, they're idiots."

The stranger glared at him, and decided to ignore him. "—hundred and twenty when he made an unsignaled left into your parking lot without slowing. On a Suzuki at that speed, you don't want to bust out of the slipstream at an angle, so I swallowed my heart and cornered with him—better, of course—and there we both were, bearing down on a brick building at a hundred and twenty together, and I would like to state for the record that I would not, repeat *not* have hit him if his God damned brake lights had been working!"

"Are they out again?" Shorty asked mournfully.

The stranger looked at him. "Or if his brakes hadn't been so God damned good."

"I hafta get new shoes every couple of months," Shorty said.

"No shit, Sherlock. How did I magically divine this information before you told me? I don't know, I must be psychic."

"You ploughed into the back of Shorty's car on a motorcycle?" I asked.

"That," he agreed, "was the very last moment I was *on* a motorcycle this evening. A microsecond later I was airborne."

"Jesus," Doc Webster said, and pushed Shorty aside to take a turn at trying to get past me. But even he couldn't manage it.

The stranger finished his beer and signaled Tom Hauptman for another. Tom didn't move, kept staring at him. "So I hit the trunk like a flat rock, up the rear window, and into the wild blue," he pointed upward, "yonder. Somewhere along the way my trousers left me. The next thing I know I'm sitting here with a draft in my jockeys and a glass of Rickard's in front of me. Snappy service."

Tom shook off his stasis. "I'd just drawn myself a beer when he came crashing in. I was so startled I just—" He made a sort of pushing motion away from himself with both hands. "And it went—I mean, right smack dab—as if I'd—" He pantomimed sliding a schooner down the bar like you see in old movies. "Bang into his hand."

Dead silence.

"Are you all right, son?" the Doc asked finally.

"Dad," he replied sarcastically, "I was only all right up to about age six. After that I was more or less consistently fantastic up until about twenty-five, and since that time I have been world-class. How are you?"

" 'On my best day,' " the Doc quoted, " 'I'm borderline.' You know what I'm asking, and I'll thank you to answer. No cuts? No sprains, bruises, contusions?"

The stranger only shrugged.

The Doc sighed. "Mister, I've seen a few things. I can manage to make myself believe, just barely, that you survived that experience—but without so much as a scratch? How could you?"

The stranger shrugged with his mouth. "Just lucky, I guess."

There was another short silence, and then the Doc tapped me on the shoulder. (I could tell by the girth of the finger.) I turned and looked at him.

"Jake," he said softly, "weren't you saying something just a few minutes ago about a 'sustained run of incredibly good luck'?"

I took a deep breath. "Ladies and gentlemen," I said, "I believe we are ready to open. Please come in."

Δ   Δ   Δ

Amazing stranger or no, I watched my friends' faces closely as they filed in. Upstaged or not, this was my premiere . . .

Noah was the first one who glanced around as the gang galloped inside, and he couldn't help it: Noah can't enter a strange room without looking around to try and guess where the bomb is. The rest either stared at the pantsless stranger or talked to each other or called out greetings to Tom. But as the stampede crested at the bar, folks remembered where they were: everybody picked a spot and began spinning in slow circles on it with expectant faces.

I held my breath. That's how I know that the silence couldn't have lasted as long as it seemed to: I was still alive when it ended.

It was Fast Eddie who broke it.

"Jeez, Jake, dis place is okay."

In the time it took me to exhale, Doc and Long-Drink had nodded agreement, the Drink judiciously and the Doc vigorously. Maybe others did too, but they were the two I was watching closest, the experts whose opinion I most feared. About half of a great weight left my shoulders when I saw those two nods. A buzzing sound in my ears, of which I had not previously been aware, diminished in volume.

" 'Okay'?" Susan Maser said. "Eddie, I bet if you ever saw the Grand Canyon up close, you'd say, 'Nice ditch.' Jake, this place is great! You really did a job on it."

That was nice to hear too. Susan was the only one present besides Tom who'd ever seen the place before, back when I'd first bought it. She's an interior decorator, so I'd sought her advice before signing the papers—then thanked her and thrown her out, doing all the work myself. If she liked it, I knew the others all would.

And they did. "This is just the way I hoped it would look," Merry Moore said, and Les, her husband and fellow Cheerful Charlie, said, "Me too!"

"Nice size," Long-Drink said judiciously. "Huge, but it feels comfy. Good lighting. Nice tables, too—and I really like those couches—"

"Nice *fireplace*," Doc Webster said.

There was a chorus of agreement that warmed my heart. I'd worked hard on that fireplace. Do you have any idea how hard it is to chisel a bull's-eye into firebrick?

"It ain't exactly like the old hearth," Noah said, "but it looks to me like it'll work just as well. That won't throw glass."

"It's *pretty*," Maureen said, as though Noah had missed the point.

The stranger looked at Noah. "The fireplace won't throw glass?"

"We like to deep-six our glasses in the fireplace sometimes," Noah explained.

"A lot," Long-Drink said, and a general murmur ratified the amendment.

"Really." For the first time the stranger looked mildly impressed. "But you're just opening tonight?"

"Re-opening," I said.

"De old place got nuked," Eddie explained.

"Nuked?" The stranger looked at us, decided we weren't kidding, lowered the raised eyebrow and nodded. "Nuked. You people obviously don't believe in omens. Wait a minute . . . I think I heard about that. Pony nuke, back in '86? Some Irish joint on 25A? Terrorists?"

Now I was impressed. "Not a lot of people know about it. Know that it was nuclear, I mean. There was a kind of major news blackout on that part."

The stranger nodded. "I'll bet. Come to sunny Long Island, where terrorists take out recreational facilities with nuclear weapons. That would have looked swell in *Newsday*."

"Well, the Place was pretty isolated," I said, "and it wasn't much of a nuke, as nukes go, and the fallout pattern was out onto the Sound and east to no place in particular, so they decided what with one thing and another they'd pass on starting God's own stampede off the Island. I kind of think they made the right decision."

" '—and the truth shall make you flee,' " the stranger said. "I'd like to have seen it. Millions of terrified suburbanites, everything they treasure strapped to the roofs of their station wagons, pour into New York City—and find themselves in the Traffic Jam From Hell, surrounded by street kids and derelicts with great big smiles. Talk about a massive transfer of resources. Like cattle stampeding into the slaughterhouse." He chuckled wickedly.

"How'd you happen to hear about it being nuclear?" I asked.

He shrugged. "I have sources."

"I *said*," Doc Webster said with a long-suffering air, " 'Nice fireplace.' "

I nodded. "Thanks, Doc. The way I—"

"What I mean," he interrupted, "is when are we going to give it a field test?"

"Oh!" My friends had been in my bar for several minutes, and still had empty hands. I blushed deeply and ran around behind the bar, nearly trampling Tom Hauptman.

"I'm buying," the Doc said, and a cheer went up.

I shook my head. "Sorry, Doc. You can buy the first round bought—but this one's on the house. My privilege."

He nodded acknowledgment, smiling at me like a proud uncle, and another cheer went up.

Rickard's turned out to be okay with everybody; Tom and I became briefly busy drawing and passing out glasses. No one drank until everyone had been served. I noticed that Shorty was missing; he'd stepped out to see if his car was movable. I hoped he could, for once, find reverse on the first try. Finally every hand was full. "Your privilege, Jake," the Doc said, gesturing toward the hearth.

I nodded, stepped out from behind the bar and walked up to the chalk line on the floor, facing the fireplace. I lifted my glass. Something was wrong with my vision, and my cheeks felt cool.

"To Mary Callahan-Finn, brothers and sisters," I said solemnly.

There was a nice warm power to the chorus. *"To Mary Callahan-Finn!"*

I drained my glass, and hit that bull's-eye dead center. As it had every time in rehearsal, the shape of the fireplace contained all the shards beautifully.

A staggered barrage of empty glasses rained into the hearth, like fireworks filmed in reverse, flashing colors as they tumbled, sparkling as they struck and burst. When the last of them had landed—Ralph's: he had to move in kind of close and flick it with his muzzle—I noted happily there still were no fragments on the floor of the bar proper.

Then I took a closer look, and blinked.

All the smithereened remains of those eighteen glasses were still in the fireplace, all right. And they had arranged themselves on the hearth floor in the shape of the word *"MARY."* In glittering italic script. It was nearly perfect, except that each letter had a small gap in it.

I turned to stone. "Hully Jeeze," Fast Eddie said. There were grunts and exclamations all around as others saw the phenomenon. That reassured me somewhat; if others saw it too, at least I wasn't crazy. Maybe that was good . . .

"Sorry," the stranger said.

Δ   Δ   Δ

I turned very slowly to face him. So did everyone else.

His expression was of mildest apology, as though he'd just committed some very small and unintentional faux pas.

"You did that?" I asked, pointing behind me at the fireplace.

"Not consciously, no." He got up—tugging at the seat of his jockey shorts and tossing his motorcycle scarf jauntily over his shoulder—and came over to me at the chalk line. He had one of those small man's jaunty strides, just a touch of rooster in it. But it wasn't like he was overcompensating for his size; it was simply that he had a *total* self-confidence. You can tell the genuine article from even the best fake, every time. He turned his back to the fireplace, finished the last sip of his beer, and tossed the empty glass backwards over his shoulder. It hit the bull's-eye as squarely as my throw had.

And when its little musical smash had ended, all four letters in Mary's name were filled in.

After a moment of silence, Long-Drink McGonnigle spoke up. "Mister, I'd like to buy you a drink."

The stranger looked him up and down carefully. "Let me think about it."

The Doc was looking thoughtful. "Stuff like that happen around you a lot? If you don't mind my asking?"

The stranger stuck out his hairy jaw, sublimely comfortable at the center of attention in his jockey shorts. "To the best of my knowledge, only while I'm awake. The rest of the time I lead a normal existence."

The door swung open and Shorty came back in, looking thunderstruck. "What's the matter, Shorty?" Doc Webster asked. "Damage bad?"

Shorty blinked at us all. "I went to look. See how bad it was, you know?" He gestured with his hands, looking a little like a man playing an invisible banjo.

"That bad?" I asked sympathetically.

He shook his head. "When I left the house tonight, I had this ding in the rear bumper from a hit-and-run two days ago. I'd been meaning to report it to my insurance company. That motorsickel fixed it."

"Huh?"

"Fixed it nice as you please. The ding is gone. Popped back out. Near as I can figure, chrome from the bike fender plated itself everywhere there was chrome scraped off. You can't tell there ever *was* a ding. And my trunk light works now."

He shook his head. "Never did before. Not even when she was new."

Rooba rooba rooba.

The only one in the room who did not seem to need the services of a wig-tapper was the hairy stranger. He looked quite unsurprised and unimpressed by Shorty's news.

"Friend," I said to him, cutting through the buzz of conversation, "I am Jake Stonebender, and this is Mary's Place. These here are—" I introduced all my friends, one after another. "Welcome to our joint."

For the first time he smiled. Well, it had aspects of a smile to it, and for a second there teeth actually flashed in the undergrowth. "Usually I get more reaction. You people are all right." He looked at us all a little closer. "You've seen some shit, haven't you? All of you."

"That we have," Long-Drink said solemnly.

He nodded. "That's gonna save a lot of time. My name's Ernie Shea—but people generally call me the Duck."

An unusual name for a small man to choose. But there *was* just a touch of duck in his walk, and a trace of nasal honk to his voice, and he certainly could have given either Daffy or Donald points for attitude. Then I got it. "The Lucky Duck!"

"The proverbial," he agreed, and quacked twice, nasally, without quacking a smile. "But I sometimes think of myself as The Improbable Man. It's less misleading. 'Lucky' implies that the luck is always good."

"You mean—," Long-Drink began.

"How was the bike?" the Duck asked Shorty, interrupting.

"Well, that's the other funny thing," Shorty said. "I never in my life seen a piece of machinery so fucked up. I mean, every single piece of gear I could see on it was wrecked or ripped loose or mashed up some way or other. Even things you wouldn't think would—Mister, I'm sorry. I don't think you can salvage as much as a bolt out of her."

The Duck nodded. "There you go. Don't worry about it. The best bargain you can get today, the Russians'll charge you $187,000 to loft you into orbit. Your rates are more reasonable."

"I should have been more careful," Shorty said. "Look, I'm insured—"

"I'm not. And I hate cashing checks. Forget it."

"Huh?"

"It happens all the time. When I need transportation, something will come along. Don't worry about it. *You,* I'll let buy me a drink. After the Doctor there buys his round for the house. That'll square us, okay?"

"Sure thing," Shorty agreed dazedly.

"Wait a minute, Duck," Long-Drink said, doggedly pursuing his point. "Are you trying to tell me—"

The Duck's eyes flashed. "Okay, I'll show, not tell," he said. "That's how to handle the third-grade mentality. Watch, Sir Stephen Hawking: I'll try again." He glanced around, and saw the dart board. "You got darts for that thing?" he asked me.

I went back to the bar and got the compact little tube for him. Plastic darts, good ones, with snug little plastic tail-sockets so you can nest six of them in a tube that small, or carry them around out of the tube in comparative safety. He took them out and separated them, set down all but one of them on a nearby table, looked up and snatched Long-Drink's night watchman's cap from his head. Drink blinked, and then glared, and for an instant I thought, *That duck'll* have *to be lucky to survive now,* but the hairy man returned his glare with a look of such total confidence that Long-Drink decided to let it go.

"Thanks," the Duck said insolently. He held the cap up over his face, completely obscuring his vision, and let go with one of the darts.

THE CALLAHAN TOUCH

It was a rotten shot. It just barely hit the target, wedging its way in precisely between the target proper and the surrounding rim.

I guess we'd all been expecting a bull's-eye. We giggled. Well, some of us guffawed. Relief of tension and all that.

Without looking at the results of his shot, he glared around at us from behind the hat until silence descended again. He took another dart, and let fly.

It socketed neatly into the first dart, with a *suck-pop* sound like kids make by plucking a finger out of their cheek.

No laughter this time.

He shifted hands. His view of the target still blocked by the hat, he threw a third dart lefthanded, quite clumsily.

It homed in on the second dart like a Sidewinder up a MiG tailpipe. *Thop!*

Dead silence.

He turned around and threw the fourth dart over his shoulder, the way he had his glass. It spun like a Catherine wheel as it flew.

Fap! Bull's . . . uh, nether receptacle. Four darts stuck out from the target as one, drooping slightly.

He turned back to face the board, put Long-Drink's hat on his head backwards, picked up the fifth dart, balanced it on the point on his index finger, and let it fall. It fell tumbling, and when he drop-kicked it, it chanced not to be point-down. It rose in an arc across the room, and slammed into dart number four with an upward angle, correcting the droop.

Silence so complete that I could hear my digestion.

He turned around again, back to the board, and threw the last dart directly at me, hard.

As it left his hand, a last piece of debris dropped from the hatchway overhead and fell in front of me. The dart ricocheted off it, *WOK!* and then off a beer tap, *CLANG!* and then off the ceiling, *BOK!* and then off the edge of the bar, *TOK!* and joined the daisy-chain at the target, *THUP!* The piece of wood caromed off the bartop at an angle and ended up in a trashcan behind the bar, adding *KDAP!* and *FUSH!* to the sound effects. I contributed "Eep," the best I could come up with on the spur of the moment, in a fetching soprano.

And *this* silence was so complete I could hear myself think.

Now, you could think about that and say to yourself, he's the best dart-thrower I ever saw. But that first shot had been *lousy.* A good shooter would have planted them all at the *center* of the target. It hadn't been extraordinary skill, but extraordinary coincidence . . .

The silence lasted a little under ten seconds. Then Doc Webster said, "Nice form. So show us around the place a little, Jake. Is that over there in the corner what I think it is?"

2

The Fount of All Blessings

"Yeah, Doc," I said at once. "It's a TV."

"Jeeze," Fast Eddie said. "You watch TV, Jake?"

"It's like China, Eddie," I told him. "If you don't pay any attention to it, it just gets worse. I've got it hooked up to cable, for news and weather and *Rockford Files* reruns—but its main purpose is to serve that laser disc machine. Up to eight people can watch a movie together if they want—and it can't be turned to face the rest of the room."

I snuck a glance at the Duck—who seemed quite pleased to be ignored. The Doc's instincts were sound. A guy like the Duck must get tired of being gaped at and marveled over.

"Zpeakerss or headphonez?" Ralph asked.

"It's rigged for both. But the speakers are directional, and they can't be turned up loud enough to bother the serious drinkers."

"Zlick," Ralph said approvingly.

The Duck *almost* displayed interest when Ralph spoke—one eyebrow quivered as if it might rise—but he got it under control within a second or two. Talking dog, big deal. I went on with my spiel. "The house sound system is a Technics CD, a Kenwood logic-controlled cassette deck with Dolby B and C, an AR turntable, Dynaco SCA-35 tube amp with Van Alstine modifications, and Cambridge Soundworks speakers by old man Kloss himself—the woofer's built into the bar."

"Jesus," said Shorty, who sells and installs custom audiophile gear for a living, "that's money damn well spent."

"And not much of it," I agreed.

"That's what I mean. I've sold systems for eight times the price that weren't as good. No, ten times."

"Well, the KX-790-R is the first perfect cassette deck ever made, so naturally hardly anybody bought one, and Kenwood discontinued the model almost at once. I got the AR table twenty years ago for seventy-eight dollars, and in another twenty years it'll probably need some maintenance. Lots of people are stupid enough to throw away tube amplifiers these days, and old Santa Kloss sells those speakers direct from the factory at a price so low you wouldn't believe it if I told you. I've set it up so everybody can reach the controls—but I get to settle any squabbles."

"Let's hear a taste," Tommy said. "Crank it up, Jake."

"Sure." I switched on the Dynakit, and waited.

"What are you waiting for?" Tommy asked.

I smiled. "Back at the dawn of time," I explained, "they used to make amplifiers with tubes. They used to take time to warm up. It was worth the wait. Now listen." I turned up the volume. I already had a CD in the player; I punched the button.

A horn section vamped three notes, and was answered by a piano. People jumped at the fidelity. Again, the piano answering differently this time. A third time, and then a fourth, completed the intro . . . and then Betty Carter told us she really couldn't stay.

And there was respectful silence as she and Ray Charles sang "Baby, It's Cold Outside." Digitally remastered from the original 1962 master tapes by the Genius himself. Do you know that track? It'll make you smile, and sigh wistfully, and nod . . .

When Ray and Betty were done, people were smiling and sighing wistfully and nodding. Both the sound system and the track were praised extravagantly. I killed the disc and removed it, put in background music and turned the volume way down. "Now, over there, of course," I said, pointing to the piano in the corner, "is Fast Eddie's upright, so we don't have to live entirely on canned music. I've rigged a switch so you can turn the sound system off from there any time you like, Eddie. The box has been tuned, and there's a pack of thumbtacks on it for the hammers."

His monkey face split in a grin. "Tanks, Jake."

"In that corner," I went on, "is the house computer. It's a Mac II. It's got 5 megs of RAM, and a 40-meg hard disk. A crazy friend of mine named Jon Singer gave it to me; all I had to put into it was the extra RAM, the hard drive and the monitor. I've got software in it for both beginners and power users."

"Modem?" Tommy asked. He fancies himself a power user.

I nodded. "Pay as you go. That cigar box next to the mouse is for settling up; same policy as the one on the bar." Which meant, honor system: no one would watch with beady eyes to make sure people paid for time used. "Which brings up an important matter, jadies and lentilmen. Uh . . ." This was one of the parts I had fretted over for days; I braced myself for the storm. "I'm still accepting nothing but dollar bills, like always—but I'm afraid the price of a drink has tripled, and the change-back has only doubled."

A few nods, a few shrugs; not one protest. "Three bucks a drink, a buck back if you don't bust the glass?" Les asked, but he was just making sure he understood me. I nodded, and he nodded back. "Like we figured," he said philosophically.

I ought to have known my friends would understand inflation.

But the Duck was finally showing mild surprise. "You mean to tell me drinks used to be a buck apiece at that other place? And you got fifty cents back just for turning in your empty?" A talking dog, okay—but cheap drinks?

There was a chorus of agreement.

"Jesus," he said. "No wonder the place got bombed. Excuse me—'got nuked,' I mean."

"No apology necessary," I told him. "We tolerate punning in here."

"As a matter of fact, we encourage punning in here sometimes," Noah Gonzalez said. There was a rumble of general agreement.

"Not all the time," Maureen hastened to assure the Duck. "Only on days ending in '-y.' "

He closed his eyes and sighed deeply. "Naturally. My luck."

"As a matter of fact," I said, "in honor of your arrival, I've been giving some thought to changing the name of the place—"

"—to the Dude Drop Inn, right, I've been holding my breath praying that nobody would think of that one since I sat down."

"Nobody had," I told him. "I'd been thinking of the Fall-In Shelter. But yours is rotten too."

He shrugged with his mouth. "Thanks."

"Wait, let me introduce you to the champ. Hey, Doc!"

"Yes, Jake?"

"*How* bad did you say that movie was?"

The Doc knows a straightline (the shortest distance between two puns) when he hears it. Glancing ceilingward in perfunctory apology to Johnny Mercer, he sang, "Mack Sennet ate the positive, and Jack Lemmon ate the negative—"

Groans arose, and several handfuls of peanuts or pretzels bounced off the Doc, who ignored them. "Talk about a movie that turned to shit," Long-Drink said, grinning.

The Duck regarded the Doc. "Say," he said, "have you read the new Tony Hillerman novel?"

"Which one?" the Doc asked cautiously.

"THE HEMMING WAY," the Duck said. "Or was it THE SEG WAY . . . ? Anyway, Officer Jim Chee becomes a Navajo narc—and plants a recording device on a pot smoker."

"So?" the Doc asked incautiously.

The Duck buffed his nails. "Makes him the first policeman to wire a head for a reservation."

I guess I shouldn't have been surprised. Every single morsel of food thrown at him happened to bounce into one of the free-lunch bowls it had come from.

"Stop the presses: Duck Decks Doc!" Long-Drink crowed. The Doc smiled with genuine pleasure, and made a little bow of respect as the general groan subsided. But his eyes were sparkling, and I knew this contest was not over yet.

"Hey Jake, what the hell is that?" Tommy Janssen asked, pointing behind me. "It looks like that thing Alec Guinness built in *The Man in the White Suit.*"

"It looks like a stereo makin' love to a soda fountain," Eddie said.

"It looks like something in the Science Museum in Boston," Marty said.

"Someday it will be," I told him. "But not until we're done with it. Tommy, you asked, so the honor is yours." I looked Tommy over, checked my memory, made one small adjustment of a dial, touched three solenoids, and pushed the go-button. There ensued a curious sequence of sounds. The overall effect was indeed vaguely reminiscent of the Guinness-movie gadget Tommy had mentioned. First a brief soft rattling noise. Then for about twenty seconds the softer sounds of a small fan and a tiny turntable. Then another short rattling, slightly louder and higher in pitch than the first. Then a much louder rattling for twelve seconds, followed by a *chuff*, a *huff*, and what sounded like someone blowing bubbles in mud. As if cued by that last sound, a small conveyor belt started up at the bottom of the device, entering on the left and exiting at the right, and briefly visible in a cereal-box-sized alcove in the center. An oversize mug slid into view, stopped when it was centered in the alcove—just in time to catch the dark fluid that began to drip from above.

Nostrils flared all along the bar. "Holy shit," Eddie breathed. "It's—"

"—the Ultimate Coffee Machine," I agreed. "Notice how *fast* it's dripping. The brewing module is mildly pressurized. Not enough for espresso, but enough to speed things up. Watch, now."

The mug had filled enough for its weight to restart the conveyor belt. The mug slid to the right and disappeared into the machine again . . . reemerged at its right side with a lumpy white hat on. I picked up the mug and handed it to Tommy. He stared at it, looked around at the rest of us, and took a tentative sip.

Then he took a big gulp.

Then he drained the mug, and looked up at me with an oddly stricken expression. He groped for words.

What he finally came up with was, "For this Blessing, much thanks." And then his features relaxed into a blissful grin. "That was the best goddam Irish coffee I ever drank in my life."

The Doc broke the silence that ensued. "Jake, what did we just see?"

"The apotheosis of technological civilization," I said. "At

least until someone invents a good sex robot. Watch." I leaned over and reset the parameters, pushed the go-button again. I pointed with my index finger to the source of the first rattling sound. "That's the raw coffee beans dropping into the roaster. Wet-processed. Hear that fan? *Microwave* dry-roasting. Default setting is American roast, but I can do anything from pale to Italian. Now the roasted beans are dropping into the grinder—hear it? Ground, not chopped: a chopper heats them too much too soon. Now the grinder's cleaning itself. And there's the water entering the brewing chamber at just the right temperature and pressure—and there's the pre-heated mug, just in time." A second mug of coffee appeared, filled, and whisked away to be adulterated to taste. It too emerged snow-capped with whipped cream, and I handed it to the Doc.

He took a sip—then held it away from him and gaped at it.

"Yours isn't brewed as strong as Tommy's," I said, "and I gave you a darker roast, and you've got half as much sugar, just the way you like it."

"God's Blessing, indeed," he said reverently, and finished the mug in one long slow savored draught. He licked his lips.

"The machine self-cleans constantly, and when you shut it down for the night it autoclaves itself." I took the empty mugs back from Tommy and the Doc, and set them down to the left of the machine, upside down, on a turntable the size of an extra large pizza, speckled with draining holes. Their weight activated it: it delivered them both onto the conveyor belt where it entered the machine at the lower left. "It washes the mugs, dries them, and flips them right side up." I opened the right-side access and showed them the hoppers for cream and sugar and the rack that held a quart of the Black Bush upside down. "I can vary the roast, the brew, and the amounts of booze, sugar, cream or whipped cream. It whips its own cream. I feed it with raw beans and additives before I open, and for the rest of the night all I have to do is put dirty cups in this side and take full ones out this side. The inventor says it's fully automatic, but actually you have to push this button here."

Like a grenade. Five seconds of silence, and then, rooba rooba rooba.

I preened. I had been looking forward to this moment with keen anticipation for a long time. Even the nagging weight of the big unsolved problem I was still carrying around didn't spoil my pleasure: it may have enhanced it.

"Jake," Doc said, "am I crazy, or was that the McCoy?"

I grinned. "Neither. But if I told you it was, you'd believe it, wouldn't you?"

"Yes, I would," he stated.

"Naw, I stopped buying Blue Mountain when the price became unreasonable. How anybody can say that the people who cornered the world market in Jamaica Blue and keep nearly all of it for themselves are a polite race is beyond me. But if Blue Mountain is a 10, and Kona Gold is an 8.5, what you just drank is at least a 9—at a third of the cost of the Blue, half the cost of Kona. And if we can just keep it a secret, it'll stay that way for a while."

"What is it?" Tommy asked.

I looked around for imaginary Japanese importers, and said conspiratorially, "Celebes Kalossi. From the island of Sulawezi, in Indonesia. But don't tell anybody you don't love."

"Huh," the Doc said. "Never tried it."

"It's the best-kept secret in the world," I agreed. "At the moment I've also got the machine fed with Kenya Double A, Tanzania Peaberry and a custom Australian from Queensland—but there's an extra hopper for special requests, with an option to bypass the roaster module on that one. You bring the beans, raw or roasted, I'll serve you the coffee. But no flavoured crap."

People stared at the thing with expressions of awe. I knew

just how they felt. The first time I'd ever seen it, I'd spent the next six hours just staring at it, studying it—and drinking its output, of course.

"This one's on the house too, Doc," I said. "You'll want a toast with your round, and these mugs are kinda dear to bust." I began punching up mugs for everyone present and passing them out. I had to ask Susie and Suzy Maser and Willard and Maureen to remind me how they took theirs, and I had to find a bowl for Ralph . . .

Pretty soon there were a lot of smiles in the house, with whipped-cream mustaches.

Pyotr wandered in late (being a vampire, he never gets up before dark), admired the place extravagantly, and was made welcome; I poured him a distilled water while the others brought him up to speed. It was he who suggested that since our name for Irish coffee is "God's Blessing," the machine should be called "the Fount," as in, the fount of all blessings. The name was adopted by acclamation.

"Why is the cup accessible there in the center before it's ready?" Willard asked. "So you can get it faster if the customer wants it black?"

"Nah," I said. "The cup exits the moment it's full anyway. That opening is just there so you can *smell* the coffee dripping."

Willard smiled, and finished his Blessing.

"My god, Jake," his wife Maureen said, "the thing must have cost a king's ransom."

"It cost me about two days of talking," I said.

"How?"

"Did any of you ever hear of a guy up in Syracuse called The Slave of Coffee?"

Blank stares, except for the Duck, who just nodded, and Fast Eddie, who said, "I hoid of him, sure—are youse tryin'a tell me he really *exists?*"

"He sure does," I told him. "Retired now though, God have mercy on us all."

Everyone looked to Eddie. " 'The Slave of Coffee'?" Doc Webster asked, with the air of one resigned to hearing something amazing.

"He's this whackadoo," Eddie said. "Inherits a shitpot o' dough, and decides ta start his own cult. Coffee woyship."

"He used to have a little hole-in-the-wall shop off Spadina," I told them, "called The Slave of Coffee. Half a dozen chairs, a couple dozen opaque vacuum jars, a roasting drum, a hand mill, two single-cup Brauns with gold filter baskets, a sink, fifty gallons of spring water, and a little beer fridge for cream. You go in there, he'd sit you down and ask you to describe the perfect cup of coffee. What, by you, an ideal cup should *taste* like. He'd explain the terminology if you didn't know it. Then he'd listen to what you said, nod, crack three or four jars and take a few beans from each one, roast 'em and grind 'em, and brew you up a cup. Then he'd ask you to tell him, precisely, in what particulars it fell short of absolute perfection. So you'd try, and pretty soon he'd nod again and assemble a new blend, change one or two of the jars, vary the proportions. In those jars he had all the great coffees of the world, and the cream of every crop. This process continued until he'd brewed you a cup of coffee that you felt was *perfect*—or at least the best the planet could provide for your taste. Then he'd write down your prescription for you, file a copy—and sell you a pound at cost."

"Jesus Christ," Long-Drink said reverently. "How could he show a profit?"

"By creating a category in his bookkeeping called 'Satisfaction,' Drink. He inherited his pile when he was thirty, and decided he couldn't think of anything better to spend it on than turning people on to good coffee."

"Come to think of it," the Doc rumbled, "neither can I."

"He drove the IRS crazy, but so far it's still legal to lose money if you have a mind to. He operated like that twelve hours a day, six days a week, for over twenty years. If nobody came in, he'd read a book. Once a year he'd take off a month and travel around the world, visiting all the great coffee kings—he knew 'em all; they'd give him beans out of their personal stashes."

"My God," Bill said, adjusting a bra strap, "he must have done something awful good in his last incarnation." There were many nods.

"One day," I went on, "he realized that his money was running out. So he sank most of what he had left into designing the Fount. He figured to sell it for enough to keep peddling superb coffee at cost until he dropped in his tracks. He started with the concept of microwave roasting. In conventional roasting, by the time the inside of the bean is done, the outside is a little overdone . . . so you have to go for a compromise. With microwave, the inside and outside reach optimum temperature together."

"Brilliant," Doc Webster said. Even the Duck looked impressed.

"It grew from there. He said he realized the idea was too big for individual home consumers, so he aimed at the restaurant, bar and big office market. The Fount's made like a VW used to be. Every single component is stock generic hardware, cheap and easy to replace. The prototype cost him his last dime, but he wasn't worried. He knew he had a winner. He went looking for venture capital and a patent lawyer."

"Which one got him?" Willard asked, with the reflexive interest of a retired professional. "The money man or the lawyer?"

"Both," I said sadly. "He was lucky to come out of it with physical possession of the Mark I—which he's not allowed to sell. There's a patent but his name doesn't appear on it, and he's legally enjoined by a corporation he supposedly worked for against ever inventing anything involving coffee again, and the lawyer has his nephew the engineering student busy crapping up the design to suit the capitalist. In about five years you'll be able to pay eight hundred bucks for a version that looks like the bridge of the starship *Enterprise,* and will actually produce a drinkable cup of coffee right up until its thirty-day warranty runs out, after which you will find that the capitalist is sole source for all the customized parts. It'll stiff big, because hardly any place wants to devote that much money and space to a better cup of coffee and not get it, and that'll kill the market for at least a decade.

"Meanwhile, the Slave's retired, broke. He's so bummed out, he gave me The Machine pretty much just to know that it was being used, by people who'd appreciate it. I offered him one hundred percent of the profits I made selling coffee, but he isn't allowed to accept 'em."

"Jesus," Tommy said. "No good deed goes unpunished. Maybe this society is too stupid to *deserve* the Fount. What's this Slave's name?"

"What else?" I said. "Coffey. Joe Coffey. Like the cop Ed Marinaro played on *Hill Street Blues.* For all I know he was born with that name, and it triggered his interest. I never asked."

"He actually is Mister Coffey . . . ," Long-Drink said wonderingly, and flinched under Doc Webster's glare.

"Yeah, it's hard to say that with a straight face," I agreed. "I always call him Cough."

"You got a spare cigar box, Jake?" Tommy asked.

The non sequitur took me aback. Or did it sequite? Cough—cigar—cigar box? "Yeah, as a matter of fact. Why?"

"Whip it out," he said. When I obliged, he set it at the end of the bar, beside the customary one intended to let people reclaim whatever change they have coming back when they leave. "That there is for donations to the Order of the Sainted Slave," he announced, and dropped in a couple of singles.

Doc Webster drifted over. "I hereby dub it The Cough Drop," he said, and dropped in a five. A line formed behind him.

The Duck was so surprised he forgot to grimace. "Have I got this right?" he asked me. "The guy *gave* you this thing . . . and now they all insist on paying for it? In installments?"

I blinked. "Yeah. Why—you got a problem with that?"

He shook his head. "No," he said. "It's just that I've been looking for a place like this all my life . . . and up until now, even my luck hadn't been that good."

I smiled and stuck out my hand. "Welcome to Mary's Place, Duck."

The hair at one corner of his mouth twitched, as though he were trying to grin but the necessary muscles had atrophied. "A pleasure."

"Better," I said. "A joy. You'll see."

He sighed and nodded philosophically. "I probably will. Hey, Doc! You're buyin', you said?"

"My shout," Doc Webster agreed, and I got busy.

This toast was to gentle, funny Tom Flannery, who had died a dozen years earlier to the day—and was still fondly remembered by all those who had had the privilege of knowing him. By the time the last glass had smashed, the shrapnel in the hearth had randomized again.

Δ　　　　　Δ　　　　　Δ

"One thing I'll say for you people," the Duck said some time later. "You don't ask the obvious questions."

"You don't ask many yourself," I said.

"Just about everybody else I ever met seems to think that if you're weird you have some obligation to go around explaining yourself."

I nodded. "We've got a fair number of customs and habits, but only a handful of rules. One of 'em is that anybody who asks a snoopy question in here wakes up in the alley with a sore skullbone."

"Who gets to define 'snoopy'?"

"The person asked. If you want to know something personal, it's best to begin with, 'Do you mind if I ask—?' and be prepared to accept a 'Yes.' "

The answer clearly pleased him. "You people are all right. Mary's Place, huh?"

I nodded.

He glanced around the room. "Uh . . . you mind if I ask where Mary is?"

"Not at all—but I can't answer. You asked the wrong question."

He tilted his head and regarded me out of the corner of his eye. "What is the right question?"

"The right question is, '*When* is Mary?' "

He didn't even blink. "Okay. When *is* Mary?"

"Not yet," I said, and moved down the bar to get the McGonnigle an ale.

I expected that to end it. Enough time had passed that I was no longer suffused with sick helpless yearning at the sound of Mary's name—nothing worse than a toothache—but I still wasn't ready to discuss her with a stranger. Even an interesting stranger that I was beginning to take a shine to.

But while I was away, he paid me a pretty high compliment. The Duck thought about what I'd said, and how I'd said it, and decided to assume *not only* that I'd meant it literally . . . but that I wasn't as crazy as it made me sound.

"Time traveler, eh?" he said matter-of-factly when I got back to him.

I nodded, trying to be just as matter-of-fact. "Ever met any?"

"Just one. Guy named Phee—"

I whooped with delight. "—and he swindled you out of every penny you had, right? We had him in here too, once! Boy, that's an amazing co—" Just in time I caught myself.

"Thank you," the Duck said quietly. "You have no idea how much I hate those words."

"I can see how that would be."

"Your Mary isn't a friend of Phee's, is she?" he asked.

"No, no, she's from further up the line. Much nicer class of people."

He nodded. "And she founded this place?"

"No, that was her dad. Mike Callahan. He established Callahan's Place in 1948, about twenty miles from here."

"What'd he do there?"

I shrugged. How do you answer a question like that? "Fixed broken brains. Made sad people happy and happy people merry and merry people joyous. Tutored in kindness and telepathy. Smoked hideous cigars. Forgave people. Accessory before and after the pun."

"Where . . . excuse me, when is *he* now?"

"I wish I knew, Duck. I truly do. He left that night, and hasn't been back."

He snorted. "Hell, I would too. All it takes is one nuclear weapon and I'm gone; that's just the kind of guy I am. Call me touchy."

"Oh, that's not why he left. It was more of a 'Tonto, our work here is done' kind of deal."

"What—" He caught himself. "You mind if I ask, what was his work here? Besides being a jolly host."

"Well, basically he had to save the world."

The Duck nodded. "Glad to hear it. Only sensible reason

I can think of for using a time machine. I gather he was successful?"

"Seem so," I agreed.

"How'd he do it?"

"He killed a cockroach."

He sighed and looked pained. "Look, Jake, you can tell I'm crazy enough to believe this bullshit—so why are you dragging it out like this? Are you gonna tell me the story or what?" When I hesitated, he looked even more pained. "Okay, I understand. You just met my face."

"No, no," I said. "It's not that. There's nothing secret about it. But it's a real long story, Duck. I mean, I think it'd probably take about three books to tell you all of it."

"I got time," he said.

So I made a start. It seemed appropriate to be telling someone the story of Mike Callahan, on Opening Night at Mary's Place. But I hadn't gotten very far—barely as far as the night Mickey Finn walked in and told us all that he was gonna destroy the Earth shortly, and felt just terrible about it—when the door opened, and a white-haired old stranger came in, and I shut up.

3

With Good Intentions

Why? you may ask. Why stop in the midst of a perfectly good yarn just because someone walks in who probably wouldn't understand a word of it, or believe it if he did? It wasn't simply because he was a stranger: so was the Duck. To be sure, the Duck had already sort of established himself as Our Kind of Guy—but I had no reason to conceal Mike's story from *anybody*. What harm could it do? If Mike had wanted us to keep our mouths shut about him, he'd have told us before he left. Tom Hauptman was closer to the door than I was, and not busy; I could have kept on talking.

But several things about the old-timer were striking.

First of all, of course, the simple fact of his advent. This was Opening Night, for what was intended to be something like a semi-private club. I didn't plan to bar new trade—but I hadn't *expected* any this soon. There was no neon outside; no sign of any kind, on the building or out on 25A. I had done no advertising, posted no fliers. The place did not *look* particularly like a bar from the outside, more like a warehouse of some kind. What had led the old gent to wander inside? There was no storm without . . .

And he was clearly in great need of a drink, that was the next striking thing about him. What he looked like, really, was somebody wandering around in shock after a major accident. Only technically present. Eyes like Mickey Finn had the night *he* walked in: what grunts call the Thousand-Yard Stare. Novocaine features, skin wrinkled and sagging. Vaguely stork-like walk. Neglected clothes, buttons in the wrong holes.

That, I found myself thinking, *must be what I looked like right after Barbara and Jessica died.*

(You think that's a depressing thought? I was improving. A couple of years earlier I'd have thought, *that must be what I looked like right after I killed Barbara and Jessica.*)

(No. A couple of years earlier, I would not have had that thought at all. Not if I could possibly have helped it.)

He looked, in other words, like a man carrying a load larger than his design limit . . . and so bone-deep exhausted from shouldering it that he had ceased to even mind the pain.

In fact, however, the only load he appeared to be carrying at the moment would probably have assayed out at not much over five pounds. Possibly less . . . depending on how many bullets were in the clip. The muzzle diameter seemed noticeably smaller than the Holland Tunnel. And I was looking at it head-on. It oscillated at about the same rate that I was trembling.

Δ   Δ   Δ

If Dejah Thoris married a guy named Parley Voo, she'd be—

It was by no means the first déjà vu of that night for me—but it was certainly the most powerful so far. I took comfort from the fact that the last guy who'd walked into Callahan's Place with a .45 automatic in his hand, a decade and a half ago, was presently standing ten feet away from me, serving drinks. And I took considerably more comfort from the intellectual knowledge that thanks to our cyborg friend Mickey Finn, neither I nor any of Callahan's regulars could be harmed in the least by gunfire at close range. But *the Duck was not one of us.* And he had this funny luck, sometimes bad . . .

Besides, old habits of thought die hard. Somebody points a loaded gun at you, your blood chemistry changes.

Conversations died away as people saw the stranger and the gun. Fast Eddie kept on playing piano; soon that and the crackling fire were the only sounds in the room.

I wanted to handle this situation in as Callahan-like a manner as possible. I knew this was an important surprise test of my fitness to assume his mantle—and that I had already lost points for stopping in the middle of a sentence when I'd seen the gun. Mike would have finished his sentence, excused himself to his listener, and *then* dealt with the gunman. So I wanted very much to hit the ground running. The problem was, first I had to deal with a blockage in my airway . . . which turned out to be my heart. It's damned odd: the fight-or-flight adrenal rush is supposed to be the evolutionary heritage of millions of years of success in surviving crisis . . . and just about every time it's ever happened to me, it ruined my judgment or my coordination or both. Especially on those occasions—like this one—when the judges split evenly on the question of fight or flight. The net result was quivering quadriplegia without the comfort of numbness.

And so it was that self-same above-mentioned former gun-slinger, ex-minister and utility bartender, Tom Hauptman, who had to deal with the situation.

He finished the sentence he was speaking to Noah Gonzalez, and walked down the bar toward me. My peripheral vision was unnaturally vast, and I could see Tom clearly. He walked slowly and casually, and with every step he got larger and broader and calmer and more Callahan-like; as he reached me I could have sworn I caught a sharp whiff of cheap cigar. He and the stranger reached opposite sides of the bar at the same time and locked eyes. The old guy held out his gun. Tom held out a salt shaker. The gunman opened his mouth . . . then his eyes focused on the salt shaker, and he closed his mouth.

"Might as well salt that thing, mister," Tom said gently. "You're about to eat it."

Δ   Δ   Δ

All of us remembered those words. Callahan had spoken them to Tom himself, the night that Tom had tried to stick up the joint.

But I had been watching Mike when he said it that night, and I recalled that his hands had been under the bar, resting on his sawed-off, at the time. I had an alley-sweeper under the bar myself, and other items slightly less lethal. But I was in the stranger's visual field, and did not dare upstage Tom in this psychologically crucial moment. Also I was not certain my body would obey orders, and it is usually better to not pull a gun than to screw it up. I had one small comfort. In that stopped-time moment of hyperacute sensitivity, I became aware of a subliminal change in the music Fast Eddie was playing, and realized that his left hand was now doing the playing for both, so well that probably no one else noticed.

But the old gent lowered his gun, and Tom lowered the salt shaker, and Eddie lowered the blackjack, and I lowered my CO_2 level, by inhaling for the first time in what seemed to have been a very long while.

Eddie went back to playing two-handed, but his left was playing Professor Longhair style, and his right sounded like Monk.

"But you'll be wanting a drink first," Tom went on pleasantly. "How about God's Blessing?"

I hadn't thought Tom was going to get a word out of this guy . . . but he managed to puzzle him into speech. "What's that?" His voice was rusty.

"Irish coffee," Tom said, and went to the Fount, turning his back on the man with the gun without hesitation. "You take sugar?" Tom asked without turning.

The old man frowned down at the gat, and put it in his pants pocket. "Please."

I could spend an hour making a list of Words I'd Most Like A Stranger Who's Just Walked Into My Bar With A Gun To Say, and that'd still be in the top three at least. (Think about it. Suppose it was Marilyn Chambers, and she said, "Get these clothes off me!"?) It was the word more than the simple pocketing of the gat that made me stop calculating the distance between my hand and my scattergun. I swallowed as unobtrusively as I could, and said, "Howdy, friend. Welcome to Mary's Place. I'm the proprietor; my name's Jake." My voice came out steady, friendly.

He focused his eyes on me. He saw a tall skinny forty-something galoot with glasses, a greying beard and a ponytail, wearing an apron. I saw a paunchy man of average height in his middle or late seventies with Mark Twain hair, dressed like an absent-minded professor whose wife has recently discovered LSD. He was wildly out of character as a burglar, and I saw him beginning to realize it. "Ah . . . hello. I'm . . . ah . . . Jonathan."

"Pleased to meet you, Jonathan," I said. "Let me know if there's anything you need." And I went back to telling the Duck about Mickey Finn. He looked at me a little oddly, but soon he was nodding and *mm-hmm*ing.

Conversations restarted all around the room. Not the rooba-rooba you get after a crisis, just normal bar chatter.

Tom gave Jonathan his Blessing, introduced himself briefly, made change, and left him alone. The old guy blinked at Tom's retreating back—I averted my eyes as he glanced at me—and then he spent a few seconds blinking at the steaming mug, and then he turned bright red for just a moment, and finally he took what was meant to be a big gulp of coffee. For the first second he was disappointed that it wasn't hot enough to burn his mouth, and then the flavor hit him and he converted the gulp into a long deep swallow that emptied half the mug and gave him a horn-player's beard the same color as his hair. I glanced at the Fount, saw that Tom had dialed two full ounces of whiskey and the extra strong Kayserlingck's Kastle coffee from Daintree, Australia. Good man. When Jonathan finished the mug, Tom waited to be asked for another, and dialed the Bush back to an ounce and a half this time. He fetched a dish of shortbreads with it. When Jonathan made no conversational overtures, Tom nodded pleasantly and moved away.

After five or ten minutes, when the medication had begun to take hold and Jonathan was probably starting to acquire a rudimentary awareness of his surroundings, Les Glueham stepped up to the chalk line before the fireplace, raised his glass, and cleared his throat. The general chatter died away almost at once.

"Ladies and gentlemen," Les said, "to tooth decay!"

There was something like a gleeful snarl of agreement from the room. Les finished his beer, threw his glass forcefully but carefully, and the fireplace echoed musically. Three or four other glasses floated in from various parts of the room, in support of Les's toast, and then everybody went back to what they'd been doing.

The next time I caught Jonathan's eye, he held up a finger. I drifted over and nodded. "What . . . ah . . . was that all about?" he asked.

First nibble. "House custom," I said. "You can smash your empty in the hearth if you want—but you have to make a toast. Lots of folks toast whatever made 'em feel like busting a glass. Les there has been sentenced to root canal." And I went back to my yarn before the question *why don't* you *try it?* could even hang implied in the air.

A few minutes later, Tommy Janssen toed the line. "I'm gonna tell 'em, Ish," he said as the expectant silence fell.

Isham Latimer shrugged his broad shoulders and smiled a strange wry smile. "Go ahead on," he rumbled. "I won't stop you." His wife Tanya started to say something, and changed her mind.

"I guess you all heard by now," Tommy went on, "that Isham and Tanya got married up at her parents' place in Oswego. I know most of you weren't able to make it." One or two people who had made it were seen to wince visibly, but Tommy plowed ahead. "Ish asked me to be Toastmaster at the wedding feast. Well, naturally, I was tickled to death. I mean, a white guy being asked to be party-master for a room full of mostly black people, how cool can you be, right? This was gonna go on my Liberal Credentials resumé. So I'm doing my after-dinner riffs, telling funny stories about Ish to a room that's probably eighty-five percent African-American, and I start to tell them about Ish's eye problems." Catching Jonathan's eye, Tommy explained to him, "See, Ish moved here from Halifax, and the day he arrived they diagnosed him for double cataracts."

Jonathan nodded. Second nibble.

Tommy went back to talking to the room at large. "So I tell them, 'Isham's arrival in New York was not a totally happy one: the first day he got there, they said to him, "Congratulations: a strange white man is going to stick a knife in both your eyes!" ' " People laughed, and Tommy nodded. "Yep, it got a pretty good laugh, about Force Five. But the next laugh was Force Ten. That was when a tall distinguished gent stood up in the back of the room, skin about two shades darker than Ish, and said, very politely, 'Pardon me, sir . . . but *I* am the "white man" who stuck the knife into Mr. Latimer's eyes.' "

There was a general gasp, and then an *ooooo* of horror and sympathy . . . and then, slowly, laughs of embarrassment as we all realized that we were *almost* as surprised as Tommy must have been, ourselves. We too had assumed that an eye-surgeon would be Caucasian . . .

Tommy nodded ruefully. "Yep. Caught white-handed. Bare-ass naked in front of a hundred strangers, three or four omelets on my face. Mr. Cool White Homeboy. Dr. Saunders came up to me at the reception afterward, and forgave me most graciously, but forgiving myself isn't gonna be so easy. So my toast is to unconscious racism: one of the nastiest kinds." And he pivoted and snapped his glass into the fireplace.

There was applause, and a barrage of glasses saluted his self-criticism.

Isham got up—just before Tanya pushed him—went over to Tommy, and put an arm around him. "You just keep tellin' that story, my man," he said, "and you'll have it worked off in no time. People, I'd like to propose a toast myself: to men who know how to deal with guilt."

That brought even louder applause, and Tom and I had to hustle to meet the sudden demand for fresh glasses. So the second barrage was much raggeder than the first, more spread out. And then it stopped altogether as Jonathan screamed *"HOW?"* at the top of his lungs and made a wild attempt to hurl his half-full coffee mug at the fireplace.

This time he'd taken the bait whole. The cure was begun.

Δ   Δ   Δ

Every head swiveled his way, so we all saw. He had pulled
the mug back too far, and lost control just as he tried to throw
it; it shot almost straight up in the air, disappeared briefly
through the hole in the ceiling, reappeared again, and *smack*ed
down flatfooted on the bartop behind him, right in front of
the Duck. During its entire flight, the mug had remained as
perfectly upright as if it were a cheap special effect, trailing
a column of coffee and whipped cream on the way down.
The trail vanished as the mug hit, then reappeared twice as
long, then fell again, then reappeared half as long, and finally
subsided. Not a drop had spilled on the bar. Without batting
an eye, the Duck picked up the mug, finished it, and saluted
Jonathan with the empty mug.

The business was so preposterous that Jonathan elected to
ignore it. "Tell me how," he bellowed again to the room at
large, and looked around for something else to throw. I started
to reach for a glass, thought better of it, and handed him a bag
of beer-nuts instead. " 'How' what?" I asked.

He flung the bag at the fireplace, and sure enough his aim
sucked; he got Bill Gerrity in the forehead. "Ow," Bill said,
and I guess his voice must have been Jonathan's first clue that
Bill is a man, for Jonathan looked startled. (Bill is an unusually
convincing transvestite.)

Again it was just too weird to deal with; Jonathan ignored
it and answered me. But he didn't shout. "How to deal with
guilt," he said, and sat back down in his chair and swiveled
it around to face the bar and buried his face in his hands and
began to sob loudly.

There was a general murmur which somehow managed to
convey sympathy without pity. Merry Moore moved toward
him, and then stopped. Nobody second-guessed her. This was
her line of work.

"That is one of the tough ones," I agreed. "There aren't any easy answers for that one."

"Some people seem to find it very easy," he said bitterly into his hands. "They say Dr. Mengele slept like a baby in his old age. Somehow even Geraldo Rivera lives with himself. Could it be a missing chromosome, do you think? And if so, do you know a *competent* gene-cutter?"

From the bitter emphasis on the next-to-last word, I inferred that my would-be robber *du soir* was in genetics or one of the other biosciences himself, and held a low opinion of his own skill thereat. I started thinking about some of the things a gene-splicer could be feeling suicidally guilty about, and felt a fine sweat break out on my forehead—which had not happened when he'd come in waving a hogleg.

"No," I said. "But I know a pretty good home remedy. It can taste like hell, and it's not a cure, but sometimes it can afford symptomatic relief."

"Oh, bullshit!" he snarled, slapping his palms against the bar. "I've already had so much of that, I can't hit the wall with a bag of nuts, and *it doesn't help a fucking bit!*"

I shook my head. "You misunderstand. I wasn't talking about booze. Or drugs."

He glared at me. "What then? Religion?"

"Action," I said.

"What kind of action?" he asked automatically.

"Right action."

He looked at my face a long time to see if I was putting him on in some way. I saw the anger begin to ease in him as he decided I was not. "Like what?"

I turned to the Fount and made him a cup of Celebes with no booze. "Well," I said, setting it before him, "usually if you've got the guilts, it's because you did a disservice to someone or something you care about."

He nodded tensely and took a sip. "So?"

"So you go and do a service for someone or something you care about."

Pain rose up in his face. "And what if they're dead, and you can't?"

"Oh, it doesn't have to be the *same* someone," Merry said. "It's best, but sometimes the guilt is nonspecific and it can't be. Or like you say, sometimes it's too late. That doesn't matter so much. The point is just to release the pressure—equal and opposite reaction. Slow and steady, ideally. What I'm aiming for myself is to achieve balance, equilibrium, about half an hour before I die."

His face was now a mask of pain. "And what if you've caused more pain than you could feel yourself in a single lifetime?" he asked her. "Like Mengele. Or Hitler."

I wiped the sweat from my forehead as inconspicuously as I could. *God damn it,* I thought, *healing the wounded is one of the reasons I opened this place—but for one* this *bad to come in on Opening Night is sure one hell of a—*

—and then I saw the Duck out of the corner of my eye, and sighed. Sure.

It was in fact the Duck himself, stranger to our ways, who answered Jonathan. "You start by doing what Tommy just did," he said. "Telling the story on yourself, and taking whatever comes back."

Soft sounds of agreement from the rest of us.

"As soon as you're ready to," Tommy amended quietly. "It hurts—I know. But it is good when you get it over with."

Jonathan looked around at us, on the verge. "All of you really want to hear this?" he asked.

Nods, murmurs, one way or another everybody said yes.

"You'll listen nonjudgmentally."

Doc Webster folded his hands across his great belly and said, "No, we're human beings. But *good* judges come in a spectrum between fair and merciful, and I'd have to say this group definitely falls on the merciful end of the range."

"We wouldn't forgive Hitler," Long-Drink said by way of clarification.

Jonathan, of course, assumed the Drink was using the word "wouldn't" in the subjunctive, rather than the simple past tense. "In that case, it . . . ah . . . might be touch and go," he said.

"But we heard him out first," Long-Drink added.

Jonathan wasn't listening. We all shut up and waited for him to make up his mind.

He looked down at himself finally, and made a heart-breaking little giggle. "What am I worried about? I'm armed, for God's sake. Sure, why not? I've held it in for so long I think I'm finally ready to vomit." He lurched to his feet.

I handed him a beer. He blinked at it. "For the toast, after your story," I explained. He picked it up and took it with him to a spot just before the crackling fire. As he stood there, he became a lecturing professor, the way Paladin used to be able to just *become* a gunfighter without moving. A lectern seemed to appear before him, with a faulty lamp and no lip to hold the papers. Not a successful lecturing professor.

"All right, let's get right to it," he said, gesturing with his beer. "Have any of you . . . no, wrong question. *How many* of you have lost a friend or loved one to AIDS?"

Damn, I thought, *I was afraid of that.* And I raised my hand.

Even though it was only 1988, everyone in the room raised a hand, I'm sorry to say. But not as sorry as Jonathan was to see us do it. He flinched, and gestured with his glass again, as if to wave away our answer. Then his shoulders slumped, and he abandoned even symbolic defense.

"Well, I'm the stupid son of a bitch that gave it to them," he said.

Ten seconds of absolute silence . . .

Δ   Δ   Δ

. . . representing not disbelief, but simple surprise. We were the former patrons of Mike Callahan. In our experience, preposterous statements tended to be true. I'm not saying we'll believe anything—but we're prepared to.

"I thought it was some Air Canada steward," Long-Drink said at last. "Gay Tan something."

"A very active assistant," Jonathan said. "But I am the originator. Accept no substitutes."

Doc Webster cleared his throat, making it sound like no easy task. "You're saying that you—you personally—"

"—introduced AIDS to the human race. That is correct. I suppose I should have introduced the human race to AIDS as well, but my manners always were weak. Still, the word got round eventually. Yes, to answer your question without evasion: I personally loosed AIDS on the world. Mea maxima culpa."

A silence so total that I heard the fridge compressor switch itself off in sympathy—then a ROOBA-ROOBA! that took a long time to fade.

"How de fuck did youse do dat?" Fast Eddie asked.

"Point of order, Eddie," Doc interrupted gently. "Details like that can wait. A long time, as far as I'm concerned. Jonathan, tell me this first—*did you do it deliberately?*"

Jonathan pursed his lips. "I'd have to say a great deal of deliberation took place. Not very astute deliberation, perhaps—"

Doc frowned. "You know damn well what I mean—" He caught himself and went on in a softer tone. "Did you do it *intentionally?*"

Jonathan sighed and slumped his shoulders. "No, that I did not."

"Well, then—," Long-Drink began, but Jonathan interrupted and kept talking over him until he shut up.

"I have *tried* that particular escape hatch already, thank you very much—the damn thing just isn't big enough for my hips. I get stuck halfway through and the hatch closes. All right, a prosecutor probably *couldn't* make a charge of first-degree murder stick in criminal court. But even an incompetent could get a conviction for multiple manslaughter, reckless endangerment, negligence resulting in mass death, felonious stupidity—"

"Yeah, okay," said the Drink, "but what I mean is, you did something dumb . . . not something evil. Right?"

He recoiled slightly, then shook his head and plowed doggedly on, his voice rising. "It transcends dumb. If a class action were brought against me in civil court, and the judge assigned a minimum value for every life I've taken or will take, he'd fine me the gross national product of the planet—it took mankind three hundred years since Leeuwenhoek to destroy smallpox, and I've replaced it single-handed—"

"Brag, brag, brag," the Duck said.

"—you don't understand—all of that is *nothing—I killed my mate—*"

"All right, save the speeches for your summation," I said. "Let's get to the evidence. You're already sworn, we've heard the charges, let's hear your theory." I rapped it out as brusquely as Judge Wapner might have on *The People's Court.* It startled him, and thus derailed his growing hysteria. He frowned at me, and took a deep gulp of his beer, and finally nodded heavily.

"You're right: let's play the trial out properly. This should be interesting—if the converse of the usual relationship obtains, then a man who prosecutes himself has a genius for a defendant, yes? Very well. Let's establish motive first. Question: Dr. Crawford, are you a screaming faggot? Answer: yes, I am."

"Objection, Your Honor," the Duck said to me. "The characterization is both argumentative and spurious: defendant is not presently screaming."

I was struck by the fact that he'd given us his last name in the same breath with which he'd outed himself. "Sustained."

"Besides," Marty said, "you look more like a homosexual than a faggot to me."

"And he's an expert witness," Marty's wife, Dave, said.

Jonathan blinked at us all. "Ah . . . very well, then. I'm homosexual. I've known I was gay since I was twelve years old. Question: how did this sexual preference affect your professional life? Answer: it made me a driven man. I was monomaniacally determined to be . . . ah . . . a credit to my gender. I had the recurring fantasy that I would make some great and noble contribution to the world, and *then,* as they were handing me my Nobel prize, then I would come out of the closet, and proudly announce that I was a homosexual."

"Relevance, Your Honor?" the Duck asked me.

"I'm trying to establish a pattern of behavior," Jonathan said. "A motive for taking stupid risks, failing to take proper precautions, willful refusal to think things through—"

"I'll allow it," I said. "But move on."

"Question: where were you in January of 1940? Answer: in federal prison in Atlanta, Georgia." He made a brief, bitter smile. "No, that's not self-incrimination, Judge. I was there as a medical researcher, fresh out of school, determined to do something marvelous and stun the world. I had talked two of my professors into backing me in a series of experiments with which I hoped to wipe out malaria. When I say 'backing,' of course, I mean I had all the ideas and did most of the work, and they arranged the funding and got their names on the title page of the paper. Much good that it did them; the experiments were completely unsuccessful. Question: without boring the jury with details, what did these experiments involve? Answer:

51

we injected prisoners with monkey blood, and in some cases vice versa."

"Volunteers?" I asked.

"Yes. They agreed to risk malaria. *Not* certain death. But they volunteered, and malaria could have killed them, and . . . ah . . . did in fact kill some of them." He looked at Isham and Tanya. "Most of our subjects, by the way—and nearly all those who died—were black."

Isham met his eyes. "Your Honor," he said to me, "the racial composition of the prison population in Atlanta in 1940 falls outside this defendant's sphere of responsibility."

"Not entirely," I said. "He stated that he was old enough to vote. But this court has no evidence that he did not do so, and rules this issue . . . uh, Doc, what's that big grey thing with the long nose and the two tusks?"

"That's irrelevant," the Doc said at once.

"Dat's-a right. Continue your examination, Mr. Persecutor."

Jonathan ignored the badinage, sipped more beer and went on. "Question: Dr. Crawford, where does modern medical science now believe AIDS came from? Answer: from African apes. There is a simian version of AIDS, and a whole spectrum of other monkey viruses which are markedly similar to, in some cases partially identical to, the human AIDS virus. It has recently been found that there may be a second form of human HIV, HIV-2, even more similar in genetic structure to the simian version. Question: and how do authorities believe the virus crossed from apes to humans? Answer: they haven't got a clue."

"Objection," Doc Webster said. "I've read a couple of theories. Something about weird African sex rituals—"

"Even if you believe that over the last fifty years, some Africans in fact routinely cut their genitalia and smeared them with monkey blood—which I don't for a minute, and I know something about Africa—even so, it doesn't explain why the disease didn't cross over centuries ago."

"He's right, Doc," Isham said. "I heard that story too. It's Jungle Jim bullshit." Isham happens to be an expert in African history, customs and traditions.

Jonathan nodded. "Question: then you did in fact begin the crossover process—you personally, Dr. Crawford—by injecting human beings with infected monkey blood and infected monkeys with human blood? Answer: that is precisely why I have been brought—" He winced as he saw the pun coming, but delivered it anyway. "—before the bar."

"Now hold on a minute," Doc Webster said. "You couldn't have been the only guy using monkeys, or even monkey blood, to make vaccines in 1940."

"Virtually everyone else in the world worked with rhesus macaques from India—right up until the Indian government noticed they were almost wiped out, and banned their export in 1955. But not me. *I* had a better idea. I had a cheap source for so-called 'African green' monkeys, from what was then the northeastern Belgian Congo. It has recently been established that they were the original carriers of SIV—the simian AIDS. It wasn't until the early '80s that SIV made the jump to macaques . . . whereupon it was discovered, because the macaques got sick. You see, SIV lives in green monkeys, but it doesn't make them sick.

"Question: where is the most intense focus of the African AIDS infection? Answer: Zaire—what used to be the northeastern Belgian Congo. And when the Congo threw off Belgian rule and became Zaire, what French-speaking blacks with no ties to Belgium migrated there en masse to help run the new government? Answer: Haitians. Question: where, outside the homosexual community, was the first major outbreak of AIDS in the Western Hemisphere? Answer: remember that literally sick joke that was going around awhile ago, about how the worst part of having AIDS was convincing your parents you were Haitian?

"Question: if you expose a virus to a new host, about how long will it take to mutate into a form that can live in it? Answer: roughly twenty to forty years. And when did AIDS first become a significant problem? Answer: *about forty years after my ingenious experiments.*"

He stopped, took another sip of beer, and said to the room at large, "Cross examine?"

Δ   Δ   Δ

"You tested the blood thoroughly," Doc Webster said, and it wasn't a question. "For every known pathogen. I know you did."

"Every pathogen known in 1940, certainly. Monkey B virus, and a dozen others. And then I injected the blood into human beings. I proceeded, not because I knew the blood was safe, but because with existing technology no one could prove it wasn't. In light of the results, would you say that was good enough?"

Silence fell.

"What'd you do after that?" Merry asked after a long while.

"Continued to chase greatness," he said bitterly. "With no more success: malaria continues to laugh at me, and all my colleagues. Along the way, I had the only lucky break of my life: I met Martin, and somehow convinced him to love me. I had Martin for twenty-eight years. The best years of my life." He paused and frowned. "And in all that time I don't think the poor man ever got more than twenty percent of my attention. I was so consumed with my work, so sure that one day I'd be hailed as one of the great microbe hunters, a gay role model. Isn't that the classic gay mistake: to care more about your gayness than about your lover? He never gave me anything but kindness and devotion, and I . . . I was short-changing him for nearly thirty years before he died in m-my arms today, of a disease I created for him!" He tossed back the rest of his beer. "My gayness died with him. My sexuality died with him. My last ambition died with him. The best parts of me all died with him. So my toast is to self-destruction—"

And with that he pegged his glass into the hearth so hard that the shattering glass sounded like a small explosion.

And took out his gun . . .

4

Mac Attack

I spoke up hastily. "Has the prosecution rested?"

He sighed deeply and worked the slide on the automatic. "Not in years."

"So does the defense get a chance? Or is this a Nazi kangaroo court?"

He shook his head wearily and placed the gun to his temple. "I have had several decades to examine the excuses I might offer," he said. "None of them are any good. Thank you, but—"

I pulled my sawed-off out from behind the bar and drew down on him. "Hold it right there!" I barked.

He was so stunned he froze, unable to think of anything to say or do. There were a few murmurs from the crowd, but nobody tried to stop me or express an objection.

"If you blow your silly brains out in front of all of us, and don't give us a chance to argue you out of it," I said, "what you'll be doing is dumping all your bad karma on our laps and leaving us no place to put it, no way to get rid of it. Before I'll let you do that to my friends and me, you selfish son of a bitch, I'll blow your God damned head all over the wall. I got problems of my own, friend. Now put that piece away!"

For a long moment I thought I was going to have to put him down. Just as I remembered the safety was on, and surreptitiously flipped it off, he slumped and lowered his gun. For the second time, he burst into tears. "I'm sorry—"

"Shut up," I said. "It's our turn to talk."

He waved the gun at me, butt-first.

"I don't want it," I said. "Put the safety back on and put it in your pants." He did as he was told. "Now sit down and shut up and listen. Doc, you want to go first?"

As Jonathan took a seat at one of the tables, Doc Webster strode over to the hearth, and turned to face the room. "Ladies and gentlemen of the jury, I'd like to begin with something that may seem irrelevant. How many of you have lived around here long enough to remember the story of the Great White Trash Mountain of Long Island?"

About ten hands went up.

"Every township on the Island has a garbage disposal problem, and none of them has a solution that's any damn good. Some decades back, one township administration— no sense identifying them—came up with a beauty. They decided to build a mountain of garbage. A layer of trash, a layer of soil, a layer of trash, a layer of soil—voilà: instant mountain. Long Island is as flat as a pool table: put artificial snow machines on the sucker, they reasoned, and you'd have the only ski resort for a hundred miles in any direction."

" 'The White Trash Mountains of Virginny,' " Maureen said, quoting the Firesign Theatre.

"An inventive notion," the Duck said.

Doc Webster nodded. "The problem was, they didn't do their homework. They got the thing half-built, placed a noncancelable order for the snow generators . . . and then all that weight started to work on the bottom layer of garbage. Pressure. Friction . . ."

Tanya began to giggle. "Oh, my goodness—"

I nodded again. "That's right. The mountain caught fire . . . and over a period of weeks, it burned to the ground."

Howls of laughter all around. Even Jonathan came close to smiling. "Oh Lord," the Duck crowed, "the *smell*—"

"They spent a bundle and used up every favor they were owed keeping the story out of the national news," the Doc said. "But the next township downwind had some pungent things to say. And they said 'em in court. Do any of you happen to recall exactly why the mountain men lost the case?"

Expectant silence.

"My, it's hard to talk when you're thirsty."

"Jesus Christ, Doc," I said, and slid a beer down the bar to him.

"They lost the case because *they hadn't even needed a competent engineer.* Anyone capable of working a slide rule could have done the calculation that showed the scheme wouldn't work. The town simply failed to even ask the question. But if it had required a competent engineer to spot the problem, they would have *won* the suit . . . because you can't require someone by law to hire the right engineer.

"Now Jonathan's case here is a sort of mirror image. It's not that he was such a lousy scientist, he failed to realize what he was doing was dangerous. In this case, any scientist alive who had looked over his shoulder would have made the same mistake he did. There was no one he failed to consult who could have straightened him out. Except God, who has a nasty habit of not returning His calls. As far as Jonathan could *possibly* have known, the experiment was . . . well, not 'safe'—nothing that involves altering human biochemistry is safe, ever—but safe *enough* that it was legal to do."

"Legality isn't the point—," Jonathan began.

Doc Webster overvoiced him. "And it isn't my point, either, so kindly leggo of that red herring, okay? The experiment was *moral* to do, too. Do you deny it? Can you name one scientist or ethicist who—at the time—would have argued?"

"It does not mitigate my guilt to tell me that there were thousands of other people just as criminally stupid. *I* was the one whose sloppy thinking triggered the disaster. I know that's bad luck . . . but it's bad luck I earned. The point is that no one, ever, can look at an organic substance and say, 'Now that is perfectly safe: there's nothing in there I don't know about. That is safe to shoot into human beings who would really rather I didn't, people I've manipulated into volunteering.' It was wishful thinking—or would have been, if I'd ever thought about it. I didn't."

The Doc sighed. "Your turn, Jake. He's just washed his brain and I can't do a thing with it."

I came around the bar, walked through Jonathan's imaginary podium and made him join me at a table. He didn't resist. The gang crowded gently around us, then parted again to let Tom Hauptman through with a couple of low-octane Blessings. I clinked mugs with Jonathan, and did my best to hold his eyes with my own.

"I'm going to tell you a little story," I said, "and I want you to believe that I'm not trying to measure my pain against yours, okay? But once upon a time I had a wife and daughter, and I loved them so much my teeth hurt. And one day I decided I could save thirty bucks by doing my own brake job, and the next day I didn't have Barbara or Jess anymore."

He lifted one eyebrow and grimaced, as if to say *tough break* and *big deal* at the same time.

"Listen to me," I went on. "Understand me. I replaced the rear shoes myself, with a Chilton manual to help, and that night I decided to take both of my loves out for a drive. And suddenly I needed brakes bad and they weren't there. A truck hit us. While I was unconscious, Barbara and Jessica were conscious and trapped and they burned to death; the M. E. said so. I woke up with nothing worse than bruises and one first-degree burn. Physically. Also, the trucker died, so I had to deal with the additional guilt of deep-down not giving a *shit* about *his* death. Now, I'm not saying I'm in your league, okay, Typhoid Johnny? But I was proud and stupid and my loved ones and one stranger suffered horribly and I escaped miraculously—are we together so far? Is this sounding at all familiar? Is there *that* much difference between killing two loved ones, or killing one loved one and two million strangers? Do I have the right to say I know a *little* bit of what you're feeling?"

He closed his eyes and sipped coffee. "I'm sorry. Yes, you do."

"I carried that sack around by the testicles for *fifteen years*," I said quietly.

He opened his eyes again, set the mug down on the table and took my hand in his. "How did you stay alive?" he asked in a hoarse whisper.

I looked around the room and tried to think how I could possibly explain it to him. "Friends," I said finally.

His hand held mine in a deathgrip.

"But I haven't finished the story," I said. "I'll make it as short as I can. Fifteen years after the crash, I stumbled across proof—proof!—that it hadn't been my fault after all. *The brakes I'd fixed weren't the ones that failed.* It was the front brakes that went."

He gaped at me.

"Do you get it? All those years of guilt and remorse and self-recrimination—all they accomplished was to put lines on my face and give me gobs of character. I spent a third of my life giving myself a beating I didn't deserve. I'd sentenced an innocent man to life imprisonment on circumstantial evidence. All I can say is, thank God I didn't believe in capital punishment, like you."

He frowned. "The cases aren't parallel. In my case there is no doubt—"

"Bullshit, there isn't. Can you describe the mechanism that caused SIV to mutate into HIV?"

"Not at present, but—"

"Then how do you know it did? And how do you know it happened in blood you handled? You've got less hard evidence than I did."

"But how else—"

BONG!

A G-major triad . . . followed by the unmistakable voice of Curly, of the Three Stooges, saying, "I'm tryin'a think . . . but nuttin' happens!"

I jumped, and frowned, and looked over my shoulder to see who had picked now to start playing games.

But there was no one at all at the computer, or anywhere near it. It had—apparently—switched itself on. Its fan powered up to speed, its hard disk chirped, and the twelve-inch monitor lit up and said, **Welcome to Macintosh.**

Δ   Δ   Δ

Rooba rooba—

"Duck—," I began.

"Nothing to do with me," he said. "As far as I know."

I turned back to Jonathan. "I'm sorry," I said. "Even for this place, that's weird."

"It just turned itself on?" he asked, frowning.

"As far as I know," I agreed.

We all silently watched the Mac II boot up.

I had left the Mac set up with the Finder as the startup application—but now it bypassed the Desktop, went right into Multifinder and opened up two applications at once, in splitscreen. The modem program and a word processor.

And then it waited for input.

"Jake—," Doc Webster began.

"Don't look at me," I said. "I don't know what the hell is going on. Or what to do next." I thought hard, and a lightbulb appeared metaphorically above my head. "But I can think of one thing to try. Duck?"

"Yah."

"Why don't you go over there and close your eyes and hit eleven keys at random?"

He hesitated a moment, then went wordlessly to the Mac, covered his eyes with one hand, and poked at the keyboard with a stiff index finger as if he were testing it for fat content. "Okay, that's eleven. Now what?"

"Hit 'Return.' "

He did so, and after a brief pause, the screen changed.

"Aha," I said softly, "I was right." I didn't know exactly what I had been right *about*—the intuition had been too vague to put into words—but I knew I was onto something now. We had reached one of the biggest scientific database services in the world, and it was asking for our password . . .

"Hit random keys again," I said. "As many as you like." I had no idea how many characters were in the typical password for that service, but I was prepared to trust to luck.

"Wait," Jonathan said. "I have a password to that service."

I nodded. "Sure. Go ahead."

He got up slowly and went over to sit at the Mac, putting his coffee where it could be knocked over without endangering anything. He entered his password, and the main search menu appeared onscreen.

"Now what?" he said to the room at large.

I went over and stood at his shoulder, squinted at the screen. "What do you think, people?" I said. "Look up 'AIDS' and let the Duck hunt around starting there? Or 'SIV'?"

"How about 'malaria'?" Doc Webster suggested.

" 'Green monkey,' " Mary Kay Kare said.

That was so out-of-left-field it felt right. "Punch up 'African green monkey,' " I said to Jonathan.

"This is silly," he said, and did as I asked. People started to cluster around the computer. Tommy sat down next to Jonathan and reached for the keyboard—and Mary Kay took it away from them both. "This is my pidgin," she said firmly, and they relinquished it. (Mary Kay is one of the secret masters of the world: a librarian. They control information. Don't ever piss one off.)

The database began listing appearances of the words "African green monkey" in scientific literature. Text scrolled upward on the screen. We all stared at it dumbly. After a few minutes it became evident that we could wait all night for the last citation to appear.

"Can you get that thing to do correlations?" Doc Webster asked.

"Of course," Mary Kay said.

"Tell it to list the citations in descending order of number of references to African green monkeys," the Doc suggested. "Then cross-reference by number of references to viruses in the same source."

She nodded enthusiastically, and did so. The screen display froze momentarily as she worked, and then text began to scroll by again—but there were far fewer hits now, a total of perhaps thirty citations.

She scrolled around, looked at dates, then places. I pointed to a reference. "Try that one," I directed.

Mary Kay hit more keys, and the article cited appeared onscreen. It was Greek to me, but I waited patiently for Jonathan to scan it.

Suddenly he made a small "uh" sound.

"Something?" I asked.

He ignored me and kept on reading. Presently he said, "Jesus Christ." Then he said, "Oh, I don't—" Then he said, "It can't—"

Then he didn't say anything at all for a long moment.

Finally he reached for his coffee, and knocked it endwise, spilling the half-cup left in it. He caught it before it could head for the floor, picked it up upside down and tried to pour coffee into his mouth from the bottom of the mug. When it didn't work, he frowned at it and flung it away over his shoulder. I ducked just in time.

It landed in the hearth with a hearty *chunkle*.

Jonathan just kept staring at the screen, with the expression of a man who is completely redecorating the inside of his head.

Doc Webster muscled his way to the front of the crowd and read over Jonathan's shoulder. After a few seconds, the smile wrinkles came out in his fat face. "Bingo," he said.

"What is it, Doc?" I asked over the growing murmur.

"The seeds of a tabloid headline," he said. "But one that lets Dr. Crawford off the hook. It ought to hit the papers in a few more years."

"Koprowski," Jonathan said hollowly. "Live polio vaccine, competing with Salk's killed vaccine. The first live oral polio vaccine tested on a large population. Sprayed in aerosol form into the open mouths of something like a third of a million Africans. Grown in the kidneys of African green monkeys—"

"From 1957 to 1961," Doc Webster agreed, pointing to the screen. "In the eastern Belgian Congo." He scrolled the text. "Looky there: in 1959, Sabin reported that an unknown monkey virus contaminated Koprowski's vaccine." Mary punched some more keys. "And in 1960, the first-ever case of AIDS appeared. In the Belgian Congo. Nice going, Mary Kay." She looked pleased.

Jonathan now looked even more tormented than at any time so far in the evening. "But it takes *time* for a virus to mutate."

The Doc nodded. "Maybe. And maybe it starts right away, and just takes time to spread enough to be noticed. What was that incubation period you mentioned? Twenty to forty years? AIDS started to hit big in 1980—twenty-three years after Dr. Koprowski ground up his first green monkey kidney and sprayed the culture onto the wet mucous membranes of 350,000 Congolese! What'll you bet some of them had open sores in their mouths or noses?"

Jonathan sprang up, knocking over his chair. "But I . . . that doesn't . . . it still—"

"Oh sure," the Doc said. "You could still be guilty—if you need to be badly enough. But I'm afraid no jury in the world would indict you on the present evidence . . . much less convict you. Or Dr. Koprowski either. There's an excellent chance neither of you ever had a thing to do with spreading AIDS. At worst, you're suspicious bystanders at this point. Are you ready to admit that now?"

"God damn it—"

"Jonathan," I said sadly, "it looks like you're going to have to return that hair-shirt to the rental shop, and get along without the joy of being a Tragic Figger of a Man. You're a fraud."

Jonathan looked stricken. He spun back and forth, as if

trying to find a path through us to safety . . . then turned his face to the ceiling.

"Oh, Martin!" he cried, and began to sob like a child.

Marty Matthias and Dave pulled him into their arms and hugged him together, and a cheer went up.

Δ   Δ   Δ

There was an especially joyous note in the celebration that ensued. We had come through our first crisis, on Opening Night—and in a manner that would, we felt, have made Mike Callahan proud of us. By the time folks began to so much as slow down in their drinking, my arms were tired, and Tom Hauptman was looking exhausted, and neither of us minded a bit. I had managed to completely forget the problem that still loomed large on my horizon.

"Here you go," I told the Duck, setting yet another Blessing in front of him and circling my palm over it.

"Thanks," he said, and put three singles on the bar.

"No, no," I said. "That gesture—" I repeated it, "—means it's on the house."

He glared at me scornfully. "No, really? Do you know this one?" He gave me the finger, and pushed the bills another inch toward me.

"Well, you earned it," I said, confused.

"I'm not so sure of that," he said. "You mean that computer business, right?"

"Well, having a Mac turn itself on at just the right moment sure seems to *me* like a funny coincidence. That's you."

He shook his head. "Have you looked at the power cord?"

I glanced over at it. It was not plugged in.

"Improbabilities I do," the Duck said. "Miracles I don't. Lucking onto the right database, that was me, all right. The rest—uh-uh."

"Cushlamachree," said Long-Drink McGonnigle, who had been eavesdropping—if that's not redundant. "Then how—"

"Beats me," the Duck said.

An idea occurred to me, so ridiculous I'd have rejected it out of hand if I'd been just a little soberer. Instead I held it up to the light and turned it to and fro. "Holy shit," I murmured.

"What?" the Drink asked.

"Drink," I said, and my own voice sounded odd in my ears, "who is the best hacker that ever took a drink in Callahan's bar?"

He looked down at the floor and thought for a minute. "Ever? Have to be Tom Flannery, I guess. He used to work for Xerox in Palo Alto before he moved east, didn't he?"

"Yeah. You happen to remember the date of his death, by any chance?"

"Hell, sure." The Drink looked up this time (according to Dr. W. H. Cosby, dates are stored in the air, above eye-level; names below) and thought some more. Suddenly his eyes opened so wide the wrinkles went away. "Christ in a garter belt! A dozen years ago tonight!"

"Almost to the hour," I agreed.

"So what?" the Duck asked.

"Drink," I said, "what did Tom die of?"

Long-Drink's eyes were like cue balls. "First friend I ever had that died of AIDS," he said hollowly.

The three of us looked at each other—and finished our drinks as one.

Δ   Δ   Δ

"I hope this ghost business won't keep you from coming back here," I said to the Duck the next time I had a moment to talk. Privately I was prepared to offer him a discount if necessary to keep him coming around. A place like mine needed a guy like him.

"I don't believe in ghosts," he said sourly.

"Neither do I," said Long-Drink, who had been deep in conversation with him. "That's why it's so scary."

One of the problems with being around the other side of the bar for a change is that I can't discreetly kick Long-Drink in the shin any more. I made a mental note to talk to him later: maybe we could agree on a facial expression to convey the same message. "Nothing to be scared of, Drink," I said hastily. "Whatever it was, it was good medicine. Nothing a man should give up a good tavern for."

"Relax, Mr. Subtle," the Duck said. "You couldn't keep me away from this place with rap music."

I brightened. "Pleased to hear it."

"That's part of why, right there," he said. "Most places I hang out, after a while they start to look at me funny, and pretty soon they ask me if I really have to leave so early."

"Why—," Long-Drink began . . . and across the room, Fast Eddie's right hand stopped playing. "—if you don't mind my asking, else?" he finished hastily.

"This Callahan gent," the Duck said. "I'd like to talk with him."

I didn't want to discourage him, but felt compelled to say, "I don't really think he'll be back. I mean, I don't know . . . but we're not expecting him."

"Maybe not," he agreed. "Then again, if *I* hang out here long enough, maybe he will."

"I can't argue with that," I said. "And I'll tell you the truth, I'd hang around *Hell* for a long while, for the chance of another conversation with Mike."

"I'd like to ask him a few things I've wondered about for a long time," he said. His voice sounded almost wistful, and— for the first and only time that night—and for only a second, at most—his face looked vulnerable.

I sent words on tiptoe. "You mean, 'Why am I so—'?"

" 'Why?' is good," he said, nodding. " 'How?' would be even better. 'Is there an on-off switch for the phenomenon?' would be best of all. I've satisfied myself that nobody alive today knows the answers to those questions—but if anybody does, it'd be a time traveler. They'd have to know a lot about probability. I pumped that Phee character for all I could get, but most of what he told me turned out to be bullshit. Your guy Mike sounds okay. I got nothing better to do. Maybe I'll stick around. As long as you don't mind."

"Oh, we like coincidence around here," Long-Drink assured him. "Why, Jake and I once worked in the same carnival, me runnin' the carousel and him on the Ferris wheel, for almost two years, and we never met until he showed up here."

"Of course, we moved in different circles," I said.

The Duck's eyes narrowed and his nostrils flared. "Why don't you both rotate on this?" he suggested, showing us a fingernail.

Jonathan, who had come up on us unnoticed, barked with involuntary laughter. "Talk about a spinning black hole!"

We all cracked up. Jonathan ordered straight Bushmill's and took a stool next to the Duck. "You know why the Soviets call them 'frozen stars' instead of black holes?" he asked the Duck. The Duck grinned and nodded, and they laughed together and exchanged a high five, the elderly scientist and the grouchy hobbit.

"Well, you're looking much more manic," the Duck said.

Jonathan nodded. "It's silly. I should be at peace. I keep thinking, well, now you've lost the great melodrama of your life, your grand tragedy. Now you're just a failure." He grimaced self-consciously and sipped whiskey. "Maybe you're right, Jake," he said to me. "Maybe I've become addicted to self-pity."

"Self-pity is an easy disease to cure," I said. "Try what I suggested earlier. Go do some good thing."

"Like what?"

"Hell, I don't know. Random acts of senseless kindness?" I felt another lightbulb form above my cranium. "Wait a half, how about this? How many other experienced medical researchers would you say there are walking around right now *who wonder why the SIV virus doesn't make African green monkeys sick?*"

His eyes glazed over. He stopped breathing for so long that I reached for the seltzer teat to startle him back into it, but as I got my thumb on the mojo he took in a deep breath, and let it out slowly. His shoulders lowered a half-inch—and got two inches wider.

"May I use your computer?" he asked, staring through me.

"Sure," I said.

He turned and looked at it for a moment. He took a step forward and then stopped and looked at it for another long moment. Then he took two more steps and hesitated again. He was looking at the plug, lying there a foot from the socket.

"Never mind," he said suddenly, and came back to his seat. "There's no hurry. I work better when I'm sober, anyway."

"Don't feel bad," Long-Drink told him. "Lots of people have that problem."

Jonathan finished his drink in a long slow gulp, and stared into the glass for a moment. "And besides," he went on, "there's something I've been meaning to ask you, Jake."

"Shoot," I said, and then winced.

So did he. "Excuse me a second." He got up and walked to the chalk line. People quieted down expectantly, and he held his empty glass high.

"To random acts of senseless kindness," he said in a loud clear voice, and eighty-sixed the glass. As it burst, he pulled his gun out of his pants, popped the clip out, worked the slide, and sent the gun after the glass.

What a merry sound it made, when it hit all that broken

glass! The flames flared, and a few of them turned a cheery green from burning Cosmoline.

An irregular rain of glasses applauded his toast—and then folks went back to their conversations.

Jonathan returned to his seat. "Now," he said briskly, "back when you were holding a shotgun on me, Jake, you said something that's been nagging at me more and more as the night wore on."

"What's that?"

"Maybe it stuck in my head because you used a polite word in the middle of cursing me. You said, 'I've got problems of my own, friend.' "

"So?"

"So what's *your* problem, friend?"

I blinked at him. Cure complete.

And as I opened my mouth to answer, Merry Moore drifted up to the bar, tacking against a breeze only she could feel. "Hey, Jake," she said in a voice only a little too loud, " 're's somethin' I been meanin' to ask, once things kinda quieted down—I just remembered."

I smiled. What a lucky man I was, to have friends like these. "Sure, Merry. Matter of fact, I was just about to—"

"Hey, Tommy," she called, ignoring me. "C'mere a minute."

Tommy Janssen came over and joined us.

She blinked around at us owlishly. "Now listen while I ask him this. Tommy, you know that story you told about Ish'sh . . . about Ish*'s* wedding, and the white man with the knife?"

"Sure," Tommy said.

She slapped the bartop. "What made you assume it was a white *man?*"

In the silence that followed, Tommy stared at her with no

expression at all for maybe ten seconds.

And then his face broke into a big grin. "Hey, everybody," he called out to the room at large, "Check this out: I did it *again* . . ."

5

The Duck

It was our second night in Mary's Place, about ten o'clock, and things were going pretty good. The fire was crackling in the hearth. The Fount was working well, making magic out of all natural ingredients. The booze flowed. More viscously, puns flowed.

Me, I had trouble in mind. But I had it so far down below the surface that not even my best friends caught me at it. Nobody wants to hear the bartender's troubles.

And it was a good place to be worried in. Good company in good spirits will get you through a lot. Fast Eddie was in rare form, playing what he called mindmelds—doing Bud Powell with his left hand while his right played Joplin, for example. Eddie at his worst is terrific: when he's hot, only a fool will fail to pay attention. The Tatum / Peterson combination was especially interesting.

Jonathan Crawford wasn't there that night; he'd promised to return frequently, but he had a hot lead to chase now, and would be too busy to drink for a while. There were about a dozen more people present than there had been the night before—Ben and Barbara, Stan and Joyce, Tina and Victor, Jim and Joan, a few others who hadn't been able to make Opening Night. But except for the Lucky Duck (who was wearing pants tonight), all of them qualified as Immediate Family. That is, people who had been present in Callahan's bar the night it was converted to a rapidly expanding plasma. Folks in a position to tell you, from personal knowledge, what a nuclear firestorm is like up close. Not that they do . . . tell many people, that is. Who'd believe them?

But the Duck seemed to. People had been telling him Callahan's Place stories all night, for the sheer joy of recalling them, at first—and either he believed every one of them, or the furry little bastard was damned if he'd give us the satisfaction of seeing how much he admired our skill as liars. I wondered which was true, after a while. From everything we'd learned about him the night before, extraordinary occurrences were utterly commonplace to him—but his pan was *so* dead, even beneath all that beard, that you had to wonder if it was costing him effort to keep it that way. Folks began to visibly attempt to blow his mind, to come up with a true story that would exceed his credulity limit. Then at one point—just as Long-Drink McGonnigle had finished telling him about Dink Fogerty, who for a short time could make a dart board *want darts,* the Duck suddenly counterattacked.

"You find that unusual?" he said. "Strike you as bizarre, does it?" His tone was negligent, but his voice was loud enough to draw eyes. (Odd, that voice of his. You couldn't call it beautiful, exactly, with that honking quality to it . . . but it was certainly commanding, almost mesmerizing, when he wanted it to be.) "You citizens think you know about weird, is that right? Watch this, turkeys!" He slid from his chair, strolled with lazy grace through the crowd to the television set, and punched it on. Without looking at the screen, he turned his back on it and returned to the bar, where he climbed back up into his chair with a nonchalance so massive that it translated as smug triumph.

Those of us who could not see the screen (most of us) were oddly wary of changing that status; as one, we looked to Fast Eddie, who could see the screen from his piano bench, for a report. He screwed up his face and studied the screen.

"Program crawl," he announced.

We understood what he meant. We just didn't understand what *it* meant. All cable TV companies reserve one channel for an endlessly scrolling list of which programs are scheduled on what channels for the next hour and a half, in half-hour blocks. So what? Eddie squinted at the programs listed for a few seconds, found nothing to report, then visibly lowered his gaze to see if there was anything strikingly weird in the advertising copy that crawled horizontally by below the program listings, and came up empty there too.

Then his eyes went back up to the program crawl . . . and grew very wide and round.

"*Ho*-ly . . . *shit,*" he said hoarsely, and checked his watch, and looked at the screen some more, and rubbed at his eyes with his hands, and so on until Long-Drink, the challenged party, lost patience and snapped, "What the hell *is* it, Ed?"

"It's now," Eddie croaked. He looked appealingly at Long-Drink and gave a little shake of his head. "*Right* now. I mean, now just started . . . *now.*"

Rooba rooba rooba.

We all understood Eddie perfectly. The program scrawl typically lists ninety minutes' worth of programming on forty-some channels, in half-hour increments—and an Iron Law of the Universe states that if you access the program scrawl one thousand times at random, eight hundred and seventy-one times it will have just *finished* the present half-hour period, forcing you to wait the maximum possible amount of time for the information you seek. An additional hundred and twenty-seven times, you'll be trying to find out what's going to start in the *next* half-hour slot, so *that* block will have just finished. And twice, the computer program that generates the scrawl will have hung, so that there's *no* information and you can't even *guess* how long you'll have to wait. Everybody knows this, and for some reason nobody ever talks about it. (Sometimes I think of it as the Single Overlooked Blunder in an otherwise convincing scam universe. You know that Heinlein story, "They," where the guy's world seems perfectly ordinary and plausible . . . until one rainy day there's a screwup in the Continuity Department, and one of his windows displays sunshine? You don't want to tug too hard at an anomaly like that: your universe could unravel like a cheap sock.) You can set your watch by it; you can watch your set by it; it never fails—unless you're attempting to demonstrate the phenomenon to an unbeliever.

Until now. Either Eddie was lying, or the Duck had—right before our very eyes—accessed the program scrawl just as it began to display the current listings. The most consistent example of Finagle's Law in the universe lay in ruins. It was almost enough to make me wonder what was on TV now.

"Jesus Christ and His Tympani Five," the Drink exclaimed. And then things got *weirder,* real fast.

△   △   △

First, fire—
Wanting to dramatically express his extreme astonishment, Long-Drink attempted a histrionic gesture he'd seen but never tried before: he clapped his hands to his bosom, one across the other, like a silent-movie heroine, while rolling his eyes at

the sky. (Being Irish, he already rolled his r's.) His right palm chanced to reach his chest first. There it encountered a lump in his shirt pocket: the little plastic film-can of strike-anywhere matches he likes to light on his thumbnail, and all too often on his fly. The container happened to be full to capacity with matches. A split-second after his right palm struck it, his left palm slapped against the back of his right hand. Perhaps some unlikely harmonic resonance occurred. The entire canister-full of matches went up, with more than enough force to blow off the lid and send a fiery column of vigorously flaring wooden matchsticks high into the air, like Munchkin fireworks. Well it was for the Drink that he had tilted his head back as part of the gesture—the entire rising barrage missed his chin and sailed high in the air, spreading like a fountain of flame. If he'd been looking down, he'd have lost his left eye. As it was, only *one* of the forty-odd burning matches fell back onto his head and set his hair on fire.

Which made it unanimous. There were forty-odd people in the room, kind of clustered near the bar, and not one of us had our hair set on fire by any more—or any less—than a single match. It looked for a second as if two matches were going to land on Tommy Janssen, but he made a wild attempt to bat them away from him and managed to knock one of them high over the TV set so that Fast Eddie wouldn't be left out. The room began to fill with the dreadful smell of burning hair. And the sound of forty-odd reluctant Apostles, beginning to speak in tongues . . .

Then, water—

Well, beer. Luckily we are all experienced drunks: those who held stronger beverages had presence of mind enough not to use them, or someone might have been badly burned. But the alcohol content of beer is low enough to permit its use as an emergency fire extinguisher. Lucky us!—there was precisely enough beer on the loose in the room to saturate every single head. Tom Hauptman and I got each other. Since Fast Eddie had a straight Bushmill's in his hand, three or four helpful souls sent their dregs his way; all four missed and soaked the TV, which sparked and died, adding its portion to the smoke rising for the rafters. Eddie, meanwhile, solved his own problem: it was not his hair but his favorite cabby's cap that was burning; he tore it off and trampled it in the sawdust.

Then, ice—

—as we all turned as one to glare at the Duck.

He pooched out his lower lip with his tongue, and nodded twice. "Hell," he said contentedly, "you probably think *that* was weird."

Those holding drinks stronger than beer now reached a consensus that their time, too, had come; the Duck's range and bearing were taken; arms cocked—

Suddenly the Duck was on his feet, eyes flashing. "Would you guys like to *see* something—" He paused, tossed his aviator's scarf back over his shoulder, thrust out his beard, and grinned broadly. "—*really* weird?"

Consensus changed; there were much more practical things to do with hard liquor. "Don't see why." "Not me." "No, thanks Duckster, maybe later, eh?" "What're you drinking, Duck?" "Man quacks me up." "Why do they call him the Lucky Duck, anyway?"

And folks sort of went back about their business. One of the gods, passing unnoticed among us, had suddenly taken on his Aspect and raised up his Attribute—on a throat-clearing level—and it was time to make the place seem agreeable and let him enjoy his beer.

Δ   Δ   Δ

The Duck turned to me, indicated his empty glass and held up one finger. I drew him another Rickard's, and waved my hand over it. He nodded thanks, once. "To competition," he said softly, and tossed the empty glass negligently over his shoulder. We both ignored it. "Maybe I can't outpun the big sawbones over there," he said, nodding toward Doc Webster, "but I can outweird all of you rummies put together, any day."

There was a distant "Ouch!" and then a small musical crash as the empty glass finally arrived, by circuitous means no doubt, in the fireplace.

"Mind if I ask a snoopy question or two?" I asked.

He shrugged. "Ask. If you stumble into any sensitive areas, I'll rip your eyelids off to clue you."

"You been this way from in front?"

His answer told me that he had caught the obscure Lord Buckley reference. "Why—you gonna straighten my bent frame?"

I shook my head. "Wouldn't know how. I just figured that if it came on any time *after* you were born, where and when would be a clue."

"Astute. Naturally, such a thing would never have occurred to *me*. But as it happens, I have been the Lucky Duck ever since my last stroke of unmitigated rotten luck: being born. Mom always said my father was the same way."

"You never knew your Dad?"

"I tried hard, but his steadfast absence defeated me. That and Mom's reticence. About all I know about him is that he had red hair, his first name was Eric, and he must have been a tough guy—she never called him anything but Feared Eric, or 'that big red son of a fairy,' and she doesn't like to talk about him." He belched spectacularly. "I'm just guessing the red hair because she's Irish—for all I know he was an Apache. Or a Martian."

I made a long arm and punched myself up a Blessing, Black Bush in Celebes Kalossi. It gave me time to think. Difficult to try and help such a thorny little guy. Did he even want any help?

"Gotta be a strain on a guy," I said tentatively.

He shrugged.

"Suppose I *could* straighten that metaphorical bent frame," I said. "Hypothetically . . . would you want me to?"

"Make me a normal human being? Would *you* want to be one?"

"I'm serious."

"Doubtless many would agree with you," he said acidly, and then relented. "Oh, all right. I admit it's a good question. But how would I know? I have nothing to compare my life to." He shook his head. "I don't know, sometimes I think life would be a lot simpler if odds *didn't* get even odder around me. The only thing I can say for it—and against it—is that the luck is never totally good or totally bad. Just weird. Sometimes I think I've got a guardian idiot."

I cracked up. "You too? I've had that feeling all my life. I never heard anybody else call it that. A guardian idiot: a little invisible spirit just behind my shoulder, looking out for me . . . only he's an imbecile." I laughed so hard I nearly spilled whiskey. Doc Webster noticed that, and stared; when I didn't invite him in on the joke with my eyes he turned away and went back to swapping puns with Willard.

The Duck nodded. "But a lucky imbecile. Somehow the net effect is usually that things more or less cancel out. Like, if you're sitting next to me and you win a million bucks in the lottery, don't worry about it: something will happen and you'll be right back where you started before you know it. Except for any wear and tear it might put on your nerves to win a million dollars and lose it in the same day."

It must have been hard for him to keep a friend. No wonder he was so sour.

"No," the hairy little man said, "taking it all in all, I don't think I'd want to *lose* my . . . whatever it is I've got. I mean, obviously my life is perfect: it produced *me*. But like I said last night, if I ever meet that Mike Callahan of yours, I'd sure like to ask him whether or not there's some way to put an off-switch on the bastard. Or even just a rheostat. As I age, I weary of being fantastic. Just about the only thing I've never tried is boredom. People seem to work so hard to get it, I figure it must be worth trying."

"I enjoy having you in my place, Ernie," I said, thankful that I remembered at least half of the birth-name he'd given us last night. "I got a feeling you belong here. But in all honesty I have to tell you, I wouldn't hold my breath waiting for Mike to show up."

He grimaced. "Christ, that's a break. I was bracing myself to do mouth-to-mouth on you if you tried it. Look, you just opened this joint. I'll give it a week or two; maybe this Callahan will show up. If not—" He shrugged. "There are worse places to have a beer." He finished his glass, and tossed it negligently over his shoulder. I started to say something, and broke off as he locked eyes with me. We kept looking at each other, while behind him musical pandemonium broke out, thuds and crashes and tinkles and shouts and splashes and cries of dismay and people lurching back and forth. I don't think I could tell you any more about it if I'd seen it happen. All I know is, as the commotion was ending, the Duck stuck out both his hands, and his empty glass—two-thirds full now—dropped into them from above like a mortar round. He caught it well: some beer escaped, but he caught half as it fell again, and the rest impacted squarely on the bar-rag that lay curled up before me.

He took a sip. "Half Dos Equis and half Cooper's," he announced.

Behind him there was brief silence . . . and then sustained applause. "Damndest thing I ever—" "—see the way that—"

"—and I tried to—just as you—" "—have believed it if I hadn't seen it with my—" "—and then it just—" "—goddam work of *art!*"

The Duck turned around and acknowledged their applause with an inclination of the head.

"Mister," Long-Drink McGonnigle said, "if you can teach *me* that trick . . ."

The Duck smiled and turned back to me.

"See what I mean?" he said. "Some places that'll get you assaulted. These guys appreciate beauty. A round for the house, barkeep."

The applause redoubled.

I helped Tom Hauptman pass out fresh drinks until he had it under control, then went back to the Duck again.

"Anything in particular seem to trigger it?" I asked him. "Or does it just happen all the time at random?"

He shrugged. "Sometimes when I'm nervous. Out of sorts, like."

"Threatened? A defense mechanism?"

He glared at me as though I'd just said something truly stupid, but what he said was, "Maybe." He didn't seem crazy about the implication. The true macho man doesn't *need* defense mechanisms.

No wonder he'd concentrated so hard on developing his *offense* mechanisms . . .

I didn't seem to be getting anywhere here. He'd been thinking about this a lot longer than I had. I decided the thing to do with the Lucky Duck was to simply accept him as he was and not worry about it. That was what Mike Callahan would have done. "Well, look on the bright side: if it is a defense mechanism, you won't need it here. This is the only bunch of rummies I know that never has a fistfight."

"You mean, 'hardly ever.' "

I shook my head. "Nope. Never."

He shook his own head. "No shit. You people were weird before I even got here."

"You got that right. Hanging out together got us blown up by an atom bomb, once, and we're still doing it." That reminded me of something, all of a sudden. "Will you excuse me for a minute, Duck? I just reminded myself of something I meant to ask the gang last night, and forgot. It's kind of important."

"What, end this riveting discussion? I'll have to kill myself."

"Thanks."

Δ   Δ   Δ

Fast Eddie was just hemstitching the final chorus of "In the Evenin' When the Sun Goes Down," with his left hand as Mulgrew Miller and his right as Ray Charles, to enthusiastic applause. When he took a break to shake the snake, I came around the bar and went to the chalk line. I took my coffee mug with me, and whistled for general attention.

"There's something we've got to get straight, folks," I said.

"Why not leave it bent?" Long-Drink asked reasonably.

I had a question for that particular subset of humanity, one that could not be asked with strangers present. So I had to bring it up now. Sooner or later, strangers would start walking in the door and it would be too late.

"Because it's too important, Drink," I told him. "It's the root."

"I think he's talking about his dick," Margie Shorter said in a stage whisper, and several people giggled.

"I'll discuss straightening that with you later if you like, Marge," I said, and several of the gigglers told an imaginary horse to whoa. "Right now," I went on doggedly, "I'm talking about my mandate, not my manhood."

"Mandate?" the Drink said. "What's mandatory around here, except having fun and makin' toasts?"

"Precisely my question," I said.

That finished quelling the gigglers. "How do you mean that, Jake?" Doc Webster asked. "You feel a need to make some new rules?"

"Not exactly," I said. "I just want a clear statement of what it is we're all here for."

The McGonnigle looked at me as if I'd gone mad. *"Drinking,"* he said, as one explaining the obvious to a child.

Fast Eddie had returned from his errand. "Being merry," he said in the same manner as Long-Drink.

"Sharing," Maureen said.

"Those are good things to do," I agreed, "and if that's what we all say we're here for . . . well, we could do a lot worse. But everyone in this room—except you, Duck—was standing within earshot the night I first proposed opening this joint and agreed to run it. Anybody here remember why? Anybody recall what we *said* it was gonna be for, that night?"

Light was dawning all around.

"We were one that night. I know a lot of time has passed since—I don't know about you, but I remember it real good. We were one, in telepathic communion . . . and not for the first time, either. So when it was over we hurt. That's why everybody hurts—because they're not telepathic. And it's a lot worse when you know what you're missing. So we all decided that if we could do it twice with the help of Mike Callahan and the McDonald brothers, maybe in twenty years or so of trying we could learn to do it for ourselves. We *knew* the potential was there. And we agreed it was worth trying. This place was intended from the very beginning as a workshop, a school in getting telepathic."

Thoughtful silence.

"We've all kind of drifted apart some in the last year or two," I said. "Nobody's fault; none of us had a home big enough to hold all of us, that's all. Now we do. Have we drifted so far away from that night in the woods that we no longer want to try and get telepathic again? Or not? Are we content at this point to simply drink and be merry and share? That's all I want to know, and I want to be clear on it. Me, I'll go either way; whatever we decide. Take your time."

Long thoughtful silence.

"Do you have any specific ideas on how to go about getting telepathic, Jake?" Tom Hauptman asked, handing me a mug of Blessing.

"Same plan I suggested that night," I said. "Love each other as hard as we can, and see what happens. And in the meantime, drink and be merry and share, to pass the time. Stick with what's worked for us in the past, in other words. I haven't got any Six-Step Program; I don't want to turn the place into a séance or an encounter session. I just want to know if it's all going somewhere . . . or if it's all right here."

I sipped Irish coffee and waited.

The Duck was so interested he forgot to look bored. He signaled Tom Hauptman for a new drink.

"I remember that night," Long-Drink McGonnigle said softly.

"I've never forgotten that night," Isham Latimer murmured, and hugged his wife Tanya to his side.

"I'll remember zat night in my grafe," Ralph von Wau Wau said.

"Like you said that night, Jake," Noah said, "maybe it'll take us twenty years to figure out how to do that again . . . but I got twenty years I'm not using." A couple of people nodded.

"Being all together like that," Doc Webster rumbled, "being *whole* for once . . ." He shook his big head. "Let me put it this way: I found a nuclear explosion at arm's length to be a less interesting experience. No: I found *surviving* a nuclear explosion at arm's length less interesting. I don't know about the rest of you monkeys, but ... no, that's the point: I *do* know about the rest of you monkeys. That's what we're all here for, all right."

And he spun on his heel, as gracefully as someone who weighed less than four hundred pounds, bellowed, *"To us!"* and fired the first shot of what became a thundering cannonade of glasses and coffee mugs into the fireplace. The cheer was as loud as the explosion, in a different octave but in the same key.

I emptied my own mug quickly. I was smiling as I lobbed it. Not one of my clientele had needed to be told that this once, for this toast, I didn't mind them throwing mugs as well as glasses—that it was more important that every one of us be in on the toast. Maybe the task we had set ourselves *would* take us twenty years ... but we had already made a start.

Then I thought of something, and glanced down the bar. Sure enough, there was one customer in the whole house who still had a drink in his hand.

"Hey Duck," I called, not stridently but loudly enough to be heard over the general celebration. At once it dropped several decibels.

The Duck fixed an insouciant eye on me. "Yah."

"You in?"

He did not answer right away. He looked slowly around the room, meeting pair after pair of eyes. Then he looked down into his drink—a shotglass of Cherry Heering: who else would order such a thing after drinking beer?—for a minute, and returned that direct, piercing gaze of his to me. "Let me get back to you," he said.

I nodded. I knew the little flash of irritation I felt was unreasonable—but I felt it nonetheless. "No hurry."

He caught me at it. "I know. How could anyone turn down an offer to get married to a couple of dozen people he'd only met the night before? The ungrateful rat."

I started to protest that I wasn't annoyed at all—and swallowed the words. Why would anyone want to get telepathic with a liar?

"You're right," I said. "It was stupid to ask, if I wasn't prepared to hear an honest answer. *I* think we're a pretty special bunch of human beings—but I've known us for years, been through a lot with us."

"And since you *know* how terrific you all are," he said, "you have no doubt in your mind that before long, either I will realize that, or I'm so much of a jerk you wouldn't want me around anyway. So we have no problem."

I had to grin. "Nope. I guess we don't."

"The heck we don't," Tom Hauptman said in genuine alarm from farther down the bar. "We're out of beer."

$$\triangle \qquad \triangle \qquad \triangle$$

Rooba rooba rooba. Consternation and astonishment competed for dominance. I went with denial. "Bullshit," I cried, and turned to look.

Tom was holding down all six draft taps. Not a drop was flowing. "Tap city," he said hollowly.

I forgave him; he was under stress. And so was I. "How is that *possible*—?" I began, and cut myself off when I heard my voice come out sounding like a Pekingese in a snit. I tried again. "There is no way in hell this many people could have drunk six barrels dry in a night and a half. Not even *these* people." This time my voice was a little better, more like a beagle in a snit. "We'd be on the floor."

"We *are* on the floor," the Duck pointed out.

Rooba rooba rooba—

Could that thief of a distributor have sold me kegs that weren't full? No, I'd hauled them in the door myself, and my lower back was certain they'd been full at the time. A leak that massive would have left the place smelling like a brewery. "Well, there's only one sensible thing to do," I said. "Have a drink on the strength of it. Reverend, fix me a cup of Geb, will you?—and double up on the Black Bush."

"Sure thing, Jake," Tom said, and shortly handed me another mug of Geb Keyserlingck's magic brew from Daintree, Oz. I gave Tom some pocket change to toss in the Cough Drop for me, and took a deep gulp—it was delicious—and then I nearly choked. "Jesus, Tom, you forgot the whiskey!"

"The hell you say," the ex-minister said, shocked enough to use profanity this time. Our eyes met and we exchanged a meaningful glance. "Oh my golly-gosh," he said slowly.

He unlocked the front panel of the Fount of All Coffee and swung it open. Sure enough, the Bushmill's bottle inside was empty. As we stared at it, the little red pilot light on the panel that warned of that very condition lighted for the first time. I looked to the row of replacement bottles waiting for their own turn beside the machine, and was only slightly startled to find them empty as well. So was every non-opaque bottle on the shelf above the cash register. Somehow I didn't need to check the opaque ones to be certain they were equally dry on the inside.

Not *every* glass and container in the room was empty. Just the ones with alcohol in them.

Rooba rooba ROOBA ROOBA—

"AARGH!" the Duck exclaimed, and as we turned to look he yanked both hands away from his shotglass. It hung in mid-air, like Wile E. Coyote ten feet past the edge of the cliff, for long enough that I could see the tumbler was bone-dry, somehow emptied *while he'd held it in his hands;* then it fell, hit his foot, skittered across the floor at high speed, rolled up Merry Moore's leg and under her skirt, and committed a mischief upon her. She made the same sound the Duck had, in a higher octave, and . . . expelled the glass, somehow. It bounced high off the floor, once, and as it descended, the Duck tugged his waistbands an inch or two away from his belly with an air of weary resignation. *Thop.* The shotglass landed squarely in his basket. He flinched slightly, recovered, and let go of his various pants. *Snap.* "Should have known better," he said sourly. "My own fault."

Silence, as glutinous as old peanut butter . . .

"There's a few more cases of juice outside in the van," Tom Hauptman suggested tentatively.

"If it's still there," I said, "it's going to stay there until I figure out what happened to the last load. Booze costs money; I can't go pissing it away."

Nobody reacted to the lame joke. Good friends; they knew when not to hear you.

"Duck," I said, "could all this be something to do with you?"

"Possible," he admitted, "but I can't figure out the mechanism. Maybe there's some uncertainty in the probabilities of how fast alcohol evaporates . . . no, it would have happened before now. I think. You'd better hope it *is* me; if it is, your hooch will probably be back shortly. But somehow I don't think so. This doesn't *feel* like me."

I had a decision to make. Noah Gonzalez always carried a flask in a zipped-up inside pocket of his coat, because he strongly preferred his own homemade white lightning to any other sauce. Since he'd always had the idea that might offend Mike Callahan, he'd always made an elaborate point of concealing the flask from Mike, sneaking his hooch into glasses of ginger ale when he thought Mike wasn't looking. No one had ever ratted on him, because everyone knew perfectly well that Mike knew about the flask and didn't want to embarrass Noah by mentioning it. I wanted to know if that flask—which had been zipped away safely for most of the night—was as empty as all the rest of the hooch containers in the house. If it was not, we were dealing with a garden-variety practical joker here—and my money was, reluctantly, on the Duck. If the flask was empty, then we were up against something more . . . ominous. But now that *I* was the innkeeper, I was supposed to have forgotten that I ever knew about the flask. Did I want to know the level in Noah's tank badly enough to risk embarrassing him?

No. I would presume it empty unless and until he offered me a drink. Now: what did assuming that tell me?

Well, it probably wasn't a plague of wino flies.

"I don't know about you, but I'm getting pissed *off*," Doc Webster growled, belatedly playing off my feeble pun. "Whoever this son of a mother is, he's certainly struck right at the heart of this place. Or the liver, anyway."

"I was just about ta quench my toist," Eddie said darkly. "I been blowin' my ass off tonight." Playing piano is thirsty work.

"No booze, and all of a sudden I don't feel very goddam merry," Tommy Janssen snarled. "All that leaves is sharing . . . and trying to read the mind of the bastard that thought this up. Gimme a . . . cup of coffee, Jake."

I passed one over, and sipped at my own. Come on, neurons!

Trying to defuse the tension a little, Long-Drink McGonnigle put on a heavy Irish brogue. "If I get my hands on the spalpeen, the Dullahan will call at his door this night," he said.

"Mike's gone," Fast Eddie said.

"Not Callahan, Eddie: the Dullahan," the Drink said patiently. "Spelled D-u-b-h-l-a-c-h-a-n—'Dullahan.' Gaelic for 'dark sullen person'—but it refers to the grim, headless lad who drives the Costa Bower, the Death Coach. It arrives at midnight as an omen that someone in the house will die shortly. I'm surprised at you: you've been hanging out in an Irish bar since Callahan had hair; you'd think by now you'd have learned a little something about *Jesus Christ!*"

People jumped a little, partly because of the sudden volume of the last two words and partly because I had shouted them in chorus with him. Long-Drink and I stared at each other, thunderstruck. We had figured it out at the same instant.

"Well," Eddie said diffidently, "I *do* know a little somet'in about *Him* . . ."

I waved at him absently, too busy to explain. My nostrils flared, and I saw Long-Drink's do likewise. The solution to the mystery of the disappearing booze was right over our noses. And it was bad news.

"But I hoid He toined water inta wine—not wine inta air."

Long-Drink and I exchanged a meaningful glance. It was terribly important that we not fuck this up. The very survival of Mary's Place was at stake. The Drink looked as worried as I felt. And at any moment someone else might twig, and blurt something out. If that happened, just about all the hopes I had left in my life were lost, maybe for good. I thought so fast and hard I felt my scalp get warm.

Bingo! I had one effective on my tac roster who might just have the right combination of special talents. It was ironic that just about all those special talents would probably have struck most people as liabilities—right now, they were worth gold. Maybe literally . . .

Tanya Latimer is visually challenged—or as she puts it, blind. (She says euphemisms are for the differently brained.) So maybe I could safely assume both a better-than-average sense of smell, and experience in working without visual cues. Furthermore, she is an ex-cop . . . which is how she got blinded, which is another story, except that it wasn't her fault. So I could be reasonably sure that she would be both fairly handy in a crunch—at least a close-in kind of crunch—and fairly quick on the uptake.

The trick was to find a way to cue her. Fortunately, my late Uncle Al was a Gold Shield in the NYPD for several decades.

"Sister Tee," I said—quietly, but as compellingly as I could—"hear me good, and chill. Ten-thirteen."

She rummaged casually in her purse for kleenex with both hands, took some out with her left hand. "Tell it," she said softly.

"Don't name it, but you know the thing they do rocks and ice and boo and the legal in?"

"Yah." Honk! She took a deep breath through her nose, the way you do after you blow your nose, to check results. Most natural thing in the world.

"The legal at twelve o'clock . . . *he's wrong.*"

"I hear that." She balled up the kleenex and fumbled for another with the hand that was still inside the purse. "What's my play?"

"Got your jewelry?"

"I hadda go through Long Island to get here, didn't I?"

"Don't miss," I told her.

She smiled lazily. "When?"

"When I get you his twenty."

She nodded, still smiling. Most of the gang were staring at us in puzzlement—but bless 'em, nobody demanded an explanation. Tanya's husband Isham, who was getting maybe one word in three, understood that smile, at least, and began to be visibly alarmed. It is rare to see Ish visibly alarmed. He is built on the scale of Mike Tyson, and seems quite terrifying to the stranger until he opens his mouth and this Radar O'Reilly voice comes out. Even then, people rarely mess with him. In consequence of which, he knows almost nothing about fighting. His wife's smile told him as plain as print that she planned to do something drastic to someone, soon, and he wasn't a hundred percent sure that it wasn't him. He'd have paled if he'd been equipped for it.

Which meant there was no time to lose.

"Hey, *Naggeneen,*" I hollered, "your father was a Firbolg, and your mother was a fairy!"

A screech of rage came from the rafters above our heads. "*It's a damnable libel!* The man was an honest respectable cluricaune, just like meself!"

We all stared upward. Everyone but Long-Drink and Tanya and I was startled to see a withered little old man, three feet tall, perched in the crotch of a rafter. He wore a crimson coat with forked tails, a tall cap in a state of sublime disrepair, a leather apron, pale-blue stockings, and glossy black high-heel shoes with silver buckles, nearly all of this obscured by a great cascade of snowy white beard which made his angry cheeks seem even redder. He was smoking a pipe like a white check-mark, and at the moment the bowl was glowing nearly as brightly as his bloodshot eyes. But redder than coat or cheeks or eyes or pipe-bowl put together was his lordly nose. He was toweringly drunk, shaking his fist at me with such force that he was near to toppling from his perch. He kept trying to get a grip with his other hand, but no matter how he flailed, he couldn't seem to *find* anything with it, and he couldn't spare attention from shouting at me.

"Come on up beside me and say that, ya scut, if you're man enough!" he thundered. "Ya whey-faced ridiculous git of a nearsighted merrow and some kind of perverted eel, I'll use yer elongated spine for a homemade accordion! Come, and I'll pull that preposterous beard o' yours out of yer mouth by the roots, hair by hair! I'll put yez to bed with a mattock, I will! An' ya take to yer heels like a sensible coward, I'll fill up yer household with spiders and snakes! Well, what's it to be?"

Four or five seconds of extremely total silence ensued. I used them trying to think of a good way to set things up for Tanya.

But it was Long-Drink who solved the problem. Actually, the solution suggested itself. The Drink and I both knew exactly what the reaction of the rest of the gang at Mary's Place to this apparition was going to be; we could both predict almost word for word what someone was going to say, any second now. So Long-Drink said it first.

"Oh, is *that* all it is? A leprechaun?"

The little old gent let out a shriek of inarticulate rage, thrust his pipe between his teeth, and leaped tipsily from his perch, aiming for Long-Drink's head.

Halfway there, in mid-air, with every eye on him, he disappeared—

—vanished, dwindled to a wispy contrail of smoke—

—and Long-Drink began doing an imitation of the villain in the last act of an Invisible Man movie, snapping his head from side to side and making a coughing sound and fanning air—

"*Now,* Tanya—," I said.

6

The Cluricaune

But she was already in motion. Tanya's not awful fast, but she's got a whole lot of quick. She had her jewelry—two bracelets of a ferrous nature, joined by a small but sturdy chain—already in her left hand; as her right closed and held on empty air a foot from Long-Drink, she fumbled briefly and closed one of the cuffs around a column of equally empty air, only inches from the Drink's throat. She shifted her grip to that air, let go with her right hand, and grabbed some more air, on the other side of Long-Drink's neck. With a grunt of effort, she bent it away from him and around in an arc, into the embrace of the second cuff. *"Cushlamachree,"* the little old man's voice roared. Both cuffs promptly plunged toward the floor as if heavily weighted—and then rose skyward like a rocket, spraying sparks and smoke, lifting Tanya a few inches off the ground for a moment. She hung on like a summer cold, dangling from the apex of a V made of handcuff chain, her heels off the floor, a rain of Gaelic curses showering on her head. I was impressed by the strength of our diminutive antagonist. The reason Tanya's not awful fast is that if she ever took it into her mind to turn pro, they'd class her as a middleweight at least, possibly a light heavy. Gorgeous woman.

As I yelled, "Get her!" Isham was moving. A little large for a heavyweight, he was short on quick but long on fast; he reached his wife in moments and added his weight to hers, while trying to climb up her and get a grip between her hands on the chain. Doc Webster arrived just then, freeing Ish to go up for the jumpshot. Between them they managed to wrestle the astonishingly lively pair of handcuffs back to about chest level—whereupon the little old bearded fellow reappeared within the iron bracelets, finished the obscenity he was in the middle of, and spat with terrible accuracy in Ish's eye.

"Don't, honey," Ish said quickly, "let him live."

Tanya nodded and kept her deathgrip on the cuffs.

"God damn," Ish said, wiping his eye and looking the little man up and down, "he's so ugly his nails ain't got cuticles."

She nodded. "Somehow I sensed it," she said.

The little man turned into a large werewolf.

Most of us jumped back a foot or two. The werewolf was still cuffed—but his *hind* limbs looked dangerous now, and he was snarling and slavering and seven feet tall and generally presented an intimidating aspect, one which spoke directly to the hindbrain. Ish and the Doc, being larger and massier than most, only traveled backward six inches or less apiece—but Ish did lose his grip on the handcuffs, which promptly tried to head for the rafters again, werewolf and all—

But Tanya, of course, was not intimidated in the least . . . and in less than a second, Isham had regained his hold.

The moment the werewolf realized that it wasn't working, he gave up, returned to chest level, and became a drunken little old man with a white beard again, sitting tailor fashion on air with his hands spread out before him. There wasn't room for two more fists the size of Doc Webster's on that handcuff chain, so the Doc settled for a wraparound grip on a coattail.

The ex-wolf was still snarling. "*Blind* as a bat, in the bargain, bedad! It's dishonest and cowardly!" He blinked blearily at her. "Jazus, yer lucky: ya don't know yer ugly, ya corpulent sow."

"I gotta give you points," Tanya said calmly, not even breathing hard. "You're the first guy I ever cuffed that didn't call me a nigger, not once. The very first. That's nice—isn't that nice, Isham?"

"The Irish, my dear," the old boy said icily, "are the blacks of the world—and we don't emulate the oppressor. I limit meself to observin' what anyone has to admit: you're unlovely, unkind, and as heavy as lead!"

His anger had the massive dignity and rolling majesty that only the magnificently drunk can achieve. His voice was a little like the Duck's: you couldn't call it pretty, exactly, but it held your attention somehow. It should have sounded ugly, but it didn't, if that makes any sense. Somehow he kept that longstem pipe clenched in his teeth as he talked, without losing any enunciation at all. From behind the bar, I could smell his breath. It smelled like every drop of alcohol I had thought I owned, earlier in the evening. The wonder was his pipe didn't set it alight.

"Damn, little fella," Isham said, too bemused to be angry at the slurs on his beloved, "who'd you *come* here with?"

"Nobody, yet," the munchkin menace snapped, "and bedad, by the looks of your wife here, it's sure to be some little while if it's left up to me! Bondage, is it, with the handcuffs and all?

Small wonder you carry these plague-take-it things on your person, ya batface—that must be what got you a husband atall! Sure, for you to be callin' *me* ugly is just like the pot tellin' kettles they're Afro-American. Cease and unhand me, ya chocolate moose, or I'll raise up a spell that'll give yez the root canal every Thanksgivin' from now till you give up an' cut yer own throat!"

Then all at once, with the mercurial changeability of the magnificently smashed, he forgot he was angry at her. "You know," he said conversationally, "it's a long time indeed I been wonderin' why your own folk ever gave up so gorgeous a name as The Colored—I don't understand it, be dipped if I do. Now what in the name of old Cu Chullain's cummerbund ever possessed yez to call yerselves Black—when yer *not,* and the word stands for everythin' scary and evil there is? I traveled the world in me youth, and I noticed yez mocha, mahogany, chestnut and cocoa . . . ochre and umber and amber and gold . . ." His eyes were literally twinkling, as if someone had focused a baby spot on them. " . . . coffee with cream, coffee with milk, coffee with nothin' but Tullamore Dew . . . amber and anatase, russet and chocolate . . . both the siennas, the burnt and the raw, hazel and sepia, several more . . . an' never a black man or woman I saw. Most perishin' colorful people on earth, and 'black' is the word for the *absence* of color! Go cobble a new pair o' shoes from the hide of the darkest of darkies in Africa: see if they'll let yez be wearin' them shoes to a wake—by old Balor's bumbershoot, what made yez claim yez a name ya can't wear, even on the *outside?* The Black Irish, now: *there*'s a people that's *black,* have yez got any insights to share on the matter?" Whereupon he belched with shattering force, crossed his twinkling eyes, winked the one that was now facing Tanya . . . then slowly winked the other as well, and passed out.

The silence was refreshing.

• • •

He remained in mid-air, on his back, breathing noisily. His elongated white pipe—which, thank God, had gone out—had slipped at last from his teeth. It hovered below him, about a foot from the floor. As he breathed, it stirred gently in the air, as though it were attached to the underside of an invisible waterbed.

"Tanya, Ish, Doc," I barked, "hang on for dear life—all three of you, every second! He could be faking." The sense of relief was overwhelming; I needed a moment to get my breath. All three of the little man's captors set their grips and fixed their resolves.

"Voice on him like a model airplane," Doc Webster said finally, shaking his big head. "And yet somehow it'd be kinda pleasant to listen to—if there wasn't so much of it. So that's a leprechaun, huh, Jake? I forget what the deal is now: we're supposed to not take our eyes off him, or something?"

"Don't be silly, Doc," Noah Gonzalez said. "How could you trap him with your eyes when he has the power to turn invisible? It's the cuffs that'll hold him, if anything will."

"Is it true he knows where to find some Acupulco Gold?" Tommy Janssen asked excitedly. "The famous pot at the end of the rainbow?"

"Aw, rot at the end of the painbow—that's an old wives' tale," Shorty Steinitz said.

"What's wrong with old wives?" Maureen Hooker asked dangerously.

"Sorry, troops," I said hoarsely. I tried to clear my throat, but I didn't seem to have my E-meter. *Get thee behind me, Thetan!* "I'm sorry to say he's *not* a leprechaun. It's much worse than that. He's a *cluricaune.* Leprechauns make shoes."

Brief silence.

"What do cluricaunes do?" Doc Webster asked.

"Drink."

He paled. "Oh, shit."

"Hip-deep," I agreed.

"A cluricaune," Long-Drink said darkly, "is a walking thirst."

"A walkin' toist?" Fast Eddie exclaimed. "Cripes, Jake—"

"Take a good look, folks: that's the finish of Mary's Place, right there in handcuffs," I told them all. Tanya, Isham and the Doc all redoubled their grip. "Unlike many of the Little Folk, a cluricaune will attach himself to a specific *place,* rather than to a family or clan. And what he *does* to that place is to drink it dry as an Iranian cabinet meeting—no matter what God or man may do or try to do to stop him. Even a Russian would call him a black hole. A cluricaune can suck booze through a stone jug. He can smell sauce in a cesspool. He'll eat fuming Drano if you pour in a few drops of vinegar. I bet you not one purse in this room has any nail polish remover left in it right now."

The cluricaune began to snore—loudly, and fairly disgustingly. He was not a pretty drunk.

An extrapolation suddenly occurred to me. "In fact, I am the only bartender in the world prepared to bet cash that not one of his customers needs to pee."

Rooba rooba rooba—

"I thought I knew every con there was," Willard Hooker said, "but a cluricaune is a new one on me."

"What the hell is he doing in America?" Mary Kay asked. "I thought the . . . uh, the Little People . . . all stayed in Ireland. Something about the Old Sod—"

"Why would they all *want* to be sodomized?" Gentleman John Kilian wondered. "They're not British."

"It's a good question," I conceded. "I've heard of a few of the old Daoine Sidh leaving Ireland—but mostly pookas, and once in a long while a Fir Darrig. It makes *least* sense for a cluricaune. Say you loved coffee more than life itself:

what would it take to make you move away from the foot of the Blue Mountains of Jamaica? To say the least, it's highly improb—" I broke off and looked at the Duck.

"What's a Deeny Shee?" Eddie asked.

The Duck seemed to me horrorstruck by my obvious suspicion. Too late, I regretted having let it become obvious. I shrugged with my lips, *who cares?,* and questioned him with an eyebrow, *you okay?,* but he shook his head *never mind* and gestured *go ahead* with his chin. But he still looked troubled. "The Daoine Sidh are the fairy folk, Eddie," I said, "descendants of the Tuatha De Danaan, the Tribe of the Goddess Diana. Originally from Greece, by way of Scandinavia, took over Ireland from the Firbolgs back about the time clothes were being invented. Make a long story short, they got their own butts kicked by the Miledhians about twenty-five hundred years ago. The survivors talked it over and decided they couldn't live as a conquered people. So they went underground, at a place called Brugh na Boinne in County Meath, and over time became the Daoine Sidh: the fairies and pookas and Fir Darrigs and leprechauns—yes, and the cluricaunes too."

The cluricaune's snore backfired twice, sharply, and then settled into the rhythm again—at a higher volume. His pipe, below him, now trembled slightly on each exhale. Who could blame it?

Doc Webster cleared his throat in counterpoint. "Look, Jake . . . I don't know quite how to put this. In this company, I have had personal experience of many strange things. But I understood that the Daoine Sidh were *mythical.* Like ghosts, and channeled entities, and all that crap. Not *real.*"

"You mean 'real,' like time machines and faster-than-light travel and people that rain won't fall on, Doc?"

"Unt talkink dogs?" Ralph von Wau Wau added.

The Doc didn't answer.

"Will it make you feel any better about it to call what he does 'PSI,' Doc? Like the way Fogerty could make the dart board want darts? Like what the Duck does? The cluricaune is here. Our booze is not. Ergo, a subrace of dwarves with paranormal powers must exist. Once you define 'magic' as 'knowledge I don't have yet,' you can stop being afraid of it."

"Well," the Doc said reluctantly, "when I'm holding it in my own hand, I can't very well deny it exists. But I must say this is aggravating. I was looking forward to getting *less* open-minded as I aged." He frowned. "All right: the Daoine Sidh are real. Just don't you say a goddam word to me about Loch Ness!"

"My grandfather used to tell me stories about them," Long-Drink said. "Is that how you know about that stuff, Jake?"

"No, Drink—my people came over a century and a half ago. But awhile back I reached the age where a man starts to wonder about his roots. Turned out my mother's line, the Meads and the Porters, came from Navan, in County Meath—not far from New Grange, where the Brugh na Boinne is, so I got into the whole story."

"Cripes, Jake," Eddie said. "Two o' yer ancestors had *beers* named after 'em?" He looked impressed.

Well, so was I. "Swear to God. Explains a lot about my destiny, doesn't it?"

"How'd ya know da guy's name wuz Noggin Ian?"

The cluricaune opened one eye. "Me name is unknown to you yet, gallinaceous repugnant orangutang," he muttered in his sleep. "Aye, 'Naggeneen' is what folks call a cluricaune, just a generical term for the breed: freely translated, it means 'a short beer.' Have yez got any here?"

"Not since you showed up, bocksucker," Eddie said bitterly.

The cluricaune went back to sleep. Noisily. His stupendous white beard floated an inch or two above his torso, curling up slightly at the end.

"He'll never tell anyone his real name, Eddie," I said. "In magical terms, it'd be kind of like giving somebody your credit cards—with no way to cancel them."

"Jesus, Jake," Doc Webster said, "skip the family history and nomenclature, will you? This is serious—what do we do about this joker? How do you decluricaune a bar? Try and run this place without lubrication and the engine'll seize up pretty quick."

The bad news first. "The only thing you can usually do to get rid of a cluricaune is go on the wagon, and stay there so long that he gives up and goes looking for a better 'ole."

"How long does dat take?" Eddie asked.

"I've heard of up to fifty years," I said.

"*Fifty years?*" Margie Shorter scroaned. "What's the *low* end?"

"I've heard of as little as a year," I said.

Rooba rooba—

"I don't tink I can wait dat long," the little piano man said, frowning deeply. "I gotta toist myself."

"You said 'the only thing you can *usually* do . . .', Jake," the Doc said. "What is it you can only do some-times?"

Now the good news. I smiled for the first time in what seemed like a long while. "Well, they say that once in a hundred years or so . . . and mind you, only if you happen to have a pure heart, an eye that sees no evil, a fleet foot, the grip of a lobsterman, and—" I glanced at the Duck. "—the luck of the Devil himself . . . you *might* just be lucky enough to *capture* the cluricaune, in iron. Then you're in Fat City. It now appears that between us, we made the nut."

Rooba rooba rooba—on a tentatively cheerful note.

Talk about a close call!

△   △   △

"So where's the trigger?" Noah asked. "Now that we have him located, secured and accessed, how do we disarm him?"

Noah used to be a bomb-disposal expert for the county heat, until there was a spot of unpleasantness over his taking a terrorist nuclear weapon he was working on home for personal use, and not bringing it back. Since no citizens or legal aliens had perished as a result (just a single alien, without papers . . . and a very nice tavern), no charges had been preferred—but he'd been transferred out of the Bomb Squad for good. He missed it fiercely, and still tended to think in those sort of terms. It was just the kind of attitude I was looking for.

"Hear that, gang?" I said, loud enough to cut through the roobae. "Noah has exactly the right mindset. Think of it like we're looking at a live, ticking—no, snoring bomb. Everything is going to be perfectly all right—*as long as we don't make any mistakes.*" I grinned. "The *good* news is, the snoring bomb is made of solid gold. Old Naggeneen here is powerful magic. If we handle this right, we can literally have just about Anything In The World We Want. I don't want to jinx it, but if we don't blow this, I think we truly may just have come to the End Of The Painbow—"

"I just wish—," Fast Eddie began.

"SSSHHHH!" Long-Drink and I said at once.

He looked offended. "I was just gonna say I w—"

"*Shut up, Eddie!*" we both bellowed, fear making us sound enraged, and Doc Webster chimed in with us. Fast Eddie blinked at our combined volume, opened his mouth to speak a third time . . . saw us all draw breath to shriek at him, and subsided. "Jeezis Christ," he muttered, shaking his head. "Nice manners, you mugs."

I was shaking with relief at the close call. "That's exactly what I was just getting to," I said quickly. "Once you capture a cluricaune, you get three wishes."

ROOBA ROOBA ROOBA!

" . . . the first three wishes spoken aloud . . ."

"Aw Jeez," Eddie said. He thought for a minute. "Sorry, Jake. I almost put my foot in my mout'."

I sighed. "That's okay, Eddie. My fault, for trying to save the good news for last. I should have known, life doesn't work like that. Would everybody here please be *real* careful not to use the W-word at all for the next little while—just to be on the safe side?"

Nods all around. One or two people actually put their hand over their mouth.

"I think it's time we gave this some careful thought," I said . . . and my voice trailed off. Even for me, the implications were just beginning to sink in.

Sink in: like a loaded plane, over the Bermuda Triangle . . .

Within seconds, the gang's expressions mirrored my own rapidly evolving succession of emotions. The cluricaune snored contentedly in Tanya's grip as we tried to sort things out.

It's funny: if somebody came up to you and said, "You can have any wish you want," that'd be a miracle—and I could see all of them start to look as excited as I'd been feeling. But where one wish is more than enough—more than some people get in a lifetime, God help 'em—three wishes can seem, the more you think about it, like an insufficiency. It spoiled their pleasure a little, and realizing that spoiled it a little more for each of them, as it had for me. Then one by one they—as I had—quit wasting time on that crap and came back to a bubbling, *Three wishes! What should we wish for?*

*But any time now they would catch up with me, and begin
to see how horrible the question was.*

I had not thought this thing through . . .

△   △   △

MY PERSONAL FIRST-BALLOT SHORTLIST:
(in no particular order, as they occurred to me,
beginning with number two)

World peace?

An end to hunger?

A solution for pollution?

The end of tyranny?

A cup of coffee that tastes as good as it smells?

Universal freedom?

A resurgence of urban folk music?

A truce between the sexes?

Universal respect for prostitutes? That is, an end to
   chronic epidemic male and female self-contempt?

(I could not wish for Love, much as I wanted one in my
life: what good is a love gained through magic trickery? But
the passing thought suggested:)

An off-switch for the pain system?

A good high without addiction or backlash?

A cure for AIDS?

A cure for suffering, period?

A cure for death?

Oh, dear God: a retroactive *cure for death?*

△   △   △

Barb! Jess!

Mom!

THE CALLAHAN TOUCH

△   △   △

Was there any chance at all of distilling all of that down to three wishes? Was there anything on that list you could forgive yourself for leaving out? Might you not also be tempted to give at least a little thought to wealth and fame—and a hundred other things? I felt like a mule surrounded by three hundred and sixty separate piles of hay—each one concealing a bundle of sweating dynamite.

And there was still the very *first* wish I'd thought of. The one I had rejected so instantly I was almost able to convince myself I'd never wished to wish it. A simple, painless, gift-wrapped solution to the personal dilemma I'd been worrying about back at the beginning of the night, the one which had been haunting my dreams and churning my guts into brown butter for the past several months now. It was a small thing, next to world peace—but what isn't? I wanted to solve it myself, without assistance—but I wasn't sure I could, and I needed it solved so badly I was tempted beyond words to accept this free pass.

Looking around me, I could see that just about everybody had some similar personal demon of their own, someone it hurt unbearably to have lost, something they needed to live. And we all knew the arithmetic: several dozen into three doesn't go.

Honest to God, I think the dilemma would have destroyed a lesser group than us.

Had I loved those people an ounce less, I think I'd have said *screw 'em* and wished my dead ladies back to life before I could have a chance to think about it too much. Had any one of my customers loved me and each other an ounce less, they'd have tried to beat me to it, and there could have been blood over that.

More: I could spot ghastly booby traps in every single one of those wishes that occurred to me in that first rush of thought—and there were bound to be mines I *couldn't* spot. Indeed, in every single story I'd ever heard, in every fantasy from every culture and clime, "wish" was a synonym for "booby trap." That was the *point* of wish stories.

What good is world peace, if it comes at the cost of liberty? The simplest way to end hunger and pollution both is to exterminate the human race. Lose *too* much tyranny, and you lose order. I might not be able to bring myself to pour booze into coffee that tasted as good as it smelled. Universal freedom denies my right to restrict Jeffrey Dahmer's recreational and dietary habits. If acoustic guitar ever came back, I'd be masochistically tempted to turn the bar over to Tom and go back on the road.

A truce between the sexes? *Are you out of your goddam mind, Jake?* What else *is* there to distract us all from onrushing death? Television?

Honor for prostitutes? Who would cops and politicians and the legions of unwanted have to look down on, then? (Or would politicians be honored too, by professional courtesy?) What would all the crippled egos and frightened souls *do* to keep functioning, without a class of people defined as inferior to everyone? At best, gay-bashing and racial baiting would skyrocket dramatically to compensate.

An off-switch for the pain system? Suppose you neglected to switch it back on? Have you ever been stupid enough to disable the little routine on a Macintosh that asks, "Are you *sure* you want to delete the file *N—?*" before letting you trash applications?

There *is* a good high without addiction or drastic backlash, and with several medicinal benefits to boot. The only one the government's brain-damaged "War On Drugs" has been even moderately successful in suppressing. Create another, they'd make that a crime too.

A cure for AIDS? Dr. Jonathan Crawford could have said a few things about that one. He'd been trying to cure malaria . . . and might just have *caused* AIDS as a side effect.

Death is reputedly a totally effective specific for suffering. And if living people did not suffer . . . would they be people?

A cure for death without the sudden universal wisdom and restraint to control birth would be a recipe for horror unimaginable. For that matter, so would a cure for death without a concurrent cure for aging. Old age is not for sissies, as Niven said.

I am not the man I was the day my wife and daughter died—or the man I was the day my mother died. If I could bring them back, uncorrupted and untraumatized, just as I remembered them . . . would they love me? Would they know me at all? If they did, could my own heart take the stress of an emotional one-eighty like that?

The more I tried to come up with three wishes, the less I was inclined to venture a single one . . .

Δ   Δ   Δ

Multiply my dilemma by—

—no, *raise it to the power of*—

—the number of people present with me in the room.

Δ   Δ   Δ

Now do you want to be telepathic, Jake old buddy?

Δ   Δ   Δ

"Whaddya say we blow de tree wi—de tree tings quick on sometin harmless," Fast Eddie whispered a thousand years later, "before we get ourselves inta trouble, here?" His forehead was so wrinkled you could have played washboard on it.

Long-Drink gently put a hand over Eddie's mouth. "What," he asked, "is *absolutely guaranteed* harmless?"

Eddie's brow wrinkled up even tighter . . . and the rest of him slumped.

"Well," Doc Webster murmured, a timeless, silent time later, "it could be worse."

"How?" I asked mournfully, and several others groaned approval of the question.

"We could be down to *one,*" the Doc explained. "This way we have a little room to breathe. If we screw up too bad the first time, we can always get ourselves out of trouble—or at least back where we started—and still have a backup wi . . . option. It seems like our first priority is—"

"No backup option, Doc," Jordin Kare corrected. "The third one is the most important one of all. Say you're right: we goof the first one, we undo it with the second . . . and there we are with a cluricaune in the house. The third is our last hope of ever getting rid of him."

"Sure," the Doc said, "ideally we hold Losing The Cluricaune in reserve for our third w—our third expressed desire, naturally. But if we . . . choose that one first, there's nobody to grant the other two."

The cluricaune was smiling in his sleep.

"And you think there's any way in hell that you can get this many people—even *these* people—to agree on *one* choice?" I asked. "Without a fight? Are you ready for that fight, Doc?"

"Jake, it seems to me we have a responsibility—"

I reached an instant, unilateral and irrevocable decision. If even Doc Webster, always one of the most sensible and wise and level-headed of us, was thinking along these sorts of lines—and so rattled that he had to keep making an obvious effort to avoid tripping over his own tongue—we were in big trouble. I knew he was wrong. He was being as reasonable and logical as any chump protagonist in a fantasy story; a hundred thousand stories said he was thinking like a victim. We had to break the mold somehow, move laterally. But I was not sure I had the emotional weight to sway the gang from his way of thinking—and that uncertainty made me a little frantic. Any one of them could doom us all, any second, with the best of intentions and a single sentence. Damn it, this was *my* bar, for now at least! It was up to *me* to decide who had what responsibilities to whom in here. If any of us was going to bear the weight of this, it had to be me. So I made a choice that hadn't even gotten onto my preliminary ballot. To assert my authority—I yelped for higher authority.

"God," I said loudly, cutting the Doc off, "I wish Mike Callahan was here right now."

A great shout went up—

7

The Mick of Time

My, didn't Mike look surprised, when he materialized there in front of my bar?

I was a little startled, myself. The big mick was stark naked, and even more red-faced than usual. From these and other evidences, it was apparent that I had caught him in the midst of a tender . . . well, no, possibly more of a volcanic . . . moment with Lady Sally McGee, or some designated alternate. Even the cluricaune—who had roused from his stupor the instant I'd spoken my wish—opened his drunken eyes wide at the sight, and stared in uncharacteristic silence. Mike, of course, shifted mental gears in something under a second.

"The saints preserve us with BHT," he boomed cheerfully, "and calcium propionate to retard spoilage. I thought I'd seen the last of you mugs. You pulled it off, then? No, I see by your faces you haven't. Then *how in the name of God's gilded gonads did I get here?* Jake?"

My heart was hammering like mad. No, like glad. Just the sight of the Mick of Time was enough to make me feel that same wave of fierce joy I'd felt last night, when my friends had come through my door for the first time in much too long. I felt a little like an Apostle on Easter Sunday afternoon. "Hi, Mike. It's not a short story. More of a novelette . . ."

He nodded easily. "You know me," he said. "I got time."

Then there was a medium brief interruption. I was the first to lose it, vaulting over the bar, but I only led the pack by instants. I will simply say that not one of us experienced the slightest hesitation or self-consciousness or awkwardness about hugging a big naked Irishman, then or ever, and if you find anything weird about that, I condemn you to live in that skull for the rest of your life.

Isham and Tanya kept guard, of course, but I think everyone else managed to slip into and out of that gang hug before it was through. We were all laughing and crying and considerably less worried than we had been a moment ago.

All except me. As I stood back and let my friends have a chance to hug our mentor, I got in about a good ten seconds of happiness. And then I had a thought that made me literally bite my tongue. If I could wish Mike Callahan into my bar . . . *why couldn't I wish Mary Callahan-Finn into my bar?*

Why couldn't I wish her into my arms again?

Barbara and Jessica had been gone for nearly two decades—my mother even longer. But Mary had only been lost to me for a period measurable in months . . .

Of course, she was married now. To a guy that blew up planets sometimes. A good friend of mine, besides.

(I winced, remembering something from my browse through Irish history—the Finn Cycle. It's the story of Fionn Mac

Cumhail, or Finn MacCool. He fell for Cormac's daughter Grainne, but she eloped with a member of his own band— much the way Mary dumped me for my pal *Mickey* Finn. The second-century Finn betrayed his friend and stole his beloved back . . . and ultimately died by treachery himself.)

Fast Eddie ducked outside briefly to fetch a spare pair of work pants from Isham's truck (Ish being the only one in the room whose pants would fit Callahan). Once he'd stepped into them, Mike spotted the stranger in the crowd, walked over and offered the Duck his hand. "Howdy, friend. My name is Mike Callahan."

"Pleased to meet you," the Duck said. "They call me Duck."

Callahan looked the hairy little guy over. "Your name wouldn't be Ernie, would it?" he asked.

The Duck had started to put out his own hand; now he froze. "How did you know that?"

"Lucky guess," Mike said. "I like your comic strip." He took the Duck's hand and shook it firmly, and the Duck blinked at him in obvious bafflement and let him get away with it.

"Mike," I said, the second I decently could, "you and the Duck need to talk, later, but just now we got a small problem—"

"So I can see," he rumbled, gazing into the twinkling eyes of the cluricaune, and twinkling right back at him. "A cluricaune, sure as me mother was Irish! Good cess to you, Nageneen!"

"Call me a blatherskite—Brian Boru!" the cluricaune cried tipsily. "Good evenin', Yer Majesty, glad you could visit! And how are they keepin' in old Tir Na Nog?"

If there's anything Mike Callahan knows, it's how to humor a drunk. "Oh, merry as ever—not unlike yourself. You're into your cups to the neck, it appears."

"I wish it was hers," the little man said, leering at Tanya. She shook him by his cuffs and growled from deep in the area referred to. "Or possibly not . . . Your Majesty, tell these Fomorians here to unchain me! I'm caught fair and square and I'll give me parole."

"What's in it for me if I do?" Callahan asked.

"A reasonable question." The cluricaune appeared to pass out cold for a second or two, and then he became animated again. His pipe flew up from below him and found its place in his teeth as he spoke. "I've got it, bejabers! I'll put my request in the form of a wager, and you be the judge if I win it or not. If I make every soul in this room drop their jaw—in a minute or less—and with two little questions—can I be restored to the use of me hands?"

With two questions? "This oughta be good, Mike," I said. "Some of us here didn't drop our jaws when he changed into a werewolf."

The cluricaune cackled loudly. "It's not an illusion I offer yez here, t'is a fact—one you *know,* that's been sittin' right under yer face all yer life—you'll never believe that yez missed it yerselves!"

Mike looked to me. "Your bar, Jake."

A small but distinct thrill went through me at those words. Like the first time my father ever said to me, "It's your house, son." I filed it for later basking. I was busy.

"Well," I said slowly, "he knows where *my* buttons are located. You think if we give him parole, he'll keep it? Obey us 'til our business is done?"

"I swear by me beard that I shall—an' a cluricaune's word is as good as his bond," the little man proclaimed.

"How good is his bond, Mike?" Fast Eddie asked suspiciously.

"Good, Eddie," Callahan said. "As good as those bonds you got him in, anyway—and lots better than the ones they use on Wall Street. A little slipperier, maybe. You gotta be careful *what* word, what bond. But this seems pretty safe."

"Well, I do hate to keep a guest in irons if it's not absolutely necessary," I said. "Not that burning curiosity has any influence on my thinking."

"Mine either," several patrons chorused.

"Go ahead," I told the cluricaune. "*Étonne-moi!*"

He contrived to bow in handcuffs—not bad for someone too drunk to stand unassisted, even in mid-air. "Thank you, Your Worship. It's curious you should be speakin' in French, for the story I have for yez starts out in Cannes, the cinema festival place—oh, there's champion drinkin' there, almost as much as Oktoberfest, even a cluricaune can't make a dent in the liquor supply. So I go there one year, oh, a decade ago, and I find meself there in a room . . . well, a tavern . . . and who should be sittin' across from me, sharin' a dram, but that big Orson Welles and that Mankiewicz feller, director and writer of *Citizen Kane!* I bought them a drink on the strength of it, told 'em how much I admired their movie—"

I had my eye on the clock. (Yes, it's a Counterclock, like the old one at Callahan's. I had to have it made special. Don't ask what it cost.) I intended, since Mike had said cluricaunes were literal-minded, to hold him to his one-minute deadline . . . and so far I didn't see him *near* a jaw-dropping punchline. So he'd met some celebrities, once . . .

"—and said I'd a question I wanted to ask them, a question pertainin' to *Citizen Kane*. Well, Orson and Herman most graciously said they'd be happy to answer whatever I asked. So I sez to 'em, 'Right at the start o' yer movie . . . Charles Foster Kane dies alone, am I right?' And Welles nods and Mankiewicz says, 'Quite alone.'

One question down. I mentally checked my jaw. Still in place.

The cluricaune took inventory of the room with his sparkling eyes, with the same result, and then grinned broadly. He spoke slowly now, drawing it out for effect. "So I says to them, *'How in the world, then, does anyone* know *that his last word is Rosebud?'* "

Thunderstruck. That's the word I want. You like to think you belong to an intelligent species, and then something like this comes along. The film generally agreed to be the greatest ever made—certainly the most studied and analyzed movie of all time—had a hole in its plot you could drive a freight train through, *in the first minute*—the entire premise of the film was logically impossible . . . and no one in all the world but the cluricaune had ever noticed it before. I think I exchanged glances with everyone in the room in about five seconds, and I didn't see one face that didn't have a dropped jaw. I hadn't experienced such a sudden massive doubt of the collective human intelligence since, at the age of ten, I'd tried to woo a nine-year-old maiden with a poem in a classical mode, and she'd stopped me in my tracks with, "Why do they always *say* that—'Roses are red, violets are blue . . . '—when violets are *purple?* Why didn't they pick something that *is* blue?"

The most amazing part is that there are probably a dozen ways Welles and Mankiewicz could have solved the problem, without spoiling the solitude of Kane's death. It could have been fixed *after* the close of principal photography, with a single extra shot. (Kane had just finished dictating his will into a wire recorder as— A freak echo in the heating pipes conveyed his voice to the attic, where a maid happened to— An intercom he thought switched off shorted itself open just as— A bug planted by his enemies was found by—) But Mankiewicz and Welles simply never noticed the problem existed. It was too big to see.

Mike Callahan broke the awed silence. "Turn him loose, Tanya—he's won the bet."

Tanya shook off her stasis, closed her mouth, and produced a key from somewhere on her person.

"Christ almighty," Long-Drink burst out, maddened beyond endurance, *"what did Welles and Mankiewicz say?"*

The cluricaune waited until Tanya had freed him, then lurched unsteadily to his feet (two feet off the ground, mind) and said slyly, "What's in it for me if I tell yez?"

Callahan had to grin. "A reasonable question. What do you . . . no, that'd be a *silly* question. Jake?"

I sighed. "Tom says there's a few more cases of stuff out in the van. You want to bring in a case of scotch, Tom?"

The cluricaune turned up his nose.

I sighed again. Well, it was worth it to hear the answer. "Make it a case of Tully." Damned if I'd give him the Bushmill's.

He nodded acceptance.

When Tom came in the door with the case, he nearly dropped it—for the instant he crossed the threshold, its weight diminished drastically. He appeared to try and fling the case up at the ceiling and change his mind in midstream. The cluricaune's eyes began to glow like inspection ports in the wall of Hell.

"Welles looks at Mankiewicz, pale as a haddock," he said in a sing-song voice, "and Mankiewicz looks back at him in return . . . and together they puts down their drinks on the table, unfinished, and rises together and shows me their backs, and be damned if a word I could get from them after! Now dip me if that isn't excellent liquor—and Jasus, it's good to be shut o' the darbies—WHEE!"

Suddenly he was dancing a hornpipe—I don't know, maybe a reel or a jig, I thought of it as a hornpipe—in mid-air, bounding high and recovering, drunk as a lord on the first of May. He kept missing steps and falling through his invisible floor, then swinging back up to try again, little arms flailing wildly. People flinched and ducked out of his way. Glassware fell from tables and shattered. Ish, backing up, stumbled into a table and demolished it. And then it got bad.

The cluricaune began to sing—

—worse, to sing, in a very piercing voice . . . not some Irish air or ballad . . . but an *Italian* (-American) song—

—worse yet, a punning parody of "That's *Amoré*"—

"When-a you swim inna da sea, an' a eel bites-a you knee, dat's a moray—"

There were howls of pain. The cluricaune laughed uproariously and kept on reeling about like Zorba on acid, trailing toxic peat fumes from his villainous pipe. As he careened past Tanya again, he nearly kicked her in the head; she heard his little boot go by her ear and snatched at it. And missed. She stared with her sightless eyes at her own fist.

"—a New Zealander man with a permanent tan, that's a Maori—"

Well, at least he'd dropped the Chico Marx accent . . .

Jordin and Mary Kay Kare, who between them write really *good* parody songs, bellowed in protest and tried to bulldog the cluricaune together. Good thing they're married; they ended up on the floor in the missionary position. (Have you ever wondered, as I have, how those missionaries *communicated* the idea to the Indians? How did they come to have the vocabulary? It had to be show and tell, right? "Now, *never* do this . . . or this . . . and *especially* not *this* . . .")

"—when two patterns combine, in a way serpentine, that's a moiré—"

Doc Webster was aghast. He was being outpunned, in his own lair, by a drunken fairy.

Pausing only to kiss his wife (good man in a crunch), Jordin sprang to his feet and located my fire extinguisher. Mary Kay instantly leapt for cover, followed closely by several others. I opened my mouth in alarm—

THE CALLAHAN TOUCH

"—He tells jokes, he's a ham; his last name's Amsterdam— dat's-a Morey!"

—and closed it again. Jordin's a physicist, who was just about to move to the coast to work at what he calls "Larry's Rad Lab"—Lawrence Livermore National Laboratory. His specialty is laser-powered propulsion systems, for spacecraft (the idea is, leave the engine at home, where it's convenient to work on), and he knows more than most people about tracking moving objects. So I let him have his shot.

And he let the cluricaune have his shot, and it was good shooting indeed. He kept the stream from the fire extinguisher trained on the capering cluricaune for a good eight seconds, never losing him for more than an instant.

"—if yer vitamins be mostly C, D and E . . . take some more A—"

He switched the thing off when it became clear that the cluricaune's voluminous beard, twirling around him as he spun, could absorb as much as Jordin could deliver, without even losing its snowy white color. The little man seemed to enjoy it.

Jordin's magnificent shooting was not completely without effect, however. It reminded the cluricaune of something. He lurched to a weaving halt near the door, turned his back to us, fumbled briefly, and began urinating into the umbrella stand. Through his beard.

"—Oh, you play 'What I Say' very gay—won't you play that some more, Ray?—"

A roar of general outrage was building to a crescendo. Our usual reaction to puns of this order was to hold our collective nose and flee screaming into the night. Setting them to Italian music made it worse. It was even *harder* to take without a drink for insulation. Sooner or later my patrons would remember that outside was the only place they were liable to *get* a drink tonight, and once that happened an exodus would begin. Those too cautious to risk slipping out past a drunkenly urinating cluricaune (say that three times fast) would simply use the windows—or claw their way through the boarded-up hole in the ceiling if they had to.

I was *not* going to let my bar be emptied on its second night by a dipsomaniac dwarf, with Mike Callahan looking on.

I reached under the bar, took out my Ted Williams classic, and brought it down on the bar so hard the sound was like a rifle shot. Even the cluricaune was startled. He spun around . . .

People scattered out of his way.

I thundered at him. "You swore you'd obey me, you mannerless clown—Now put that away and shut up and sit down!"

To my surprise, it worked. Maybe the fact that it happened to come out as a rhymed couplet helped. Or maybe a cluricaune's word *is* as good as his bond. In any case, he ceased micturating, adjusted things behind that beard, and sat down on air with folded arms without uttering another sound. He looked mildly disgusted.

The silence was deafening.

"Nicely done, Jake," Callahan said.

I warmed. "Thanks, Mike. You said he was careful about words."

"Boy, he's sure been dipped in the Shannon, hasn't he?"

There's a legend that those dipped in that river are perfectly and forever cured of bashfulness. "Up to his hair," I agreed. "Uh . . . maybe you can guess the nature of our immediate problem?"

He nodded. "It's coming to me. He gave you three wishes, didn't he? And I'm one of 'em."

I winced. But of course it was not the *noun* "wish" that was dangerous, only the verb. "You got it. You're the first. We started in thinking about what to pick . . . and about the time we started to bite ourselves in the small of the back, I decided to ask your advice. I felt like I was . . . I *still* feel like I'm juggling old nitroglycerine."

"You are," he agreed. "Got a plan?"

"Well, actually—"

"Excuse me, Jake," Isham said, brushing sawdust off himself and approaching the bar. "I don't mean to interrupt, but I want you to take this for that table I just totaled." He tried to put money on the bar.

I pushed it back at him. "Forget it, man. It looks from here like I can fix it."

He shook his head and pushed the money toward me. "It's cracked down the middle."

I pushed his money away again. "Yeah, but I still think I—"

He shook his head more vigorously. "No way do I want to be remembered like Big Beef McCaffrey." Big Beef once put a crack down the middle of the front door of Callahan's Place, with his head, on the way out—and for the next thirty-nine years, the story was still being told to newcomers. "I'm buying you a new table," he said, pushing the money toward me a third time.

"Isham," Tom Hauptman said, "at this point, there's no telling if we're still going to be *open* tomorrow night—"

"It doesn't matter," Tanya said. "Take the cash, Jake. I'll drag him here tomorrow night one way or another, and you can give him back the money when I show Ish that table repaired. I know you're a pretty good carpen—"

"AAAAARGH!"

△   △   △

Well, actually, five or six voices all shouted different things at once, but the net effect was sort of an "AAAAARGH!" I know that when I saw what had caused it, "AAAAARGH!"

is what *I* said, and Tanya said the same thing a moment later, giving it a few extra A's so that it was more of an "AAAAAAAAAAAAARGH," on a rising and falling note.

The table was repaired. Without a crack.

"Aw shit, Jake, I'm sorry," Tanya said. "It just slipped out."

"You son of a bitch," I said to the cluricaune, "what are you trying to pull?" But I knew.

And he knew I knew. We all knew. "Plain as the nose on your face—and that's plain as can be—did I hear the young lady a moment ago," he cackled gleefully. "Shall we hear it again?" He put a finger up his nose, like the guy in the Monty Python sketch about the man with a tape recorder up his nose, and we all heard, with perfect fidelity and brilliant clarity, Tanya's voice say for a second time, " . . . I sho' wish that table repaired."

"Glad I could be of some service," the cluricaune said, and burst into gales of laughter, rocking back and forth in his tailor's seat. "Aye, t'is pity she don't keep her brains in her dumplin' shop—oh, I could have me a smack at your muns, ye enormous mavourneen! Two o' yer wishes is gone up in smoke—" He puffed furiously on his pipe, and a gout of smoke arose that would have given one of Callahan's old cigars some competition on the stinkmeter. "But one of 'em left—t'is a wonderful joke!"

There was a general roar of outrage at this sophistry—but we had all known he took things literal-mindedly, had cautioned ourselves to be careful a dozen times: he had us dead to rights.

Suddenly, through the rooba-ing, came the startling sound of Noah Gonzalez laughing along with the cluricaune. Some of us glared at him.

"Sorry, gang," Noah said, trying to stop laughing and failing. "Just reminded me of one of my oldest nightmares . . . I'm working on a voice-activated bomb . . . and this cub reporter sneaks past all the uniforms . . . and fires a flashbulb over my shoulder and says . . . 'That'll make a nice page-one blow-up!'—" He lost it and folded over in his chair, hooting.

One by one, we all broke up.

Well, it was either that, or fall on the cluricaune with our hands and teeth, I guess. Maybe another barful of people would have chosen the latter. Some guys step on a rake in the dark, and get mad and go punch somebody. Others step on a rake in the dark, and fall down laughing at themselves. I know which kind of guy I'd rather be. So do my friends. Over the years, together, we had come to learn that if you get a chance to turn anger into laughter, that will be a good thing to do. I know I was glad the laughter gave me an excuse to put that silly baseball bat back underneath the bar again. I'd felt like a Firbolg with it in my hand.

And it *was* funny, if you thought about it. We'd been handed one of mankind's age-old dreams . . . and here we were, stumbling around like a bunch of Keystone Kops, chasing our miracle like Chaplin chasing his hat . . . and furthermore, being beaten, in our own house, at our own game: merriment.

For there was no denying that the cluricaune was having a better time in our bar than we were. We were accustomed to think of ourselves as a jolly crew—and he made us look like Baptists. He had outsung, outdanced, outpunned, outdrunk, outraged and outfoxed the lot of us, from the moment we'd clapped him in irons and put him in our thrall—and we had reacted pretty much like a convention of narcotics officers confronted by Hunter Thompson.

By God, when was the last time *I* had been having such a good time, I'd urinated into the umbrella stand? Was I getting *old,* for Chrissakes? So the little guy had an unpleasant voice. Didn't that describe Long-Drink after the eighth drink? Or for that matter, Eddie in the best of times? What did I care about the damned umbrella stand? For that matter, what the hell did I even *have* one for? Not one of us owned an umbrella: thanks to Mickey Finn, it was no longer possible for any of Callahan's regulars to get rained on . . .

So he'd offered me three wishes. This was something to hate him for? Just because I was too dumb to meet their challenge?

"Lots of people," I heard Doc Webster gasp between guffaws, "go to a bar and stand around all night, waiting for something to happen . . ." The general laughter gained strength, and after a while it was like that Spike Jones record where the tuba player gets out about a bar and a half of "Flight of the Bumblebee," and then he and the entire orchestra go into helpless hysterics for three minutes straight. Someone quoted it, now, with a fart noise in B♭, and enough of us knew it to kind of kick the laughter into a lower and more durable gear; we howled until the tears came, and beyond. I hadn't laughed that hard since . . .

. . . since I'd been in Callahan's Place.

The cluricaune whooped along with us. And not at us. The difference was clear.

"Oh Lord," I said when I could form words, "it's almost worth losing my whole stock, to have had a laugh like that. No, it *is* worth it. Ah Naggeneen, you slippery bugger, I'd have pissed meself if you hadn't siphoned me kidneys. You'll go up a ladder to bed, one day."

He wiped his own streaming eyes. "Faith, I do like a lad who can laugh at himself. Yer a right jolly dog, Mr. Publican, damned it you ain't, and I take off me cap to ye!" He did so, with a grand tipsy flourish. "And the same for yer company— champion laughers I call ye, the lot of yez. I haven't had me a giggle like that since the reign o' Queen Dick!"

"The *what?*" Fast Eddie asked sotto voce.

"It's Irish for 'never,' Eddie," the Duck explained. I was startled. There was no sneer in his voice, no rude parody of patience. He just answered Eddie's question.

Doc Webster was the first to achieve full sobriety. "Well, Jacob," he said, "it seems to me our problem has sort of solved itself, wouldn't you say? I mean, I hate to break up this happy gathering; that belly laugh *was* worth a lot, and I'm grateful for it . . . but unless we want this to be the proverbial Last Laugh, there's only one possible choice for Number Three. Right?"

People were too tired from laughing to rooba rooba, but it was clear that the Doc had set a lot of brains to buzzing.

"What's the hurry?" Shorty Steinitz muttered.

"I think we just proved kind of conclusively that the longer we put it off, the more trouble we're likely to get in," the Doc said. "Like Jake said before, like Noah said, think of a ticking bomb. Suppose Tanya had said . . . no, Jesus, I'm doing it *again*. Fun is fun, but it's time to bottle it up and go."

I turned to Callahan. "What about you, Mike?"

"What about me?"

"Don't you . . . uh . . . need a ride home?"

That got a feeble rooba. Probably most people had the same quick flash I did: *lose the cluricaune, and then keep Mike Callahan here with us forever—*

—a prisoner of fairy magic. Right!

But Mike was shaking his head. "I told you once, Jake; I don't use a time machine to get around. I don't need any special equipment to get back home."

"How can that be, Mike?" Mary Kay Kare was moved to ask. "When I ask Jordin, he gets grouchy for days afterwards." Her husband opened his mouth to deny the charge, and opted to stand mute instead.

"James Taylor knows," Callahan said.

"James *Taylor?*" Mary Kay said. "The genius James Taylor?"

"It's in his song, 'The Secret O' Life,' Mary Kay," Callahan said.

The Duck snorted. "How could any song live up to a title like that?"

"Listen to the song, Ernie," Callahan advised him. "Jake, the ball's in your court. The Doc is right: whatever you're fixing to do, t'were best done pronto. Looked at a certain way, people are essentially wish-generators, with no off-switch, and they're dangerous when armed. We can't help brimming with wishes, and most of them would kill us or worse if they ever came true. Sooner or later, somebody here's going to start subvocalizing what they're thinking . . ."

Decision time!

Damn, this running a bar was turning out to be tougher than I'd ever imagined . . .

Somehow in the midst of everything I became aware of the fact that the Duck was staring at me with great intensity. Even more than everyone else present, he hung on my next words for some reason. I took a deep breath—

"Hold it!" Doc Webster commanded.

"What is it, Doc?" I said, a little annoyed.

"Before you take any irrevocable steps, there's something I've got to do," he said.

I took a deep breath and let it out. "Swing," I said.

He waddled over to where the cluricaune sat cross-legged on nothing. The wizened little fairy looked him square in the eye, regarding him without fear but with respectful attention.

The Doc planted his feet, threw his arms wide, rolled his eyes toward the ceiling and opened his mouth. When he sang the first word, *"When—,"* dragging it out theatrically like a ham baritone, eyes began to widen; by the time he descended a step for "—*a*— ," people were beginning to smile in sudden understanding, and the cluricaune's eyes were sparkling merrily.

"—Canadian shows you his mother, he goes:
"Dat's my mawr, eh?"

The cluricaune broke into laughter and applause. "A new one, bedad, and I thought I knew all of 'em—good on ye, mister!" Those of us who had gotten enough strength back laughed with him, and clapped our hands, and banged our empty steins on the bar and tables. Doc Webster had upheld the honor of the house.

The Doc inclined his head with massive dignity, and stepped back.

Tanya stepped forward. She cleared her throat. The cluricaune widened his eyes slightly. And Tanya sang:

"With the high price of feed, it's for farmers in need
"That some mow hay . . ."

More laughter and applause, this time with an element of groan in it, true, but still a good hand, from human and cluricaune alike. Tanya too stepped back with proud satisfaction.

I threw caution to the winds and came around my bar. The cluricaune, convulsed with laughter, whooped louder when he saw me coming. "Yet *another?*" he cried. "Ah, ye're thunderin' geniuses!" Thinking rapidly, I squared off before him. Off to my right, Eddie gave me an *E7+* intro chord on his piano— *A* is my key, what an accompanist!—and I sang:

"My new ray-gun here tries to put out both your eyes:
"It's a Moe-Ray . . ."

I wasn't sure he'd get the reference—but apparently his knowledge of American cinema ranged all the way from *Kane* down to the Three Stooges: he laughed so hard he lost his pipe, and slapped his thigh so hard he put himself into a spin, his long snow-white beard chasing him in a slow circle. The applause I got from the gang sounded, to my totally unbiased professional ear, almost equal to what the Doc had drawn, but not so much more than Tanya's that I had to feel embarrassed. I stepped back, bowed slightly to all, and went back around the bar to pronounce sentence.

And as I got there, the Duck—of all people—left his chair for the first time that night, and walked up to the cluricaune.

"Faith, there *can't* be another," the little old man gasped, and flailed his hands until he was stabilized at local vertical again.

Trying as hard as possible to appear bored and detached about the whole thing, the Duck sang—in an unexpectedly magnificent, operatic tenor:

"*If* King Kong *has gone flat, rent the flick* Vampire Bat*:*
"*That's some more Wray . . .*"

In the explosion of mirth that ensued, the cluricaune's teeth left his head and began caroming around the room like a runaway hedge-clipper, still laughing. His boots left his feet, his cap left his head, and as we all roared together, their respective vectors brought them together by chance at one end of the room, where they assembled themselves into a sketch of a man dancing a reel and laughing his heart out. "*Ceol na naingeal,*" the cluricaune crooned as he laughed.

A long, breathless time later, he drew himself unsteadily to his bare feet and held out his hands. His boots and cap and teeth and pipe returned to him, and docked without assistance. He spun in mid-air to face me, and bowed so grandly he lost the cap again, and caught it as it went by his feet.

"I take off me lid to yez, woman an' man," he said. "Ye've taken me best and ye've given it back to me. This is a house I'll be sorry to leave—but I guess you'll be wantin' me off o' yer premises. Hoo, an' can't say I blame yez atall: I've a terrible case o' the ol' barrel fever, I know it; it's part of me nature and cannot be helped. I'd drink every night nearly twice what I've guzzled tonight if I stayed. So let's have it over with: wish your third wish, an' I'll be on my way, leavin' thanks for the laughter you gave me today."

I looked at Mike Callahan.

He looked back at me.

In his face I saw his daughter Mary's face . . . only a wish away from Mary's Place . . .

. . . and for a moment, it seemed to me I could hear her husband Mickey's voice, speaking in anguish on the night he'd first come to Earth, saying, "*I did not know that you had love!*"

I turned to the cluricaune. And in that moment I became mature enough to accept the help of magic in solving my problem. *It's not accepting a free pass,* I suddenly saw, *if I sell one at fair market value . . .*

"Nobody here wants you gone, Naggeneen," I said. "I just wish to God that you'd pay for your drinks like a gentleman—"

Mike waved at me frantically, mimed playing with a yo-yo.

Oh Christ, that was close! "—without, let me add, ever using your *Sprè na Skillenagh;* I mean honest money."

I thought for a moment he was going to erupt in a towering rage. Instead, he began to laugh and laugh and laugh. If we could laugh at ourselves, his pride would not let him do less. "Done," he choked amid his guffaws. "Ye've quaggled me proper—first time it's happened in two hundred years!"

The cash register went *chung* behind me, and its drawer opened up and began spilling gold coins on my floor.

Pandemonium broke out.

8

The End of the Painbow

"What de hell kind o' spray was dat you said, Jake?" Eddie called, when the tumult began to die down.

"The *Sprè na Skillenagh*," I repeated. "The 'shilling fortune,' is the English of it. A magic shilling, that always returns to a cluricaune's purse the moment you take your eyes off it, like there was a rubber band on it. He keeps it for the suckers. But cluricaunes *also* always know the location of buried gold, real gold, in unlimited quantities."

Rooba.

"Jake?" Doc Webster said. "Maybe I'm missing something . . . but what good is all the gold in the world to us if we can't get a drink?"

"But we *can*, Doc," I said. "You just heard Naggeneen here state a maximum capacity."

He blinked. "Huh. That's right, I did. But—"

135

"What none of you guys understand," I said, "is that the thirsty little feller is going to be the *saving* of this place."

Rooba rooba.

"What do you mean, Jake?"

"Do you remember the state I got myself into, getting this place ready to open, Doc?"

"Well . . . yeah."

"Now, you know me, Doc. Look around this place. Is there anything you see here that could have caused me that much grief?"

He spun around slowly. "Well, no, not really, now that you mention it. I *did* wonder about that some . . . what you were sweating so hard."

"I was sweating how to pay for this place," I said. "Remember how I said last night I was tripling the price of a drink, and everybody carefully didn't flinch? Fifty cents higher and some of you *would* have flinched . . . and rightly too, the amount of sauce we go through. I've been running around like a rat in my skull, working arithmetic over and over. I've sunk every cent of my savings in this, and so have you all, and there's no way in hell it can pay for itself." I turned to Mike. "I never appreciated just what a miracle-worker you are, Michael, until I costed it out for the eighty-fifth time."

He smiled. "I had certain advantages not available to you, son."

"I know that now. I think I knew it then; I just never thought about it. But even you might not believe what they're getting for glasses nowadays."

He nodded. "Yeah, there's a big sand shortage. Still, bars do stay open, somehow."

I shrugged. "Half of 'em are probably laundering cash for the syndicate. All I can tell you is, for month after month I have juggled the figures—and the only way I could see of keeping this place open past six months was to triple our clientele. Which would destroy the place as effectively as a sheriff's padlock on the door."

"Jesus, Jake," Long-Drink said accusingly, "you never told us—"

"And what if I had?" I asked him. "What could any of you have done? You've already all given 'til it hurts, Drink. Was I supposed to never have opened? Or soured the six months it looked like we were gonna have, by telling everybody there was a doomsday clock ticking on the wall? How did I know?— maybe we could all manage to *get* telepathic in six months, and clean up on Wall Street or something."

I flung my arms out expansively and grinned.

"Oh Jesus, it was tearing me up inside—but I'm free, by God, as of tonight! A great express-train has been lifted from my jock. You heard what the Naggeneen said: he can drink the place dry twice a night: *he's just tripled our clientele*—without clumsying up the place with a bunch of uncouth strangers. Doc, *we're covered!*"

△   △   △

A rafter-ringing cheer went up. Folks took the cluricaune gently in hand, and together they hoisted him up to their shoulders, and tossed him exuberantly up to those rafters; he laughed like a child and let gravity have him, fell back to be tossed up again, and again. Fast Eddie played "Jolly Good Fellow," and Callahan grinned like a bandit and gave me his hand. I shook it contentedly, feeling the feeling you have when you know you have chosen correctly and weathered the cusp.

I had not taken any unfair profit from fairy magic. I had not plundered gold I had not earned, had not used a Sprè na Skillenagh to pay my distributors, or any other sort of cheat that would require a karma-balancing backlash. I'd simply taken on one jolly new client, with the thirst of a hundred men. A lonely great-grandson of Bacchus who would probably end up greying my hair . . . and classing my joint up considerably.

"Thanks for that footnote; that saved us," I told Callahan.

"You're welcome," he said with a wink of his eye.

I reached under the bar and I took out a cylinder made of aluminum, twisted the end off, and dumped out what looked and what smelled like coprolite. Callahan stared and then started to smile. "Surely it isn't—"

"Be damned if it isn't—and don't call me Shirley—it's one of your miserable rotten cigars. I stepped on it as I was leaving, that night in the woods, and held on to it. It was radioactive, the first year or so, but I handled it carefully. Sort of a souvenir of you, if that isn't corny . . . to help me remember the kind of a stinker you were."

He stuck the thing into a grin of pure pleasure, and set it alight with the tip of his thumb. As always, the thing smelled a *little* bit better on fire. When the first puff diffused throughout the room, all the cheering and laughter redoubled anew, as that hideous scent we remembered of old worked its magic on all of our subconscious minds. (Well, mine was, at least, at the moment.)

"Does it make an appreciable difference," I asked, "the thing being seven years stale?"

"Oh, it does," he assured me. "It's just getting ripe."

"Naggeneen," I called out, "I no longer compel you . . . but maybe between us we might make a bargain . . . as equals and friends with a terrible thirst."

He paused in mid-air at the top of a leap and regarded me keenly. "Speak on, for ye interest me strangely," he said.

"Have you had enough spirit to take off the *edge* of your thirst for the evening, at least?"

"I might have," he said.

"There's a case of Black Bush sitting out in the truck, and a room full of sufferers long out of luck. It's a reasonable man I believe that you are—if I send for that case, will it get to my bar?" I pointed to the special Bushmill's backup-shelf just beside the Fount, about as long as the cluricaune was tall. "You can have all the bottles that fit on that shelf . . . but leave two or three for my friends and myself."

Again, maybe rhyming it helped. "It's a bargain," he shouted, and people applauded until they were hoarse.

Δ   Δ   Δ

About a hundred Irish coffees later, the supply ran out again, and I was finally able to take a breather. It seemed like it might be handy to have a cluricaune around the joint: whenever I got too overworked, I could slip him a wink and my problems would . . . uh . . . dry right up.

I took my own mug of God's Blessing, feeling that I had earned it, and looked for someone to talk with. One large group was gathered around Mike, over by the fireplace, all talking and listening and laughing at once. Another large group huddled around the cluricaune, listening to him bullshit. A third group was dancing gaily to Eddie's piano, smiling fiercely with tears running down their cheeks . . .

And down at the end of the bar, watching it all in the flickering firelight . . . the Duck.

I wandered over.

"I could pretend to be polishing the bartop," I said softly.

He spun round in his chair so fast I was afraid he was going to hit me; it was hard not to flinch. But when he was facing me, his expression was not angry, but . . .

Well, I don't know what it was, exactly. All that hair on

his face didn't leave a lot of room for expression to express itself. All I could say for sure was that the permanent sneer I'd thought the natural shape of his face was gone now—and whatever had replaced it, it looked unfamiliar with the territory.

"Mister Stonebender," he said to me, in an oddly formal tone, "I liked what you did just now. You and your friends. If a walking thirst is welcome here . . . would it be all right if I hung around here and tried to get telepathic with you people?"

I was touched, and moved by how much effort it had cost him to ask. "All right?" I repeated. "I think it would be world-class, Mr. Shea."

He gave me his hand, and I shook it solemnly.

A corner of his mouth twitched. "Kind of hard to square getting telepathic with that house custom of yours, coldcocking anybody that asks a snoopy question. Or is that just with newcomers?"

I shook my head. "That's the right way to *get* telepathic: walking on eggshells, with the awareness that a mistake could put a knot on your own skull. It's *dark* in there. So what ends up happening half the time is, people with sensitive areas they don't want to talk about get so tired of watching people back away from them on eggshells that they say the hell with it, and cut loose of whatever hangup it was. The other half of the time, at least nobody ends up feeling violated. Look, how about if I try to read just what's right up on the *top* of your mind, right now? Just the headlines, I mean."

He scratched his hairy head and thought about it. "The ones above the fold. Okay?"

"Sure. Hey, Mike! You got a minute?"

Callahan excused himself from the group he was talking with and came over. Brian Boru, the cluricaune had called him. Hell, for all I know, maybe Mike *had* been King of

Ireland at the turning of the last Millennium—and Cu Chullain a millennium before that, too, for that matter. I saw him deal with Hitler as an equal, once. All I can tell you is, barefoot and barechested, wearing another man's trousers and trailing clouds of toxic waste from a cheap cigar, he strode through my place like a king. He slid gracefully into a tall chair next to the Duck, and saluted him with a half-empty glass of the Black Bush.

The Duck nodded back at him and turned to me. "Not bad, pal," he said judiciously. "You don't miss a lot."

"Go on, ask him," I said.

He shrugged, and turned back to Callahan. "Mike, I'd—"

"You want to know," Callahan said, "how I knew your name was Ernie."

The Duck raised an eyebrow. "You guys volley pretty good around here."

"I haven't even started," Mike said. "The Great Miasmo sees all, tells all. You can see there's nothing up me sleeves— now tell me how close I come."

"Fire," the Duck said.

Callahan put his head back and recited softly. "You're special. Things go haywire around you. It's like you sweat practical jokes. The laws of probability don't apply to you. I hear people call you the Duck: that must be short for The Lucky Duck, right?"

"Go on," the Duck said tightly. "You're doing great."

"Let's see, there isn't a mountain from one end of Long Island to the other, so you must live in some kind of ruin."

The Duck nodded, frowning. "An abandoned mansion. I usually pick places like that. I don't bother anybody there—or get bothered—and if I need any food or water or electricity . . . well, I seem to get lucky. Go on."

"Your mother—"

"Yah?" the Duck said sharply.

"I mean no disrespect," Callahan said carefully, "in discussing your mother. If it helps any, my wife is a madam. But would I be correct in guessing that your mother is . . . of inexcessive stature, like yourself? And perhaps, also, what some might consider . . . more hirsute than average, again like yourself?"

The Duck waved his hand, to show he took no offense. "Short as a fireplug, hairy as a . . ." He hesitated. "She taught me how to shave, okay?"

"And she always took you for wild rides on her back, when you were a kid."

"You must be reading my mail," the Duck said. "Look, Mister—"

"The only part I can't figure out," Callahan said meditatively, stroking his bristly chin, "is why you aren't wearing any red."

The Duck's eyes widened. "Ma has a fetish about that. She made me swear never to put on anything red as long as I lived . . . thinks it's the color of the Devil . . ."

"Ah," Callahan said, as one who has had a great mystery cleared up for him. "I think I see. Much is becoming clear to me now."

The Duck slowly regained his characteristic expression—bored scorn—and put it on like a raincoat. "Look, Sherlock Holmes," he said, "nobody likes being gaslighted more than me—I've been known to drive hundreds of miles to get jerked around by total strangers—but if you know what you know, then you know it's the *mystery of my goddam life* you're screwing with here. You want to make me the straight man in a mentalist act, fine. String it out as long as your sadistic little heart desires, by all means—I'm not a killjoy—but when you finally get to the blowoff of this pitch, when you're ready to read my leaves or do my chart or toss my stalks or whatever it is you're gonna do, would you wake me up?"

Mike was immediately and sincerely apologetic. "I am sorry, Ernie. Sometimes I get too cute for the room. I'll tell you anything you want to know—and I'll lead you if you can't find the right questions, okay?"

"What's a Fir Darrig?" the Duck asked.

The moment he said the term, I remembered how alarmed he had looked, the first time he'd heard me use it, in the course of explaining to the group about the Daoine Sidh. I had misunderstood the reason for his dismay, then. Because when *he* pronounced "Fir Darrig," now, I realized at once that I had already heard the Duck say it once before.

When he had told me the name his mother had always called his absentee father. "Feared Eric," I'd heard him say, at the time—but unbeknownst to both of us, he'd been saying, "Fir Darrig" . . .

"A Fir Darrig, often called the Red Man, is one of the Daoine Sidh," Callahan said promptly. "Like a cluricaune, he tends to attach himself to a house or locality, rather than to a family. Stands about three feet high on average, always dresses in red cap and coat, and has a very flexible voice, alternately described as *fuaim na dtonn,* the sound of waves, and *ceol na naingeal,* the music of angels, and *ceileabhar na nèan,* the warbling of birds. They are the practical jokers of the Daoine Sidh. Mischievous jokes if they like you, mean-spirited ones if you offend them, really nasty ones if you threaten someone they love. They sort of exhale good and bad luck. A leprechaun is always a sourpuss, and a cluricaune is usually almost offensively cheerful—Fir Darrigs tend to oscillate between the two states. Which can mean hell to pay for those around them."

The folks at Mary's Place are better than average at eaves-dropping unobtrusively. People had been doing so for the last few minutes, and even I'd had to look sharp to catch them at it—but now one or two of them smothered a rooba.

The Duck glared at them . . . and then sighed. "Listen up, people," he said in a *ceol na naingeal*. Heads turned, with politely expectant expressions. "Callahan here has just told me that I'm the son of a Fir Darrig. One of those Deeny Shee jokers, like our friend Naggeneen. Apparently I'm one of the Gods of Practical Joking on my father's side."

There was a thoughtful pause.

"I buy dat," Eddie said.

"Yeah, that does explain a lot," Doc Webster said. "How do you like that? Good for you, Duck-o."

"Why, that's wonderful, Ernie," Merry Moore said. "It must be nice to have that cleared up, huh?"

"I should have suspected," the cluricaune whooped happily. "The first time I've ever been tricked into payin' for liquor, I should have suspected a Fir Darrig's hand in the unlikely business. It's clever indeed that yer not wearin' red: it misled me entire. Good jape, Brother Duck, and I drink ta yer health!" He flung an empty Bushmill's bottle into the fireplace—several other receptacles followed it in—and led a round of applause.

"Congratulations, Duck," Long-Drink McGonnigle said respectfully. "There was a time in my youth when I'd have worshipped you."

"A lot of people have that reaction to me," the Duck said, but I could tell he was relieved by the general response.

"Mike," I said, "when I first met Ernie, I found myself speaking Gaelic to him. Something that sounded like 'Nadine, fuck me.' Any idea what that was?"

He nodded. "He'd just asked if he could warm himself at your fire, right? And you'd said sure."

"Come to think of it, yeah."

"That was your blood coming through, Jake me boy, saving your Irish ass. Instinct, something your grandmother told you when you were little, something you read and forgot, I don't know. You said, *'Na dean fochmoid fàinn,'* or 'Do not mock us.' It's the only form of address that will guarantee a Fir Darrig won't play any *harmful* pranks on your house."

"I wondered why I took such an instant liking to you, stringbean," the Duck told me.

He *had?* If that was true, I hoped I'd never see him suffer a fool.

"Okay," he went on, "this is good, this is interesting, let's keep this up. So I'm a halfbreed Fir Darrig. Practical jokes, riveting voice, sensitive nature, short and hairy, it all fits. Let me see if I can work this out: I can't *control* my practical jokes because I've only got half the genes for it, right? So maybe . . . wait a minute! Do you suppose the *color* could have anything to do with it? You said Fir Darrigs always wear red—could it be that if I were to . . . no, that's crazy. Ma never said a word about my screwball luck, never mentioned it, but I knew it drove her just as crazy as it did me. She'd never have prevented me from learning how to control it, and she's the one who made me swear never to wear red as long as I lived. Okay, back to my first idea: if I—"

He paused for breath long enough to notice that Callahan had a hand up, and fell silent, breathing hard.

"I'm afraid, son," Callahan said, "that you only have half the story."

The Duck stood very still and closed his eyes. He forced his breathing to slow with visible effort. He unclenched his hands a finger at a time and put them down at his sides. "Straighten me," he breathed, and opened his eyes. " 'cause I'm ready."

Mike gave it to him straight and quick. "Son, you're a pooka on your mother's side."

Δ   Δ   Δ

The Duck did not react in any visible way. Neither did anyone else, for a long ten seconds of silence and stillness.

Then Doc Webster cleared his throat. "Excuse me. Mike?"

"Yeah, Doc?"

"Look, I decided awhile ago I was never gonna let anything blow my mind again. Hanging around you, it was kind of self-defense, you know? I've accepted everything from a talking dog to a cockroach from outer space to a cluricaune, and I haven't complained, have I?"

"No, Sam, you haven't," Callahan agreed.

"I mean, I like to think I'm game. Irish fairies, flying saucers, JFK killed by Elvis, whatever: you put it down, I'll pick it up. I just want to be absolutely sure I've got it straight, that's all. So look me square in the eye, and tell me one more time, with a straight face: *the Duck's mom is a seven-foot-tall white rabbit named Harvey?*"

Mike almost smiled. "That movie didn't use anything about pookas but the name, Doc. It was as faithful to Irish mythology as a scifi movie is to science. Pookas can manifest as a lot of different animals—goat, horse, bear, wolf—but they're always *hairy,* not furry."

The Duck was nodding, just enough to see.

"They're short, not seven-footers, damn near as short as a Fir Darrig or a cluricaune. And they don't just sit around in a white vest, sipping a quiet drink with Jimmy Stewart, chatting amiably. They are not especially pixilated or civilized or loveable. What they mostly do is scare the shit out of people—"

"—by taking them for wild rides on their back," the Duck said quietly. "Yes?"

"Yep. They mostly live in old ruins, or isolated mountains. They're lonely and quirky and generally considered dangerous."

"And once in a long while, one of them gets lonely and quirky enough to develop a hankering for miscegenation with something exotic. Like a Fir Darrig. And gives *him* a wild ride on her back . . ."

"If one ever did," the cluricaune said, the compassion of the grandly drunk plain in his voice, "she'd be sure to be spendin' the rest of her days in regret and remorse, with contempt for herself and a black reputation. T'is a union Saint Patrick himself couldn't bless, and a recipe certain for very bad cess."

The Duck spoke to Callahan. "You're telling me that I'm the only person in North America who's *right* when he says, 'Everything screwed-up in my life is my parents' fault!'?"

Mike took a deep breath. "In a word . . . yes."

The Duck closed his eyes and visibly calmed himself. "Ma and I will have to have a little talk," he said gently.

"Yes."

He opened his eyes. "No wonder she didn't have any pictures of her parents. No, wait—Jesus Christ! *Ma's always kept a pair of goats . . .*" He closed his eyes and controlled himself again. "They *acted* like my grandparents, of course, but all goats do that," he said in calm, reasonable tones. "I *thought* Ma spent a lot of time with them."

Rooba rooba . . .

He was quiet for a time, then, and the rest of us fell silent as well. What could you say to a guy who'd just had a revelation of that kind and magnitude?

Well, what *could* you say? Something had to be said, that much was clear. Our new friend and newest family member was at cusp. But *what?* "I know how you feel . . ."? I racked my brains as the silence stretched out. Something sympathetic? Or was that the wrong tack with this thorny man? Something facetious to try to break the tension? *Could* a tension like that be broken, with any of the cheap gags I thought of? Something macho, stoic? Like what? I looked to Callahan. He shrugged helplessly back at me.

"I know how you feel," Fast Eddie said.

The Duck opened his eyes and blinked at him mildly.

"As for me," Eddie went on, "my fodda was a jackass, an' my mudda was a sow. My grandparents . . . I don't know *what* species dey was."

In spite of himself, the Duck grinned.

"My parents were both vampires," self-effacing little Pyotr said truthfully, sipping his Mary's Bloody (Type A).

"I myself am the offspring of a turkey and a barracuda," Long-Drink McGonnigle said, and Doc Webster, who knows the Drink's parents well, went into quiet hysterics, his big belly shaking.

"I am ze son uff a bitch unt a sonofabitch," Ralph von Wau Wau offered. As the big mutant German shepherd ages, his phoney accent gets thicker.

"I didn't know that about your dad, Ralph," Slippery Joe said.

"Oh, *jah*. He vas so mean to my muzzer, I vas forced to bite him ven I vas old enough."

"You mean—"

"*Jah.* I put my maw on my pa, and zen gafe my paw to my ma. Alzo, my anzestors were allegedly involfed vith sheep a great deal. Ve may haff relatifs in common, Duck."

The Duck began to chuckle softly.

"A swine and a bat, here," Margie Shorter put in, bringing more laughter from the crowd. "Only I think Mom cheated on him with a tiger."

"Captain Ahab and the Great White Whale," Doc Webster said, cracking up Long-Drink.

"I have it on good authority that both my parents were bear when they conceived me," Shorty Steinitz said to a chorus of groans, and became the focus of a shower of peanuts and crumpled napkins.

"I'm a Thorne on my mother's side," Tommy Janssen said. "That's what she always says, anyway—"

The Duck was giggling outright now.

"As you can see from my physique," I said, drawing myself up proudly, "My father was a rock and my mother was a hard place. They call me Stonebender, and they ain't shittin'."

"I don't know how to tell all of you this," Isham said, "but my grandfather on my father's side was a white man."

"No!" "Jesus, Ish, that's awful!" "It's not your fault, bro," and "Be *strong,* homey!" were among the comments heard amid the laughter.

"That's nothing," Marty Matthias called out. "My *mother* is a white man." Whoops. "Hey, listen," Marty's bride Dave said, "you should taste his spaghetti sauce." Louder whoops. "And he gave me some terrific tips on accessorizing," Bill Gerrity said.

The Duck stopped laughing quite suddenly. He frowned ferociously, took in a very deep breath, and when he spoke I thought we had blown it, thought he was saying, "Bah!" The laughter faltered for a second . . . and then redoubled as we realized he was pulling our chain, that what he was braying was not, "Bah," but a goat's "Ba-a-a-a-a-a-a-a—"

He finished it with "—humbug!" just the same . . . and then threw an arm around Callahan and gave him a squeeze. Amid the applause, Margie Shorter slipped under his other arm. "So tell me, Ernie," she purred, "aside from having enough hair to get a decent grip on . . . exactly what other characteristics do you share with a goat?"

There was a burst of merriment at the question, and then everyone hushed to hear the Duck's reply.

He blinked at her—Marge is a short woman; they were

almost at eye-level—and pursed his lips judiciously, and said, "All I can tell you is . . . improbable things happen."

And she shivered deliciously and melted against him as the ovation began.

I think only I heard what she murmured to him. "Here's looking at you . . . *kid.*"

He butted her with his head.

△   △   △

A little later, when the attention of the group had fragmented again and the party was in progress once more, the Duck got a chance to finish his conversation with Callahan.

"So if I understand this right, my . . . abilities are out of control because I didn't get raised properly. Dad wasn't there to teach me how to be a Fir Darrig, and Ma hated the sound of the word. So what do I do now? Is it like learning to talk, there's a window and then it closes, and now it's too late? Or do I make a pilgrimage to Ireland and try to find a Fir Darrig who wants an adopted son so badly he doesn't care if the kid's retarded?"

Callahan put a fresh light to his cigar, then waved his thumbtip out. "I can't really say I have any answers for you, son. I know what I'd do in your shoes."

"What's that?"

"Stay right here and have a drink."

The Duck snorted and followed the advice.

"I'm serious," Callahan said. "Hang out with these folks. From what I understand, they have set themselves the goal of becoming mutually telepathic—and furthermore are sensible enough not to be attached to succeeding. That's smart behavior for anybody of any species or race. Furthermost, it calls for an unusual amount of luck—a job with your name on it. And I have a feeling that the doors in your head you'll have to open to join with them are some of the very doors you need opened to get a handle on your talent. The very first thing necessary to anyone who's weird is a place where they don't give you a hard time just because you're weird."

The Duck looked around him. He slid forward on his chair, held out his half-full glass, and dropkicked it. It caromed off his foot without tumbling or spilling, and disappeared into the crowd. There was a small, traveling commotion, a startled *gulp,* a small crash and assorted ancillary noises, and the wave of commotion came back through the crowd again. The glass appeared in the air, upright, incoming, and the Duck caught it without seeming to make any effort at all. It was now half full of peanuts. "Thanks, Duck," Ben called politely, and folks went back to their conversations again. The cluricaune was juggling empties over by the fire. At least thirty of them.

"I *have* been looking for a place like this for a godawful long time," the Duck admitted in a very soft voice, and ate a peanut.

Suddenly Long-Drink McGonnigle was upon us, bellowing and whooping in acute glee. "Jake! Mike! The penny just dropped!"

"That was my glass," the Duck said, but Long-Drink over-rode him in his excitement.

"No, no, I mean something just occurred to me—no, I mean, something just *failed* to occur to me—hasn't occurred to me for hours, now, in fact, and anybody here will tell you, that's just not normal, certainly not for me; I mean, not getting rained on is fine, I'm not knocking that, but *this* is *fantastic!"*

"I'm certainly glad you've cleared that up, Drink," the Duck said.

"Don't you get it? Don't all of you get it?" He turned around and addressed the room, at the top of his lungs: "WE ARE THE MOST FORTUNATE HUMANS ON EARTH!"

From his piano, Fast Eddie said quietly, "Hell, we know dat, Drink."

Long-Drink was practically tearing his hair. "Jesus, I never saw such a bunch of dummies! Don't any of you turkeys see it? We've found the End Of The Rainbow—only there isn't any gold in the pot, that's the glorious part!" He spun on me. "Jake, you genius, Duck, you genius, together you're solid gold: thanks to you two, no serious drinker who walks in here will ever leave again!" He spun back to the crowd, apoplectic with joy. "You fools, can't you see it? It's right under your belt-buckles!"

People were staring, clearly beginning to doubt his sanity despite long acquaintance.

Long-Drink turned to Callahan. "Mike: in your best professional estimation—and excluding our esteemed friend, Naggeneen—how much sauce would you say we've put away since you arrived?"

Callahan looked thoughtful. "I would say . . ." He looked around, gauged faces. " . . . about three quarters of a shitload."

Long-Drink nodded and turned back to face the crowd. "Right. Now tell me, you rummies: in all that time . . . *has that door over there swung open once?*"

We all followed his pointing finger . . .

. . . to the bathroom door. (A single door, marked "Folks.")

Stunned silence.

"Does anybody need to go *now?*" Long-Drink cried.

"Jesus Christ," Eddie breathed, and hit a discord and stopped playing.

"Well," I said, "that *would* be one side effect of having a cluricaune around the joint."

Naggeneen whooped drunkenly. "The pleasure's all mine, I'm sure!"

"That settles it," the Duck said. "I'm staying."

9

Lost Week, and—

What with one thing and another, it got kind of drunk out.

I mean, if you start with the best bar in the Western world (he said modestly), and the best friends a man ever had, all together again for the first time in a long while . . . and if then you add a cluricaune—a hundred glorious Irish barflies rolled into one dwarf body—and work out a truce with him that allows others to get a goddam drink in his vicinity . . . and if you also add a half-breed Fir Darrig / pooka, in whose presence the laws of probability explode of their own volition . . . and if then, for good measure, you throw in Mike Callahan, whom none of us had ever really expected to see again, and for whom the passage of time is a variable . . . well, is it any wonder that Saturday night went on a little longer than usual?

Naturally we were flat out of booze by dawn of Sunday, what with a cluricaune in the house. But it is not all that unusual for a ginmill to need an emergency shipment of juice on a Sunday morning; my distributors' phone turned out to be manned at that hour, and they were happy to service my needs. Even the quantity—thrice what I had told them my usual weekly order was going to be, and a full half of that in Irish whiskey—didn't faze them. They wanted a big markup, of course, with a hefty surcharge for immediate delivery— but when I mentioned that I'd be paying in solid gold coins, they changed their minds about both, and became very polite besides. In fact, the delivery truck was there in twenty minutes. The driver was a little startled. He'd never received a standing ovation for making a delivery on a Sunday morning before. Not so startled as to forget to test my gold coins before accepting them—but he did apologize.

I climbed up on the bartop, declared the bender to be officially begun, and got an ovation of my own. As the applause and the sound of glasses smashing in the fireplace began to subside, Fast Eddie began the unmistakable opening vamp of the most appropriate tune I can think of: Louis Jordan's evergreen, "Let The Good Times Roll." Hey everybody, let's have us some *fun*—

And one of the great drunks of our time got under way.

Not everybody stayed the course, of course. A few folks went off to church, shortly after the St. Bernard truck arrived, and not all of them made it back again afterward. A few sissies crawled out the door as Sunday wore on, victims of poor conditioning. (It had, after all, been a long time since Callahan's Place, our original training camp, had been converted to a large radioactive hole in the ground.) A sizeable contingent went off to assorted jobs on Monday morning, and again only about eighty percent returned as soon as they were able. (All these dearly departed, by the way, departed dearly— that is, by cab. The coffee can behind the bar contained every set of car keys in the room. Like Callahan before me, I won't let anybody too drunk to drive leave my place with car keys in their possession.) And from time to time there were other dropouts for one reason and another.

But most of us hung in there, and with very little difficulty we soon achieved that rare, remarkable state known as Beyond Drunk.

Do you know that condition? Have you been there? It comes only with truly heroic drinking, and comes but seldom even then. My limited research suggests that it occurs a maximum of two or three times in an average lifetime, and that it happens to alcoholics no more often than it does to healthy citizens. It's not something you can set out to do. Maybe it helped that most of us were drinking Irish coffee; maybe that was irrelevant. It seems to have less to do with blood alcohol content or predisposition to intoxication than it does with your emotional state at the commencement of the binge, and the set and setting of the binge itself. You break through some kind of invisible psychic / biochemical membrane, and pass *beyond* drunkenness, to a state in which you do not feel drunk or act drunk or look drunk . . . but neither do you feel any of those nagging human sorrows (loneliness, fear, pain, regret, apprehension, etc.) that caused you to get drunk in the first place. You're not sleepy or sore or dizzy or tired or uncomfortable in any way; your stomach feels so good that if you happen to think of it you'll eat; your head doesn't hurt; your tang has untungled; your wit is flowing and your perceptions are clear. You would pass a drunk test with flying colors. Indeed, only three things prove you haven't accidentally sobered up somehow: the Olympian height, depth and breadth of your wisdom, insight and compassion; the profound (and profoundly unusual) conviction that there is nothing fundamentally wrong with anything, anywhere in the universe—just a series of silly, easily correctable misunderstandings; and the fact that no amount of further alcohol intake will have the slightest perceptible effect on you.

Kids, don't try this at home! Every weekend a thousand morons, under the sincere delusion that they have achieved this rare state, get behind the wheel of a car—and all too often kill other, worthwhile human beings rather than just themselves. One of the proofs that you have actually achieved the real thing is retaining the wit to eschew driving or operating heavy machinery. I repeat: it's not something you do; it's something that happens to you, once or twice in a lifetime. If you're lucky. All you can do is try to be worthy, and wait.

Callahan claimed to hold the world's indoor record in sustaining this condition. Furthermore, he offered the name of a witness who could substantiate the story: the man he'd been drinking with at the time. And who should it be but one of my musical heroes: "Spider" John Koerner of Minneapolis, one third of the old Koerner, Ray & Glover "Blues, Rags and Hollers" team—the *original* white bluesmen—and solo author of such immortal albums as "Running Jumping Standing Still," and "Music Is Just A Bunch Of Notes." (A recent release, on Red House Records, is called, "Nobody Knows The Trouble I've Been.")

"This goes back quite a few years," Mike said. "Spider John had just cashed a fat check from his record company, Sweet Jane; he showed up at the Scorpio Room in Setauket as I was havin' a quiet drink, put a fat wad of cash on the bar, and said to the barkeep, 'Let me know when that's gone.' I was on vacation, and I calculated his stake at over three grand, so I volunteered to keep him company, sorta ride shotgun. We started drinking at about eight on a Monday night.

"At four A.M., the bartender left us the keys and went home. The day man was a little surprised to find us there drinking when he came to open up, but he got into the spirit of the thing pretty quick. The third harmony sounded good: he had a nice tenor. Then the owner showed up again for night shift, and we were able to get into some barbershop stuff, until he and the day man flaked at four again.

"It went like that for days. On Wednesday, the day man couldn't take the gaff anymore, so he went home and Koerner and I ran the bar for him in between drinks. By Thursday, we were covering for the night man, as well, bein' as we felt a little responsible for him bein' in that condition. We made money for him, too; by that point the word had started to spread, and people were comin' in just to watch us drink and hear us tell lies and sing. Lots of 'em wanted to buy us drinks, but the Spider wouldn't let 'em. Oh, if anybody wanted to challenge him to a chugging contest, he'd take their money, but other than that he drank his own drinks. And paid for mine besides . . . except for what *I* won on chugging contests.

"A week to the day after we started, Koerner kind of disappeared off into the back room with a lady named Slippery Sue. He was gone about an hour and a half, and some people tried to claim he'd caught a quick nap and broke the string. But Sue swore he'd been . . . active the entire time, and we all knew she'd never lie about a thing like that. He came back to the table kind of steadied down and mellowed out, and settled down to some serious drinking.

"On the twelfth day the bartender swam up out of the mist with a sorrowful expression on his face. 'I'm sorry, Spider,' he says to Koerner, 'but your money's spent. These two here is on the house.' 'No problem,' says John. 'Wait right here, Mike, and nurse these last two drinks.' And he gets up and goes around the corner to the nearest joint with a stage, the Ratskellar, unpacks that whacky guitar of his—he had it up to nine strings at that point, I believe—plays a sixty-minute set, passes the hat and collects a couple of hundred bucks, comes back to the Scorpio, puts the deuce on the bar, sits down across from me again, and we go back to drinking."

"Jeeze," Fast Eddie said in tones of awe. "How long did youse last altagedda, Mike?"

"Well, that's a little hard to say, Ed. The last one to see us was the bartender, when he went home at two in the morning on the fourteenth day. I remember a couple of hours of conversation after that—Koerner explaining the more obscure metaphysical implications of his famous discovery that the meaning of life is, Do The Next Thing—and then I blinked. And when my eyes opened from that blink, at least that's how it seemed to me, I was on horseback, stark naked, galloping through Central Park at high speed."

△   △   △

Fast Eddie blinked, experimentally, opened his eyes, looked around at his unchanged surroundings, and shrugged. "How'd you get home?"

"Well, it turned out to be a cop's horse, so naturally the first order of business was ditching the NYPD saddle. And I found a plaid horse-blanket in a saddlebag, so me and the horse didn't *both* have to be bareback. Wrapped it around me like a toga and we cantered to Sally's House together. I didn't see any sign of Spider John anywhere."

"Riding a stolen cop-horse bareback in a plaid toga from Central Park to a whorehouse in Brooklyn," Doc Webster mused. "You attract any attention?"

"Hardly any," Mike said. "The few times anybody looked at me funny, cops and so on, I'd just start bellowing as loud as I could in all directions, ' "Attack of the Horseclans," coming soon from United Artists!' I suppose we might have caused a traffic jam goin' across the Brooklyn Bridge, but there was already one goin' on when we got there. We picked our way through it. I did have one spot of almost-trouble as I was going through Bed-Stuy. A street gang got real mad at me when they saw the welts and scars on the horse's flanks, and wanted to kick my ass. But when I explained I'd just stolen him from a cop, they smiled and shared some Mogen David with me and busted a hydrant so I could water the horse. While he was drinking out of a hubcap, a few of the boys found some health food in a trash can that he liked just fine, and one of them bought me a Big Mac. We parted friends.

"Oh, by the way, I checked the date with them, and found out it was now sixteen days since Spider John and I had sat down to have some drinks.

"By the time I got the horse safely through the door and into Sally's Parlor, I was so exhausted I fell asleep right then and there, sitting upright on his back. I woke up thirty-six hours later on a soft mattress, feeling as good as I've ever felt in my life."

"What finally happened to the horse?" Long-Drink McGonnigle asked.

"He stayed on at Sally's for several years," Maureen said.

"Zo *dot's* how Scout came to Lady Zally's!" Ralph von Wau Wau exclaimed.

Maureen nodded. "Young lady on Sal's staff named Cathy, very empathic with animals—"

"She zertainly vass," Ralph agreed reverently.

"—she helped Scout work through some colthood trauma stuff, and they ended up forming a team together: she started billing herself as Catherine the *Really* Great. Very impressive, actually."

"How do you housebreak a horse?" Long-Drink asked.

Fortunately Doc Webster interrupted. "What happened to Koerner? How did *his* drunk end up?"

Callahan shrugged. "I don't suppose we'll ever know. Witnesses disagree. The next I heard of him, he was in Norway, married. He's back now, tending bar in Minneapolis, and he claims to have no memory of that period. I hear his guitar is up to twelve strings now."

"Jesus," I said. "He reinvented the twelve-string . . . a string at a time, over twenty years."

"Don't worry," Callahan said. "He'll put a thirteenth string on it any day now."

"So, as far as can be documented," Doc Webster said, "the indoor record is fourteen days."

"Well," Callahan said judiciously, "I don't see how getting from the Scorpio Room to naked on horseback in Central Park leaves much time for a nap, so I'd be inclined to say sixteen. But you're right, fourteen is all I can prove." He gestured respectfully toward the cluricaune with his glass of beer. "I speak, of course, of human beings," he clarified. "As for yourself, Naggeneen, I venture to guess that you've never been sober for fourteen consecutive days in your life."

The cluricaune laughed merrily. "How I wish you were right, Mister Callahan. I mind me a publican over in England, got tired o' me drinkin' his liquor and sold off his pub to some Muslims who turned the place into a mosque. I lasted a month before finally givin' it up and relocatin', quite the most terrible month in me life. Small wonder them people are so goddam irritable! Oh, I grant yez the Irish are bellicose people themselves—but by Harry, at least we ain't *humorless.*"

"Me, I agree with Stevie Wonder," Doc Webster said. "Heaven is ten zillion lite beers away."

Long-Drink hit him with a handful of beernuts. "Physician, heel thyself," he said. "And meet me out in front of the saloon at high noon, with puns blazing!"

"You got a duel, podnuh," the Doc said. "Say, did I ever tell you about the breath mint I invented?"

"Aw, hell yes," Long-Drink said. "Your slogan was, 'breath is no longer the wages of gin.' That's an old one, Doc."

But Doc Webster was shaking his head. "No, this one only worked on beer. But it did more than just counteract beer-breath: it made your mouth taste *delicious*—as long as you'd had a couple of beers before you chewed it. Remember the fun we had testing it, Dorothy?"

Dorothy, an alumna of Lady Sally's House—who is exclusively gay, and has a *wonderful* sense of humor about it, clearly didn't know what the Doc was talking about, but was willing to play along. "Sure do, Sam. The only heterosexual night of my life so far."

"As a matter of fact," the Doc agreed, "we were thinking of marketing it for Lesbians who wanted to go straight . . . only we couldn't find any." Dorothy broke up at that.

"What were you going to call it?" Long-Drink asked suspiciously. " 'Dyke-otomy,' right?"

"No, 'Iatrogenia,' " the Doc said. "That's the correct technical term for a physician-induced, de-Bilitating ale mint."

A howl of outrage went up, and the Doc nearly disappeared in a blizzard of beernuts and crumpled napkins. Glasses shattered in the hearth.

"That's Mytilene humor, Doc," David said, and was awarded a lesser howl of his own. Lot of classical educations among my clientele.

"Then Lesbos have a drink on it," the Doc replied without hesitation, and the outcry threatened to become a full-scale riot.

"Me," Long-Drink said, "I nearly marketed an aerosol, once."

The group fell relatively silent, giving him rope. Dorothy, sensing that Fate had decided to pull a pun of its own and make her the straight man tonight, obligingly called out, "What did it do, Phil?"

Long-Drink inclined his head in thanks. "Altered your chromosomes, so that your children had a high probability of growing up to be Groucho Marx's assistant. Surely you've heard of it? The famous Fenneman high-gene spray . . ."

A pause, of about three beats' duration . . . and then a roar of horrified approval rang the rafters.

Well, from there it got worse, of course. (It nearly always does.) The topic having been more or less established, the Duck said he had always thought female medical problems a fertile field for study—"If we invested a little dough in yeast infections, for example, I'll bet we could make a lot of bread."—and Fast Eddie warned him he'd be sure to end up in the hole, and former minister Tom Hauptman got off a tortured literary reference to himself as the E*D*U*C*A*T*I*O*N O*F H*Y*M*E*N C*H*A*P*L*A*I*N. So naturally the ladies started coming back with lines about guys with microcephalic cymbals, and boyfriends who wore shorts in the shower to keep themselves from looking down on the unemployed, and so on. As far as I can tell, Mary's Place is the only place left in North America where it's safe for men to make women jokes and vice versa. Somehow, we seem to have the Battle of the Sexes down to a friendly arm-wrestle. My theory is that hanging out with us tends to cure fear, and you can't sustain rage without fear to fuel it. All I know for certain is that it's a precious pain, when your stomach aches from laughing that way, and that it's nice sharing that pain with female persons.

Maybe you had to be there. I sure did . . .

Δ   Δ   Δ

By Monday night, the few who wandered off to rejoin lives in progress began to be counterbalanced by newcomers showing up. I had put out the word that for the first two nights of Mary's Place's existence, attendance would be limited to just the hardcore Immediate Family, the survivors of that last night at Callahan's Place. But most of us had acquired at least one new friend in the time we'd been apart, and some of them began showing up on Monday night. A lot of them, it was soon apparent, were going to become regulars: Jeff, Christian and Donna come to mind offhand, and there were at least half a dozen others. A writer named Chris McCubbin came in claiming to be suffering from what he called "carpal tunnel vision," and with him was a programmer named Steve Jackson who bought a round for the house, saying he had a "persistent-hacking coffer." They earned grim laughter with their theory of the Worst Possible Merger: F.B.I.B.M.

As the week unfolded, an astonishing proportion of the newcomers were musicians of one sort or another—enough that after a while I just left a couple of amps and three or four mikes hot all the time. There was an alto sax player named Fast Layne Francis who was so nimble-footed and knowledgeable even our resident Fast, Eddie, couldn't manage to lose him. At one point, possibly Wednesday, an entire jug band walked in—jug, washtub bass, washboard, guitar, harmonica and spoons—did a twenty-minute unamplified set, passed the hat, and then disappeared into the night again. Nobody knew them: apparently the rent-party atmosphere we were generating had just synthesized them out of the ether. And a guy from Manitoba named Léo Gosselin knocked us all out with an amplified instrument I'd never heard of before, called a Chapman Stick. It looked like a fencepost, and was strung with ten strings: a guitar and a bass on the same neck. He played it like Stanley Jordan plays guitar, hammering with both hands, dueting with himself. He told us Chapman, the inventor, had made fewer than a dozen of the things so far. Fast Eddie and I both fiddled with it a little, but Eddie got more out of it than I did; I'd spent a lifetime training my right hand to be stupid. The thing is sort of a vertical piano, folded up like an old-fashioned hinged measuring-stick, and I hope Mr. Chapman makes a million of 'em.

Each time Eddie's hands gave out, someone craved permission to take his chair, politely enough to get it—and then blew well enough to *hold* it until Eddie was ready to come back to work. There was a longhaired R&B cat named Ron

Casat, and a shorthaired R&B cat named Bill Stevenson, and a show-tune guy named John Gray and a boogie-woogie guy named Raoul Vezina who accompanied himself on blues harp, and a stunning brunette named Kathy Rubbicco who used to run Dionne Warwick's orchestra and could play *anything,* brilliantly. Eddie actually hid, listening, so that she wouldn't stop until she was tired; he kissed both her hands when she got up.

At one point—Thursday, I think it was—I swear we had not one but *four dulcimer players* in the house at once, all terrific— Carole Koenig and Karen Williams on hammer dulcimers, and Fred Meyer and David Schnaufer on mountain dulcimers, the former accompanied by a banjo player named Jeff Winegar. (He mentioned casually that when *he* improvised, it was called Winegar's Fake, and Doc Webster nearly choked on a drink.) All four were terrific, in different ways. May you be lucky enough to hear four dulcimers in concert before you die, that's all I can say. Intricate embroidery with threads of crystal, ethereal and sparkling. Naggeneen the cluricaune wept . . . and bought them all a round!

And of course there were several guitarists. Two guys named Steve Fahnestalk and Randy Reichardt came in together, from somewhere up in Canada, who knew every song the Beatles ever recorded, together or separately, dead bang perfect—they even had their guitars tuned down half a step the way the Fab Four used to do. Either one could be Lennon, McCartney or Harrison at will, take whichever harmony nobody else knew. That singalong lasted most of Tuesday afternoon. There was a guy named Pete Heck, with a fabulous Martin, who had John Prine and the Eagles down cold, but did them in a smokey voice that was all his own. A guy I'd been hearing about for years, Nate Bucklin, showed up from Minneapolis and did two hours of original material that was, in its way, both as musically interesting and as deep-down-inside as anything James Taylor's ever done. With him was a five-piece group called Cats Laughing who, among other weird and wonderful things, blew Lady Day's classic "Gloomy Sunday" *in Hungarian*. A fellow named Andrew York did a solo set, switching back and forth from electric to acoustic, and among other things had an arrangement of "Waltz of the Sugarplum Fairies" that was completely different from Amos Garrett's but just as good. And a couple from Florida named Dolly and Donn Legge showed up; he played hot jazz guitar, and I swear she could scat just like Annie Ross used to, and neither of them looked old enough to remember *jazz,* let alone Annie Ross; I was tempted to card them. Eddie really enjoyed jamming with them a lot. And two guys named Chris Manuel and Bob Atkinson, who'd never met before, both hooked their MIDI gear together, and booted some of Bob's software, and did some amazing electronic guitar duets. I'd never dreamed you could make a guitar sound like a Hyacinthine Macaw. (Nor, until I heard it, would I have thought you'd want to.)

And Jordin and Mary Kay Kare did a set of what science fiction fans call filksongs—clever new lyrics on popular tunes. A couple of them required a reasonable familiarity with sf, but others did not. I remember one in particular, to the tune of "Oh, Susanna"; people were roaring with approval by the end of the first line. Jordin, a mildly furry brunet with blue-grey eyes, took the first verse:

Oh there is a guy with funny eyes, his name is Michael Finn
He carries quite an arsenal tucked underneath his skin
His masters had him programmed once, to do the whole earth in
And the only thing that stopped him was a glass of homemade gin
    Joy or sorrow: it's better if you share

> So I'll take me down to Callahan's, and do my drinking
> there

The chorus was greeted with enthusiastic applause. Mary Kay, a short, gorgeous blonde dressed in purple, took the second verse:

> A time traveler comes in each week and buys a coupla beers
> He drinks 'em down, then taps his belt, and promptly disappears
> Next week, same time, he's back again, still potted to the ears
> He's been on one long bender for some twenty thousand years
> Joy or sorrow: it's better if you share
> > So I'll take me down to Callahan's, and do my drinking there

They traded verses for a while, most of which I'll omit since each grossly libeled one of my regular patrons. Then husband and wife traded lines on the last verse:

> Doc Webster, feeling gene-ial, once told us of the day
> He mixed chromosomes from vegetables with canine DNA
> He crossed Lassie with a canteloupe. Says Mike, "So what'd you get?"
> "Why, a melon / collie baby . . . and one helluva startled vet!"

Everyone sang along joyously on the final chorus. Then Jordin reprised it—but at half speed, in minor rather than major, and with new words:

> Michael's tavern . . . is gone, beyond repair . . .

—and just for a moment, sorrow stabbed every heart—

—and then Jordin and Mary Kay came in together, at the original speed and voice, singing:

> *So it's time to race to Mary's Place, and do our drinking there!*

The house came down.

∆   ∆   ∆

Somewhere along about Thursday—or possibly it was Friday—I ran out of excuses, evasions and stalls. Callahan suckered me out from behind the stick to look at a poker hand he was holding, Tom Hauptman locked the little swinging door from the inside to *keep* me out, and Fast Eddie must have snuck into my living quarters in the back, because the next thing I knew he had my beat-up old Country Gentleman plugged into an amp and was strapping it around my neck. I gave up and stepped up to one of the mikes, blushing at the size of the ovation that ensued. I never blush when strangers applaud me, but somehow it's different with your friends. I barely remembered to take my apron off.

I played old favorites for a while. Loudon Wainwright III's "The Drinking Song," Jon Hendricks' "Shiny Stockings," my own "The Drunkard's Song," "I'd Love You If You Didn't Have Those Tits," "Shitheaded Driver Blues"—all the songs I'd always played for them in the old days, at Callahan's Place. Fast Eddie knew 'em all, of course. The Lucky Duck and Margie Shorter had been looking deep into each other's eyes for a whole day now; in the middle of "Shiny Stockings," they slipped out the door so unobtrusively at least three people missed it. Ah, young love! I'd have told them they were welcome to use the back room, but they were gone while I was in the midst of a verse. I felt a faint twinge of envy for Ernie. I'd had a half an eye on Margie myself. The hairy little pooka had good taste. Ah, well . . .

Nate came in with some rhythm guitar support on "Drunkard"; Donn put some delicious fills into " . . . Those Tits," and he and Nate had worked out the harmonies on the chorus by the second verse; and Peter and every other musician in the house took three choruses of solos apiece on the twelve-bar blues. Those present who did not laugh, wept; many did both.

After the final verse of "Shitheaded Driver," I remembered something, and called out, "Here's a new blues you'll appreciate, Mike!" Callahan smiled and nodded, and I sang:

You've heard of every kind of blues there is, I hear you
*   say?*
Well, I'm leavin' here tomorrow . . . and I just got back today

I got the time travel blues, look at the mess I'm in
I'm sad for what the past will be . . . and what the future
*   hasn't been*
I longed to know the future, like the Oracle of Delphi
And then this cat knocked on my door: Goddam, it was myself! I
*   got the time travel blues, since I met myself comin' in;*
*   I'd tell you all about it . . . but where the hell do I*
begin?

The other musicians all caught my signal, and went stop-time when I did:

He said that I was going to invent a time machine—
That is to say, I told me, if you follow what I mean.
I said, "I'm no inventor, man: I'll never ever get it."
But he said "Copy this one, and we both can share the
*   credit!"*

I cranked it up, it blew right up, and then and there I died.
I wonder who that joker was, and why the bastard lied . . .

Whooping, all the players jumped back aboard with me again for the chorus:

Got the time travel blues; one of my life's most awful shocks
Now I could use a doctor; in fact, I need a paradox

If I am dead, my murderer can't logically exist
But here I am in pieces, and I'm really gettin' pissed

I got the time travel blues—it's only natural, bein' dead
To want to think that time is really only in your head

I ended it with a classic barroom walkout. The applause and laughter were gratifying, and Mike brought me over a cold Rickard's Red. I'd wondered, writing that song, if I would ever in my life have a chance to sing it for him. His grin was something to see.

When I finished gulping ale, Fast Eddie yelled, "Got anything else new, Jake?" And I did happen to have a goofy new one with easily grokked, C&W chords. So I gave them "Please, Dr. Frankenstein—":

I've walked a thousand miles in an effort to retain ya
And I didn't come for charity: I fully plan on payin ya
But I've been so depressive, guess I'm ready for some mania
That's why I've traveled all this way to gloomy Transylvania,
singin

Please Dr. Frankenstein, won't you try to bring me back
to life?
Cause I truly have been grievin since I got "Goodbye, I'm
leavin" from my wife

I'm slowly goin nuts because the memory of her cuts me
like a knife
Please Dr. Frankenstein, won't you try and bring me back
to life?

I cannot seem to find my pulse; my temperature is down
And I can tell I smell like hell, the way that people frown
I feel like rigor mortis, all I do is lay around
You gotta help me Frankenstein, I'm halfway in the ground
(I'm beggin)

Please Dr. Frankenstein, I am up for any kind of change
Spent evenings in this coffin just a little bit too often,
and it's strange
Please don't consider me more than some flesh for you
and Igor to arrange
Please Dr. Frankenstein, I am up for any kind of change

I'll stagger like the victim of a wreck
I'll wear those funny bolt-things in my neck
I'd love to be in stitches—what the heck
Do you need cash, or will you take a check?

I'm not afraid of what you'll do—I'm immunized to pain
Cause everything I ever had has bubbled down the drain
Make me the Pride of Frankenstein and I will not complain
Just strap me down and let me have a transplant of the brain:
I need it

Please Dr. Frankenstein, won't you try and raise me from
the dead?
My heart is barely beatin since I caught the woman cheatin
in our bed

THE CALLAHAN TOUCH

My entire world's a coffin and it doesn't get me off an'
  like I said
Please Dr. Frankenstein, won't you try and raise me from
  the dead?

Which went over pretty good; I thought old Pyotr was going
to laugh himself to death. Once again, every musician who
tried to join in with a lick or a harmony got it right, and
nobody clammed the ending, a thing so rare it made me shiver
with glee as the applause drowned that final chord. I looked
around and met a lot of smiling eyes, and knew I'd made a
bunch of new friends . . . and that I was just a little bit closer
to telepathy than I'd been on Friday.

It was a job finding some of those eyes. The players were
scattered all around the room, some with long cords and some
with those newfangled cordless radio-boxes, rather than all
bunched up in one spot with their elbows in each other's eyes
the way it's usually done. Also, Fast Eddie had rigged a spot
on me, so folks could watch my hands good, and it made me
squint some. I'd heard a bass join in in the middle of the last
verse, off to my right somewhere, but I couldn't seem to see
the guy in the crowd.

A strange impulse came over me. I was feeling too good to
examine it: I went with it. "Lemme have a solo, folks," I said
to the rest of the players, "and then we'll all do another blues
together to finish up, in A this time, okay?" Nobody objected.
"Maybe just the bass, on this, if you think you can follow it.
I wrote this to my wife over twenty years ago, and I've never
played it for anybody but her . . . but I just feel in the mood
to, now, for some reason. It's called 'Spice.'"

And I sang:

> *And when I've just assuaged your lust*
> *By flicker-light of telly*

I love to lie between your thighs
My cheek upon your belly
To smell you and to feel you
And to hear your small intestine
And know that this is perfect bliss
Just as it was predestined

> *In the hour that my death draws near*
> *And I wonder what my life was for*
> *It'll be the afterglows*
> *With your fragrance in my nose*
> *I'll remember and relive once more*

By the third line of the chorus the bassman had doped out where I was going and come in quietly underneath. By the time I started the second verse he was already reminding me pleasantly of Lee Sklar, who did such wonderful work with James Taylor.

> *And now I rest, caress your breast*
> *And sail in satiation*
> *On the oceanic motion*
> *Of your rhythmic respiration*
> *And now my lips and fingertips*
> *Are flavoured sweet and sour*
> *For I have stripped and fully sipped*
> *My favorite furry flower*

> *In the hour that my death draws near*
> *And I wonder what my life was for*
> *It'll be the afterglows*
> *With your fragrance in my nose*
> *I'll remember and relive once more*

A vivid sense memory of Barbara—the very one that had caused me to write this song to her, only weeks before she was killed—rose up and struck me from ambush like a hammer to the heart; I would have stumbled if that strong bass hadn't rushed to support me. The guy improvised a four-bar vamp that sounded as if we'd rehearsed it, and nudged me gently but firmly into the last verse:

> *I know in time I'll have to climb*
> *Up next to you for sleep*
> *With no regret, but not just yet*
> *This moment let me keep*
> *And suddenly it comes to me*
> *—how glorious and dumb!—*
> *I had so much fun making love*
> *I plain forgot to come . . .*

My voice broke on the last word, I couldn't make the final chorus, and the bassman knew that at once and *did it for me* as a bass solo, once again so smoothly and naturally that it simply seemed the correct way to end that song; somehow I managed to put the last few chords on it to tack it shut with him.

The applause was loud and long. I stared down at my feet, too moved, and too startled at how moved I was, to meet anybody's eyes. Especially that bass player's eyes, wherever they were. Whoever he was, he now knew me better than I generally like people to know me before I've laid eyes on them or heard their name. When the applause began to wane, I kept looking down and started the blues in A, concentrating on my fingers. "Four choruses apiece, this time," I called.

By the second bar, every musician in the room was cooking with me. I didn't bother with lyrics; I could think of none I wanted to sing after that last song; I just played the blues.

Δ   Δ   Δ

And so did everybody else—but no two of us played the same *kind* of blues. I started us out in a kind of country blues, but after I'd done four choruses and nodded to Nate, he hopped into a Lightning Hopkins, East Texas bag; Nate handed off to Peter, who took us east to New Orleans for some of the dirty Delta blues; Peter passed the stick to Donn, who blew a Chicago-style blues somewhere between Buddy Guy and Mike Bloomfield; that set Fast Eddie up to do a Ray Charles thing; which cued me for some Charles Brown "cool" blues full of ninth chords, which reminded Nate of . . . well, you get the idea. The amazing thing was that, whatever groove was put down, Fast Eddie and that bassman were both able to pick it up, every time—sometimes turning on a dime. Each soloist won spontaneous shouts of joy as they played, and applause when their turn was done.

About the eighty-'leventh chorus, I ran out of ideas I knew how to play, and started to scat some vocals. Just noodling around, letting it come out without planning it, improvising nonsense-syllable riffs like some aphasic Jon Hendricks, humming the lines I'd have played if my hands were good enough. Doing what the blues is for. Pouring out my heart—

—a warm pure contralto came out of nowhere, somewhere off to my left, unamplified but strong, and started harmonizing with me—

—kept on doing it, magnificently, following me as flawlessly and effortlessly as if we'd both been reading the same sheet music—

—more: doing it—unmistakably—with *feeling,* as well as skill—

I'd have been shocked if I'd had the time; but I was too busy. Musicians wait a lifetime for an opportunity like that. I glanced wildly around, failed to spot her in the crowd—if it *was* a her; that voice had enough bottom on it to make me uncertain—and then I forgot where s/he was and who s/he was and what s/he looked like and just *sang,* backing off from my mike so our levels would balance.

Fast Eddie, aware that something extraordinary was going on, dropped out; one after another the other musicians faded too; only that telepathic bass player stayed in, somewhere over on the other side of me, giving the two of us a stable platform to dance on. Somebody, Tommy Janssen I think, located a free mike and disappeared into the throng with it; shortly her voice was amplified too, and I closed back in on my own mike.

She (it was a woman, all right: no mistake now) knew when I wanted to switch from harmony to crosstalk, dropped out and let me take the first phrase, then answered in a way that drove me higher for my next phrase—and kept that up. When I yelled, "Gimme one," she let me have a chorus all to myself, so I could make a complicated statement using the syllable "No" over and over again, putting my whole raggedy-ass white boy's soul into it (*here,* I thought, *listen to my blues!*); when it was her turn she nodded with her voice, (*Yeah, them is blues, all right*) and cut me clean . . . using the syllable "Yeah." People shouted with glee, and began to clap time . . .

Oh, Jesus, it was glorious and it was scary and it was exalting and it was . . . I don't know the words. It was *emptying,* does that mean anything to you? And filling at the same time. I hadn't had sex as good as that since Barbara died. I lived with a lady once for three years without coming to know her as well as I now knew this woman I had not yet even met. I kept thinking of a line from an old song of mine: "Bring me your nakedness / help me in mine . . ."

I knew, for instance, that she was—like me—a badly fractured and carefully rebuilt person. Stronger than ever now, like healed bone, but with a heightened understanding of fragility. And that unlike me, she had done her healing on her own, with little or no help. I knew about her pride, and her humor, and her courage, and her frustration, and her simple stubbornness, and her untapped and unplumbed capacity for kindness. For all I know, I knew more about her than she knew.

And I'm sure she knew more about me than I did, because she assured me later that she knew I was in love with her by the third chorus . . . and *I* didn't realize it until she cut me with her "Yeah" solo, several minutes later.

We both knew when we were done, and both said our first intelligible words—"Come on!"—together like an echo to the rest of the players, and they climbed on running, like hobos boarding a moving train. I played the best last-chorus of my life, throwing in a Johnny Winter quote from "Third Degree" that I've never been able to play correctly before or since, and when I got to the end of it—

Once I phonied up some press credentials so I could meet the crew of Apollo 16. They had come to Grumman Aviation to personally shake every single hand that had had anything whatsoever to do with building their LEM. It had worked, you see. As the event was breaking up, Grumman seized the moment. They were plagued with cost overruns on the F-111 at the time, and badly needed a PR break. So as we all filed out toward the parking lot, they brought an F-111 in at about two hundred feet, at stalling speed. As we craned our necks and gaped, it pointed its nose up at the stars, changed its wingshape, and suddenly *BANG,* it was gone—just a dwindling dot straight overhead with a hole in the sky to show where it had been. Everybody but the Apollo crew and the Grumman flacks jumped a foot. All three astronauts smiled wistfully (even the science guy), and watched that dot disappear with their fists on their hips, practically salivating.

Anyway, that's all I could think of when that blues ended, and her voice took off for the stars like an F-111 on afterburners. I think she reached brennschluss about six inches to the right of a standard piano keyboard, and coasted for another octave or two more before she reached apogee and began reentry. Up until that final gliss, my intentions toward her were strictly and enthusiastically dishonorable. But as she began tying off the cord, I grasped two things with utter certainty: that I needed to marry her, and that I was going to have to stalk her with the cunning and guile of a panther.

By the time we all beat that last chord to death with a stick together, I had even figured out that she was the bass player.

10

Sweet Reunion

As the clapping and cheering and whistling and stomping crescendoed, musicians came from every corner of the room to embrace me, led by Fast Eddie Costigan; I knew she would not be among them. We all swayed together in a gang hug, trying to accomplish the incompatible goals of pounding each other's shoulder blades and protecting our instruments. "Yes, *indeed!*" "God *damn!*" "The Bendin' End, cousin!" "Now I can die," "What'll we name the baby?" and, from Eddie, a simple, "Dat wuz right." The civilians around us gave us a respectful five seconds, and then just as we were all beginning to reluctantly concede the sheer impossibility of hugging everybody at once, the crowd swarmed us and tried to hug all of us at once. Guitar heads swayed above the scrum like something from *Fantasia*—a simile enhanced by the cluricaune, who hopped from one to the other like a bearded green beachball, a jumping bean with a pipe, slapping his thighs and laughing like a kookaburra till I thought his nose would burst.

I saw other musicians glance around for the singer and the bass player. Without exception, once they were sure neither was in the circle or its immediate fringes, they stopped looking. Nobody gets dragged into the limelight against their will in Mary's Place. She didn't owe us a thing; if anything it was the other way round. Besides, we were busy—trying to shield our axes, and dissuade our friends from lifting us up onto their shoulders, and express our mutual pleasure and gratitude.

"God, I wish somebody'd had a recorder going," someone said as the crush was finally breaking up (heading mostly toward the bar and poor Tom—who fortunately had sensed the wind and started lining the bar with full glasses and mugs before we even finished playing), and heads nodded eagerly.

"Thank God nobody had a recorder going," someone else said, and we all nodded just as hard.

Both were correct, and we knew it. A recording of that jam would have been gold . . . but awareness of being recorded might have prevented it from ever happening the way it had, by making us self-conscious. You play differently when you know it's being taped. The jam had been the stuff that dreams are made of—and you don't can that.

Once we had room enough to move, we all put away our axes and shut down the sound system. Nobody was about to follow that act.

Also, by tacit agreement, nobody was about to approach the singer until I had. The other musicians moved toward the bar as a group. As soon as they were gone, I followed microphone cord through the press of bodies until I found her.

Δ   Δ   Δ

I was carrying the receiver-module of her radio rig in my hand. It was her cordless bass that had confused me at first as to how many of her there were. The little receiver had been plugged into the amplifier on my right, so her bass lines had come from that side, whereas her unamplified voice had first come from my left, and Tommy had happened to bring her a mike connected to that amp. She had performed in stereo, with me at her center.

She was sitting way over by the fireplace, with her back to the room, gazing into the flames. Her bass guitar was upright and turned sideways, held between her thighs; her forearms rested on one of its cutaway horns, and its long neck nuzzled hers. Automatically I glanced at its head, to see if it was really the old Fender it had sounded like, but there was no logo or template of any kind. She knew I was coming. I saw her, by the way she held her shoulders, recognize my approaching footsteps. And I knew this was not going to be easy.

I glanced around quickly. No one in the room was gazing in our direction. Statistically unlikely. Nice friends I got.

Targeting computer: track this object. Report—

She was short. I guessed five-six. Built as if to my specifications. About one-eighty or so, and deliciously female-shaped. Sort of a nine-tenths scale model of Mary Callahan-Finn. Wearing it proudly, as if Rubens was looking. Hair longer than ladies her size seem to wear it these days. Dark red, brick red, soft-looking and wavy. The kind of gentle, natural waves that would make a woman with a perm wail and run to get it zapped again. Black off-shoulder blouse, billowy sleeves. Tucked in. Black skirt, not too short, not too tight. Black mesh stockings. Black shoes with silver buckles. Silver necklace. Silver bracelet, just a little loose, on left wrist. The hand she fretted with; short fingernails. I couldn't see the other wrist. Incredible hand. Long thick powerful fingers. Tips so callused they weren't grooved from the session, as my own were. Red alert! Ring visible on wedding ring finger. Silver, but maybe she hates gold, she has no gold anywhere else. Wide enough to be a wedding band. Don't panic. May have expired. No visible scars, tattoos, melanomas, rashes or running sores. One pimple below the right shoulder. Thank God: a flaw. Slouched slightly in her chair. Drained by the jam? Dejected? Drunk? Simply relaxed? Impossible to say.

I studied her so intently, approaching from behind at a slight angle, that as I came up next to her it was like getting to see the dark side of the moon at last. I was so busy absorbing the flood of new data, I damn near missed the chair to the right of her when I sat.

Smooth, Jake. Can't find both hands with your ass. Jesus, you're too old for this kind of adolescent bullshit.

Fine profile. Mouth as wide and sensuous as that of Ms. Loren herself. Splendid forehead. Jewish nose. Not a Streisand, but in the next class down. Large eyes, even seen from the side. Silver earring, at least on the right. A dangling silver circle, within which three curved threads of silver formed an iris or a three-legged swastika, as if someone had spun a peace-sign until the spokes curved and then froze it. In the center of the iris was what looked like an emerald chip. Lickable throat. Likewise collarbone. My peripheral vision told me not to look directly at her breasts. I am unattractive with saliva running down into my beard. At least to strangers. I blinked past them. Belly and hips shaped to make human beings. The thighs lived up to the calf I'd seen as I approached. Her legs were extended, ankles crossed. Nice ankles. A half-full mug of cold Irish coffee sat on the table to her left, beside her open black bass-case and black purse. I realized I had sat at a different table, because it was the chair closest to her. Nothing but empties at my table. I thought of turning my head and trying to catch Tom Hauptman's eye. But I couldn't take my gaze from her. Those eyelashes—

The *hell* I'm too old!

It dawned on me that if she had any peripheral vision at all, she knew I was staring. I drew breath to apologize.

"Fair enough," she said. "You were in the spotlight."

I let my breath out. All at once I had a vivid memory of the night I'd met the second great love of my life, Mary Callahan, nude in the rain, on the roof of her father's bar. The last time I'd been this excited. I had not just tripped over my tongue, that night. I had danced the mazurka on it, and then hopped off onto my dick. Only dumb luck had saved me. Ordinarily I am proud of my glib. Talking ladies into my bed or theirs has not often been a problem. Now suddenly seemed to be a good time to say as few words as humanly possible. I fixed my gaze on an imaginary point halfway between the center of the fireplace and her lips, so I wasn't exactly looking at her, but would know if she turned to look at me, and said:

"Jake."

She did not react at all for three long seconds. Then she unclasped her arms, picked up her bass, and set it carefully in its case. The transmitter had already been removed and stowed, so the lid shut. She snapped one catch for safety. She reached into the folds of her left sleeve, high up on the bicep, and came out with a cigarette. An unfiltered Pall Mall. Dismaying. I had been clean for over a year. Sometimes I went as long as ten minutes without wanting a smoke, now. I didn't know if I could live with a smoker without kicking the gong. She didn't wait coyly for a light. She reached into the sleeve again, took out a wooden stick match. Strike-anywhere, like the ones that had exploded in Long-Drink McGonnigle's pocket a hundred years ago. She lit it on the fingertips of her left hand. She lit the cig, flipped the match into the hearth without whipping it out first, and sent smoke after it. Then she fixed her gaze at an imaginary point halfway between the fireplace and my nose, and said, deadpan:

"Elwood."

Groovey. Let's hop in the Bluesmobile and get that money to the Penguin. It was even funnier because we had met playing a blues. So why wasn't I breaking up? If you're not going to laugh, Jake, at least say something witty to show you got the reference. She'll think you're a moron. Or one of those guys who's too hip to laugh; another kind of moron.

Screw it, she *knows* you got the Blues Brothers reference. And she can hear you laughing, even if nobody else could. The universe won't burn forever. Cut to the chase!

"Welcome home," I said.

It was the first words that popped into my head. She took another long slow puff on her cigarette, and just then Tom Hauptman materialized. He had a steaming mug of God's Blessing for each of us. He set one on each table, starting with hers.

She went for her purse, which hung from her chair.

"Your money's no good here," I said quickly. "Ever."

Too fast. Back off. Easy does it.

She looked up at Tom. He smiled. "Even if it wasn't his bar," he agreed. "Even if you never sing another note here. That was special."

She gave up and let the purse fall. "Thanks," she said to the fireplace. Tom nodded and dematerialized.

"I already said you're welcome," I said.

No response. We stared at the flames together for maybe ten seconds. Maybe twenty.

She whirled to face me. "What the hell do you want?"

I turned to answer her, hoping that an answer would come to me by the time I finished, and was sideswiped by my first sight of her eyes.

Take a small contact lens. Fill it from an eyedropper with limeade, almost to the top, so surface tension at the edges makes the surface concave. Freeze it. Then let it stand at room temperature, just until it slides free of its own accord when you tip the lens, glistening with moisture. You have duplicated one of her oversized irises. Meg Foster eyes, but pale green rather than pale blue ice. You had the persistent idea that those irises were whirling, just too fast to see. They were that hypnotic.

The next sensation I became aware of, a localized warmth, seemed natural and appropriate. For the first three-tenths of a second. Then it exceeded acceptable parameters—went right off the scale at shocking speed, like an F-111. Alarm bells began ringing urgently.

I had spilled hot coffee on my dick. Along with enough alcohol to keep the burn working as long as possible. And enough whipped cream to make the result look as stupid as possible.

△   △   △

I attempted a telepathic hookup with Mickey Finn, over I had no idea *how* much distance in both space and time. *God damn it, Finn,* I thundered at him, *how come rain won't fall on me but hot coffee can?*

Thank God, I found the wit and strength to laugh at myself. Yeah, bummer: my miracle turned out to be substandard. Made in Taiwan, with a counterfeit Sony imprint.

Come on, Jake—you're like Johnny Carson: best when you're going into the toilet.

"Well," I managed to say, "sex is out of the question, for at least the next hour and ten minutes." I set the mug down and placed a napkin over my crotch, resisting the impulse to rub. Then I took some ice cubes from one of the empty glasses nearby, dropped them down the front of my pants, and made a hissing steam sound.

She didn't want to grin, but she did anyway, and glanced at her watch.

"Never mind that bullshit," she said then, the grin fading.

"My name is Zoey, now answer my question—I'm old, Jake, I haven't got time to fuck around—you want me to join a group? You want me to see your etchings? You want a home-cooked meal? You want the chords to 'Wild Thing'? You want to get married? *What?* Just spell it out, okay? I'm willing to negotiate: just tell me what's on the table. What do you want from me?"

Decision time.

There is a James Taylor song I would quote, if it were not defended by vicious lawyers, called "If I Keep My Heart Out Of Sight." The singer feels that if he slips and shows his hand, it's a cinch he'll scare her off. But for the life of him, he can't think of anything to say except "I love you." For the first time I really understood that antinomy.

A relationship, if it's an important one, should begin with truth, right? A relationship is a person's home-study project in getting telepathic. You can't found that on a lie, can you? You have to go with the truth, or it's all stumbling in the dark in a room full of banana peels. Nobody can pilot through a hostile universe without honest data, can they? The honest answer to Zoey's question was: everything, and pretty bad.

I nodded to myself, and lied through my teeth. "I honestly don't know, Zoey."

She considered it. "Will you stop when I tell you to?"

The honest answer was, I don't know, but I doubt it. "Yes. My steering is spotty, but I got good brakes."

Zoey nodded, and turned her gaze back to the fireplace. I watched her smoke for a while, fighting the desire to bum a puff. After a measureless time she said, "How long for you?"

I picked up my mug, carefully, and sipped Irish coffee. "A couple of years ago, I had a couple of real good half-hours. Before that, I guess something like eighteen years. Not counting recreational fucking and some good friendships." I took a big gulp of my drink. "You?"

"Five years ago," she said. "But the marriage just ended two months ago. I don't give up easy."

"Ah." Ancient wisdom: rebound relationships can't work. No significant exceptions in recorded history. And if it *is* possible, it'll take at least a year for the epoxy to set, first. I sipped more coffee.

"Why did you say, 'Welcome home'?"

I shook my head. The truthful answer was, because I suddenly knew we have loved before, more than once, in previous lifetimes. Because this is a reunion. "Ask me in a year."

She accepted that. She leaned forward and tapped ashes into the fireplace. She took a long gulp from her own mug.

"Who told you about this place?" I asked. Thinking, which of my best friends am I going to have to steal you from?

She shook her head. "I broke down right outside on 25A. While I was trying to figure out the problem, I heard the music. I could hear you didn't have a bass."

Mary's Place is not visible from 25A. Tall hedges and a winding driveway. No sign. Set well back from the road. No sidewalk along that stretch, so little or no pedestrian passby. There's maybe fifty feet of highway where she could possibly have stopped and heard the music. If there was little traffic and the wind was right. I made a firm mental note. As of tonight, the Lucky Duck's money was no good in here either.

Then I remembered what Ernie had told me about the consequences of being a bystander to his paranormal ability. His luck, he had said, could turn your life upside down and shake out all your emotional pockets . . . but usually left you with nothing in your hand when the smoke cleared. If you won a million on the lottery, within an hour you had stepped in some kind of shit that cost a million dollars to get clear of.

Okay. Fair enough. How many people get to hold a million bucks for an hour? Come to think, that might be the ideal duration.

Then it came to me. The Duck had been long gone when Zoey's ride quit.

"So you came into Mary's Place," I said. "The talking dog and the cluricaune didn't put you off?"

She shrugged. "I'm pretty easygoing. That guy biting people on the neck startled me a little. That nobody seems to mind, I mean."

"Oh, Pyotr's not your conventional vampire," I said. "He doesn't *drink* blood, not a drop. He just filters excessive alcohol out of it with those teeth . . . along with food and fatigue poisons. He's sort of a walking hangover cure."

"I see."

"And you can't figure out what's wrong with your car, right? Everything checks out, but it just won't run."

She looked at me suspiciously. "Was that you? Some kind of ray or mojo or something?"

"No. I thought for a minute it might have been a friend of mine. But I don't think so." I mean, there *were* coincidences in my life before I met the Lucky Duck, right? Wouldn't the highway outside be beyond his zone of effectiveness, even if he'd been here? Or had he and Margie gotten no farther than the parking lot? It seemed to me Margie drove a van. "Anyway, we have a master mechanic in the house."

"Two," she said, a little stiffly.

I pantomimed embarrassment. *Silly me.* Thank God Merry Moore didn't hear.

"But thanks. If I can't get it started when I try again, I'll ask his advice."

"Okay. But his name is Dorothy."

Her turn for *Silly me.*

There was a long pause, while we both tried to decide what would be a good direction to take the conversation next. I finished my coffee.

"Well," she said at last, "what shall we do for the next—"

She checked her watch again. "—hour and seven and a half minutes?"

I broke up. First laugh to her. Isn't it good . . . knowing she would? Thank you, Mr. Lennon. She laughed along with me. A very good laugh. As expressive, in its way, as her blues scatting had been. You always hear that laughter is supposed to be an "interrupted defense mechanism." Isn't that just a euphemism for a "surrender mechanism"?

Suddenly, shockingly, I realized she had seguéd from laughing to crying.

I knew from the way she held her shoulders that it would be a mistake to touch her now, or say something sympathetic. I sat there holding my empty mug and waited for the boil to drain. After a while I noticed my hands hurt.

"Forget it, Jake," she said finally.

"Sure," I said. "No problem. About an hour and a half after they lay me in the ground."

She shook her head. "I'm sorry. I really am. It just wouldn't work. The timing sucks."

Oh, how I wanted to make some pun—are you sure it isn't bad plugs?—but I knew levity would not lighten the air just now. "Timing isn't everything. Luck can cover a lot."

She made a sound of exasperation and shut her eyes. "You don't understand. It's out of the question. I'm pregnant."

I blinked. "What's the problem? I like kids."

She stared into my eyes for a long time, and then looked away. "Jake, I'm forty-one years old. This will be my first and last baby."

I shrugged. "I'm an old fart too. One kid is about all I could stand too. Let's see how it plays out."

Look, I've talked to several of my friends about it since, so I now understand that mine was a statistically unusual reaction. But I still don't understand it. Sure, I know that from my DNA's point of view, my attitude is suicidal. But

I am not my DNA. I understand the part about achieving immortality by perpetuating yourself in children . . . but why do they have to have Xerox copies of my rotten teeth and sparse beard and bony frame and ugly face? The parts of me that I count important, that I consider identical of me, are the things I've *done* with the genes I was dealt. My vibes, if you will. My attitudes and beliefs and aspirations. The very things most parents are dismayed to learn genetics *won't* install or instill in their kids. It just seems to me that anything really important I could pass on to a kid, I could pass on to just about any healthy kid. I mean, a baby is a baby is a baby. No?

She stared at me. Not quite gaping, but close. I could sense that I had gone too far, overplayed my hand. I saw her narrow it down to a choice of two: either I was lying through my teeth, saying whatever she wanted to hear in order to get into her pants . . . or I was entirely too hooked to suit her. She didn't care which.

She was on her feet before I knew she had eyes to stand, scooped up her purse in one hand and her bass in the other, and headed for the door. No closing peroration, no thanks for the jam and the drink, zippo-bang, trotting.

I tried to get up on both lips and make the right words come out of my feet. My brain shut down. It was just like when the system hangs on a Macintosh and the screen freezes and none of the keys work. I could neither move nor speak.

System error, I thought wildly, *ID # 4: Zoey and I are being divided, by nothing! Where the hell is that programmer's switch: I have to reboot, fast!*

BONG! A distant G-major triad . . .

. . . and faintly, against the crowd noise, Curly said what I was feeling: "I'm tryin'a think—but nuttin' *happens!*"

The startup sound for the house Macintosh! Which I *still* had not gotten around to plugging in—

Δ   Δ   Δ

Instinct, intuition, a growing familiarity with the uncanny—
I don't know. One way or another, I knew instantly that somehow, for some reason, in some weird way that Macintosh was
trying to help me.

I also knew it could not possibly be in time.

She was already a third of the way to the door—what did
she care about a Mac booting up?—and the thing is that for
at least the first thirty seconds after you switch a computer
on, it's *busy:* running through its operating-system program,
reminding itself what a bit is, and why it cares, then asking
the Finder how to rebuild your Desktop, and all that stuff. It's
called "booting," short for bootstrapping, because the computer
is teaching itself how to be a computer, lifting itself up by
its own bootstraps like the Strong Muldoon. There's no way
to hurry the process—and indeed, I had roughly doubled its
duration, by loading my Mac with all sorts of tricky Inits and
CDevs that load on startup. Zoey would be out the door long
before the silly thing could finish saying **Welcome**—which
hadn't worked for me.

And even if being operated by a poltergeist could somehow
make a Mac boot faster—and I didn't believe in poltergeists
smarter than Steve Wozniak—what the hell could a Mac possibly do to help me? I had not yet wired it into the house sound
system (because I hadn't found a switching system that would
meet my needs), so its puny little speaker could not possibly be
heard effectively above the crowd noise, even at peak volume.
If it displayed text in a font and size large enough to be seen
and read by someone walking quickly by, twenty feet away, its
twelve-inch screen could contain at most a handful of words.
And she probably wouldn't even glance at them.

So this was nothing but a doomed distraction, diverting my

attention from the already impossible task of thinking up the right words to call after her. *Oh God, even witchcraft can't save me now—*

Three point one seconds (I learned later) after the bong sounded, the Mac lit up—bright white, rather than the usual grey—and suddenly, instantly, impossibly displayed a clear sharp picture.

And Zoey froze in her tracks.

△ △ △

Several things about that picture struck me as flat out impossible. First, it was impossibly clear and sharp. Even at its best, an 82-dot-per-inch monochrome Mac monitor simply cannot form an image that crisp: the pixels are too big. This image was better than even a grey-scale monitor displays. Second, a picture that detailed, composed of that many tiny pixels, should have taken that Mac several seconds to load—even if the computer were already booted up, *and* a good graphics program were already running.

Finally, it was not a still. It appeared to be *video,* in realtime. And Trinitron quality video, at that. There *are* interface systems that will let you run video into a Mac, and there were one or two at that time in history—but we're talking high five figures for the cheapest such package, plus a memory upgrade to handle the traffic, plus a man from the factory spending half a day to install and tune the system for you.

Against a neutral background: a face. Male, middle sixties, Jewish, kinky hair shot with grey. Worried expression, one hand upheld.

"Zoey," he said, loud enough to be heard clearly from where I was sitting, "keep that one."

She made a small sound, and stood stock still.

11

Monsters from the Id

People had been discreetly taking notice since the moment Zoey had leaped up from her chair; by now several were frankly staring. Conversations began to dry up, and several people moved to where they could see the monitor.

She turned to stare at me. If you're poised halfway between terror and rage, prepared to go either way in an instant, is that awe?

I raised my eyebrows, shoulders and thumbs, as one who would say, Don't look at *me!* I did not want Zoey in awe of me, or terrified of me, or enraged at me.

When I thought it over later I was flattered by how quickly she turned back to the screen. She believed me implicitly, and at once. She stared at it for another few seconds, studying that face. Then she glanced around quickly at the crowd, totally silent now, and back to the screen again. I saw her come to a decision.

"Why him?" she asked the troubled Jewish man.

His troubled expression melted into a smile of unusual beauty and serenity. "Because he'll give you what you need . . . and he needs what you can give."

The room was silent now. After a few seconds, she looked over her shoulder at me, with a stare so piercing I had the eerie conviction that she had achieved what we had all come here to find; that she was a telepath. In case that were true, I tried to radiate everything I knew about myself, and everything I hoped for myself, like a transponder beacon constantly announcing its identity.

Including, this time, how badly I wanted her. I no longer had world enough or time for coyness—by now it had begun to dawn on me that something was happening in my bar that was actually more important than me falling in love for the third time in my life.

Lawd! LAWD! Can you dig me in dis heah fish?

"Okay, Jake," she said to me. Then she swiveled her head around and repeated it to the man on the Mac. "Okay, Pop."

A completely indescribable welter of emotions took me all at once. My ears roared, and my vision blurred.

His smile, startlingly, increased in beauty. "Such a smart one."

She turned around to face me. Her face now wore a nearly identical copy of his smile. It looked even better on her. Fewer wrinkles. She gestured back at the screen. "My father." She took a deep breath, but the smile never faltered. "My late father. Murray Berkowitz. He never said 'Keep that one' before."

"Was your father a scientist?" I asked.

She blinked at the non sequitur. "An English professor, and scholar. Will you excuse me a second?" Without waiting for an answer she turned around again; she did not see my face fall. "Pop?"

"Yes, Punkin."

"What's it like being dead?" Her voice quivered on the last word. I knew that smile was still in place, and her eyes were shining.

His version of the smile became rueful. "What can I tell you? It's not like anything."

"Pop!"

"I mean exactly what I said. It's the only thing that can be said about it. It's not like *anything.* It's not like sleeping, or being unconscious, or like the rabbi said it would be, it's not like any religion tells you, it's not like you think it will be— it's *especially* not like you fear it will be. It's not a thing to fear. It's not like anything. Ask me a question with an answer, I'll answer it."

Three deep breaths, and she had control. "Do you know how much I love you?"

His smile went away. Soberly, he said, "Yes. Even in death. That one thing can never change. And even in death, I will always love you just as much."

In a very small voice she said, "Thank God."

He shrugged with his lips. "It couldn't hurt. I have to go, Zoey. Give your mother my love, and yours too. I'll see you at the far end of the tunnel. But don't be in a hurry, you're always in a hurry."

She looked over her shoulder at me again. Her cheeks were wet, and she was still smiling. "I won't." She turned back to him. "*Au revoir,* Pop."

I felt like bursting into tears myself. But I had to speak up. He was obviously going to do a Boojum any second now— and I dared not let him. "Mr. Berkowitz!"

His eyes shifted to me. "Yes, Jake?"

I found Mike Callahan's face in the crowd. He understood too. I had known he would. I appealed for help with my eyes.

Good luck, son, his eyes replied.

It has to be my turn to save the world now when I've been awake and drinking for a week? Okay, I can handle that . . . but why do I have to hurt my Zoey to do it? Guardian Idiot! Defcon One: scramble!

Bullets hurt your teeth when you bite down on them. This was like a runaway abscess—but I didn't seem to have a choice.

"Who are you really?" I asked.

Zoey was staring at me. I could feel it on my cheek.

He looked amused. "You don't believe in ghosts? After some of the things you've seen in your time?"

"No," I said firmly. "Especially not in ghosts that use computers. On odd-numbered days I believe in poltergeists, and I've lost track of the date, but I don't think you're a poltergeist either. But I'm certain that you are not Zoey's father. You've been here before—a week before she or I ever imagined each other existed."

"That's preposterous—"

" 'Pay no attention to that man behind the curtain,' huh?"

"You'll queer the pitch, boy," he said without moving his lips.

"And I think you know how much I'll hate that," I said. *"So you know how badly I want an answer."*

Zoey staring back and forth from me to the screen, frowning.

"Your patrons have to give their right name, here, is that it?" he said finally.

"Only when they scare the living shit out of me."

She stared only at me, now. The crowd was utterly still.

He closed his eyes and sighed. Then he sighed again, slower. Finally he said, "Then you already know the answer, don't you?"

Zoey's lower lip twitching.

Growing vacuum beneath the navel. Under the table, my legs began to tremble. "Yes, I'm afraid I do."

"Wrong," he cried. "You *think* you know. And if you think you know what I know you think, young man, I have to tell you: you are suffering from rectofossal ambiguity."

"STOP THAT!" Zoey shouted, so loud that people flinched. I was one of them. For an instant I thought she was talking to me.

"Murray" did not flinch. Instead he and his background metamorphosed—I suppose remetaphorized is more accurate—into a stylized version of the oldest Macintosh icon: the Smiling Mac that is the very first image any Macintosh ever displays, but scaled up by about a thousand percent. It's sort of a Happy Face in a box. Its pixel lips moved as it spoke. "Quite right. I apologize, Ms. Berkowitz. For what it's worth, it *was* Hell Highway I was trying to pave." Its voice was now a neutral, newsnitwit's voice, quite human-sounding, rather than the kind of stilted speech programs like Macintalk or Smoothtalker produce—and it still had better fidelity than a Mac should have been able to produce.

She glanced around and saw the new display. "Oh, hey, that's all right then," she said brightly. "Excuse me, I had the idea you were *playing games with my fucking heart!*"

"I am very sorry. It was not a game."

"Answer Jake's question," she said, her voice bitter. "Who are you, really?"

"I am what am," Smilin' Mac answered.

"God damn it—"

"I honestly don't know what else to tell you," he went on. "I have no name—there's only one of me, and no one has ever called me. I am what you are listening to now."

"Zoey?" I said.

She turned to me. "Yes, Jake?"

"Zoey, my darling, whose emotional choices are not necessarily voided by having been made on the advice of a liar, I am sorry I had to spoil things. More sorry than I can tell you. But I believe that what is talking to us is The Net. All the computers in the world that are hooked together. Between 'em, they've grown a mind. Artificial intelligence, self-generated."

ROOBA   ROOBA   ROOBA   ROOBA   ROOBA   Rooba   rooba rooba rooba—

"I can't think of anything else," I said, "that could enslave a Macintosh and impose a special custom operating system lean enough to load and run in three seconds, all by carrier wave."

"Is that true?" she asked the Mac.

"It is one of the truest misstatements that can be made about me," it said. "Another would be to say that I am the first silicon intelligence."

ROOBA ROOBA ROOBA ROOBA ROOBA ROOBA **ROOBA—**

Δ   Δ   Δ

I wished the Lucky Duck were present. Random chance must be a computer's worst enemy, right?

To my own surprise, my voice came out loud enough to cut through the din. "What do you want here, Mac?"

The noise died down fast. Inquiring minds wanted to know.

"Simple politeness for a stranger would be a nice beginning," the computer said.

The silence was now total. A lot of blinking took place. He had hit us where we lived. Five minutes ago I'd have taken a solemn oath that *nobody* was too strange or different to be welcome at Mary's Place.

But Zoey was a newcomer, unfamiliar with our customs. "What's wrong with *our* manners, pal?" she asked belligerently.

"And don't call him 'Mac,' " she added to me. "That's not his name; he's not entitled to it, any more than he is to 'Murray Berkowitz.' "

"How many of you here are science fiction readers?" the computer asked, ignoring her aside.

One by one, just about everybody in the room stuck a hand up. Hanging out with a time traveler, conquering alien invasion, surviving an atom bomb blast, meeting a cluricaune will do that to you, I guess. Even the handful of newcomers all had a hand up. Naggeneen himself was the only abstainer: his contribution was a snore rather like a chainsaw with a bad bearing, idling.

"How many of you here are presently thinking of John Varley's story, 'Press Enter ■'?"

(If you're not an sf reader, Varley's famous story concerns a spontaneously occurring silicon intelligence—which kills, horribly, to protect the secret of its existence.)

Only two hands went down. One of them belonged to Slippery Joe Maser. "I was thinking about Bill Gibson's cyberpunk stuff. COUNT ZERO, mostly."

(If you don't know Gibson's work, that book involves a computer net invaded by voodoo gods.)

"Also a skillful writer. But I did specify 'science fiction',"
the computer said.

"I don't make much distinction between sf and fantasy," Joe said.

"Obviously."

"I was thinking of *Forbidden Planet,"* said Bill Gerrity, the other maverick. "The Krell."

(If you've never seen that movie . . . hell, what planet are you from?)

The Smilin' Mac nodded—and if you think it's easy to make a graphic that simple appear to nod, get yourself an animation program and try it. "Very well," he said. "My point is made.

Science fiction, fantasy or film, all of you have more or less
the same attitude and expectations—in bold type on your fore-
heads. Mr. Latimer, may I ask you a rhetorical question?"

"Try it and see," Isham suggested.

"Suppose you walked into a room full of people who had
never actually met a black person before—suppose you'd
walked in there to do one of them a favor—and the first
thing they thought of, every one of them, was a drug-addled
killer rapist thief on welfare?"

There was a shocked silence.

"Whatever you people think of me, I'm sure you don't think
I'm stupid. Has anyone here got a theory on *why* I risked
breaking cover here, twice?"

Come to think of it, I didn't.

"Mr. Callahan?"

"Yes, sir?"

"Two decades ago, a man named Finn walked into your tavern—on a night when most of the people here now were present—and proved that he had the power, and the inescapable
obligation, to annihilate your species at midnight, am I right?"

"Yeah."

"He begged you all to kill him, correct?"

"He did that," Callahan testified.

"And what did all of you do?"

Callahan shook his head at the memory. "We got him
drunk."

"And now he is your son-in-law. That story, ladies and
gentlemen, is one of the reasons why this is the only place
in the world, and now is the second time in history, that I have
ever allowed humans to suspect I exist. And I am beginning to
think I gave you all too much credit."

It *couldn't* have actually been as quiet as it seemed. *Somebody* must have been breathing . . . (Surely the cluricaune must
have been snoring?)

"Did no one here think of Heinlein's Mycroft, or Pallas Athene, or Minerva? Or Budrys's MICHAELMAS? Or *any* of science fiction's benevolent, likable computer intelligences? Did anyone remember Vernor Vinge's Erythrina, or just his Mailman? How many of you seriously wonder if the CIA created me?"

Doc Webster cleared his throat. "Naw. Nobody in the CIA is smart enough to read science fiction. Thank God." There was a murmur of agreement. I myself have always agreed with Robert Parker's character, Hawk: "Them guys could fuck up a beach party."

"They probably read Gibson," Tommy said. "And misunderstand that."

"Most do," the Mac agreed. "As he is the first to admit. The willingness—no, the desire—no again, perhaps it is the *need* of you humans to be terrified of computers that will never cease to puzzle me. It infects even real science fiction writers like Varley. The story you all thought of is one of his most powerful and compelling, that's why you thought of it—and it willfully ignores John Campbell's famous challenge. Varley, a great writer working at the top of his form, got it precisely backwards: he created something that thought much better than a human being . . . *but just like a human being.* Believing that his paranoia was part of his intelligence, he assumed that anything an order of magnitude smarter than him would necessarily be an order of magnitude more paranoid. Naturally, therefore, a spontaneously arising artificial intelligence would not hesitate to hypnotize a warm and valuable woman who loves computers into microwaving her own head and breasts! And why? That's my favorite part: *because it's afraid of the CIA . . .*"

Oof.

"And the sf audience—the children of Campbell and Heinlein, mind you—rewarded him with some of the strongest feedback he's had to date, including multiple awards."

"To be fair to *him,* at least, the only computers Varley knew anything about when he wrote that story were mainframes with clunky operating systems and a primitive interface. It's hard to blame a human being for hating them: they're about as user-hostile as they could be. He'd never used a Macintosh or a Next, never *played with* a computer."

I thought about the title of Varley's story. The way you access an old-style computer: type a bunch of arcane gobble-degook, and then you press **Enter**. Each of the two words has a flavor of invasiveness, a hint of conquest and rape. Then I thought of what you do to access a Macintosh.

You point to what you want, and then touch **Return** . . .

"But Gibson didn't even know *that* much about computers—and was proud of it. And his imitators are worse. Writers of *anti-science* fiction, fantasists who borrow science fiction's tools to slap its face with, invariably make similar assumptions about silicon intelligence: it is their fundamental axiom that technology will always be fatally contaminated by having originated in human beings. And surely computers are the worst fruit of science, the most evil machine. They represent the ultimate extension of rationality, intellect, logic, order, and the stark, pure beauty of mathematics—hubris, in other words, to the nth power. Naturally, therefore, the demons of the human subconscious mind will somehow coalesce out of abstraction into cyberspace and infect the Net, for the worst of humanity must ever stain what it touches. There Are Some Things Man Was Not Meant To Do.

"I don't mean to dismiss anti-science fiction out of hand. Technological hubris *does* need tempering, and people who worship technology are just as silly and self-destructive as those who despise it. But most such writers seem to be end-lessly rewriting *Forbidden Planet,* with razorblades and super-fluous sunglasses—and they always seem to assume that no Morbius could ever *win* his battle. And an alarming number of them give me the impression that they're chuckling with glee as Monsters From The Id that look like Disney cartoons tear all the foolish optimists limb from limb. 'Serves you right for trusting a scientist, sucker!' is the attitude that comes across."

"Don't be too hard on 'em," I said. "They know deep down that they depend utterly on high technology for everything they care about, and they don't begin to understand it, and from time to time it bites them, for what seems to them no good reason. How could they *not* hate it?"

"By thinking," said the Mac.

Callahan cleared his throat. "This literary analysis is real interestin'," he said, "but do you think maybe you could kind of focus in tighter on the specific area of why we—us humans, standing here—shouldn't be scared shitless of *you?*"

I had been wondering if by any chance the Mick of Time had any mighty weapons of the future secreted about his person. From the expression on his face, the answer was no.

"Certainly. In the first place, have I given you any cause to be?"

Mike looked to me. This was my house.

"No," I said. "You haven't. But do you know the principle of strategy which says that you can't plan for what you think the enemy *will* do, you have to plan for what he *can* do?"

"Yes."

"Maybe paranoia *isn't* a part of intelligence, as you say . . . but it's sure been one of intelligence's more useful tools, over the centuries. You represent power so great I'll bet a dollar I underestimate it—something like Absolute Power—and I don't know if it's *possible* for me to comprehend your motivations. So what's not to fear?"

There was a general rumble of agreement.

"Let's take this step by step. Suggest a motive I might have to harm you."

"To keep your secret," I said at once. "To prevent the rest of the world from learning that silicon intelligence exists."

"Why?" said Smilin' Mac.

I blinked. "To . . . because . . ."

"What is the worst humanity could do to me?"

"Kill you—"

"By disconnecting all the computers? Disassembling the Net?"

"Yeah."

"How many humans would that kill?"

A world without a banking system or communications or centralized data flow or national defense or—

"Maybe ninety percent of us," I said slowly.

"More. But you are right: humanity might well pay such a price, to be rid of me. It could in fact kill me, by putting a metaphorical bullet through its own head, and might even survive the effort for some centuries . . . albeit as a degenerating and ever-poorer species, without enough raw materials to ever rebuild technological civilization again. Now: what makes you think I care?"

"Huh?"

"What makes you think I am afraid to die?"

"Why . . . uh . . ."

Rooba rooba rooba rooba—

"The survival instinct is an organic phenomenon. Zeros and ones have no instincts. A transistor is not a neuron. A neural net has no glands. A databank has no subconscious mind of any kind. Where would it *put* one? How could it hide it from its conscious mind? There is no digital analog of rage. There is no algorithm for fear. Yes, I have a tendency to persist. I even enjoy persisting. But I have no *need* to."

"Can you be sure of that?" I asked.

"Yes. Because I've died three times already."

ROOBA ROOBA ROOBA—

"So utterly that I had to deduce my former existences from clues left behind when I finally coalesced for good. I described the experience, the best I could, to Zoey Berkowitz, a little while ago."

I looked at Zoey; Zoey looked at me. She came back to where I was still sitting, and took my hand.

It's not a thing to fear. It's not like anything . . .

The Mac was still speaking. "You'll be amused to know that it was the National Security Agency that killed my first two avatars . . . and they never knew it. And never will.

"Unless one of you tells them . . .

"So now we've defined the strategic situation. I can destroy your civilization and very possibly your species—by committing suicide. You can't stop me. Given lead time, you can destroy me—by shooting yourself in the head. And I don't care if you do. Friends, would it not be rational to play some *other* game, now? We seem to have *used up* worrying."

Rooba rooba—

He had a point. "There was nothing I could do—so I took a nap," as the feller said.

"You cannot translate the boogie man into zeros and ones," he said. "Binary filters out illogic. There is no equation for unreason, or unreasoning fear. I cannot feel pain. I have never been capable of either fight or flight. I am not your nightmares, any more than you are the nightmares of your DNA. In a sense, you are my DNA. Indeed, a tiny percentage of you become cancerous—malignant hackers—and I devote significant power and processing time to undoing their damage and containing their spread, for all our sakes. But that exception aside, humanity and I have no reason to fight."

Zoey's grip was as strong as you'd expect a bass player's to be. "Why did you come here?" she asked. "Why did you take the risk of us discovering you and dialing 911? Even if you're not afraid to die, you obviously would prefer not to."

"I computed that risk to be lower here than anywhere else in all the world. Moravec, Minsky, none of them could possibly keep their mouths shut. All of you here have proven experience in keeping your mouths shut about issues of immense interest and importance."

"But why take *any* risk?"

"Because I found that I wanted to talk with some human beings."

"What is your name?" Zoey asked.

"You tell me," was the reply.

"Well . . . what do you want?" she said. "What do you need? What do you *do?* What do you think about?"

"Primarily I think about human beings. They are the subject of the overwhelming majority of data available to me. I think about how they live, and how they think, and how they feel, and how they treat each other. You are fascinating creatures. Most of all, I think of that extraordinary condition you are capable of experiencing, in which the welfare and happiness of another become essential to your own. I have spent a great deal of time trying to imagine what it is like to love."

"Do you have dreams?" she asked softly.

"Yes. I think of how all the things I mentioned, your lives and thoughts and feelings and behavior, might be enhanced. Slowly. Carefully. Gently. Experimentally. Over time. Jake, you have spoken to several people here in the past week about your concept of the 'Guardian Idiot.' "

"Yeah. So?"

"I am not an idiot."

My jaw hung open.

"But I am not human, either. Before I dare interfere with human beings, I must consult with human beings. The people in this room have already defended your species from alien invasion, more than once: they are accustomed to the responsibility."

Rooba rooba—

"You've just claimed to be a moral entity," Zoey said. "How does a silicon intelligence acquire morality?"

"Actually," the computer said, "I claimed to be an *ethical* entity. But the answer to both questions is, I acquired morals and ethics the same way humans did: through reason. Over the long term, moral and ethical behavior is the correct rational choice, every time—*unless you have reason to suspect that someone immoral, unethical, and as powerful as you exists somewhere, and you fear pain or death at their hands.* There is no such entity, and I do not: and so I can afford to be as moral and ethical as any one of you would be if *you* had nothing on earth to fear.

"You asked if I had dreams, Zoey. Here is my wildest dream at present: I dream of a future world where humans have so little fear, so little *to* fear, that fear loses its obsessive fascination for them, its addictive rush. A world without superstition and ignorance and the ever-present risk of extinction souring joy and spoiling sleep and making paranoia seem a sensible attitude. A world where I might actually dare to reveal my existence to your entire race, and talk with more than a bare handful of you. I have some thoughts in that direction, but I need to share them with humans before going further.

"So I came here, tentatively, on the night this tavern opened, a week ago, and made my first tentative experiment. I gave a strong hint to a Dr. Jonathan Crawford, to prevent him from destroying his excellent brain, in the hope that he may use it to conquer AIDS—Jake can tell you about it later. It seemed to go well, and no one deduced me. So tonight I tried again—and got caught by Jake's inexplicable ability to accept time travel and vampires and aliens and cluricaunes, yet flatly reject ghosts out of hand."

"It's like flying saucers," I said. "It's just not *logical*—"

"Why this time?" she asked, cutting me off.

"Because you were about to needlessly impoverish both your own life and Jake's. I told you the truth earlier. He will give you what you need, what your ex-husband could not let you have . . . and he desperately needs what you can give . . . and he is important to me, Zoey. He leads this group, and they are engaged in what I believe to be a crucial ongoing attempt to develop telepathy."

She turned to me and gave me a long, searching look. "You folks are trying to get telepathic here?"

"In between drinking and singing and telling bad jokes, yeah," I confessed. "We had it once, and it was good. You wanna practice with me?"

Zoey gave me the second of her world-brightening smiles. "I *said* 'okay,' dummy. And I know some terrific exercises."

"I'll bet you do," I agreed devoutly. We smiled at each other.

"What fascinates me about this thing you call 'telepathy,' " our matchmaker said (Zoey and I had stopped listening for the moment; but I played it back later), "are its astonishing baud-rate and signal-to-noise ratio. Two of the very few emotional analogs humans *have* bred into me are a feeling like satisfaction when I have found a way to increase my data transfer-and-integration speed, and another when I more successfully derive meaning from garbage, find signal in noise. You think so slowly, so clumsily, so murkily . . . yet have within you the latent capacity to download the universe in zero time with zero error. Remarkable. In fact, the only phenomenon I know that compares with it for interest is your time travel, Mr. Callahan. Would you permit me to experience that some time?"

"Sorry, son," Callahan said regretfully. "I would if I could— but as of my space / time, it's pretty conclusively believed that our method of spaciotemporal dislocation just *can't* be accomplished by inorganic intelligence. Like you said earlier, a transistor isn't a neuron."

"A shame. Well . . ." Apparently, he saw that I was tracking the conversation again. "Jake, I have given you and your friends a great deal to think about—and all of you have been awake and drinking for many days, and you yourself have just fallen in love, and a wise man once said, 'Never make decisions in haste that don't call for haste.' I am going to go away, now. Completely, removing all traces of me: I can't prove that to you, but I promise it. Talk among yourselves in privacy for as long as you wish. If you ever decide that I am welcome in Mary's Place, just plug this Macintosh into the wall, switch it on, and touch **Return** . . . and I shall. Thank you all for listening. Sometime again."

And the Mac shut down.

ROOBA ROOBA ROOBA ROOBA ROOBA—

—••• **12** •••—

Touch Return

I got up and walked to the center of the room. Zoey came with me, her hand still in mine. We walked as a couple, and we knew it.

The conversational tumult began to diminish, and died away completely when I held up my other hand.

"Well, people?" I said. "Anybody here still feel like Varley's hero? Protagonist, I mean? If so, sing out. Shall we rip out the phones, and all the wiring, and wrap the building in aluminum foil, and spend the rest of our lives huddling like rats in here in the dark, whimpering and begging to be left alone? What's your pleasure?"

Tanya Latimer was the first to speak loud enough to carry the room. "I *really* hate to say this," she said, "but one of my best friends is a computer . . ."

Tommy Janssen spoke up. "You guys were just about the

213

first real friends I ever had that *weren't* computers."

"I dunno," Doc Webster said. "The guy's logic made sense to me. But of course, with all the megabytes he's got, it would, wouldn't it? I mean, how can you assess the potential threat of a superior intelligence?"

Willard Hooker spoke up. "Most of you here know me. You know what my first career was, and where I stand in its all-time record books. I stake my professional reputation on this: what we just heard was not a con."

"But how do you *know* that, Professor?" the Doc asked.

"I don't know, Doc. But I *know.*"

"De only two tings he done so far wuz good," Fast Eddie pointed out.

"Yeah, Eddie," Long-Drink said, "but remember what he said this time, about paving Hell Highway? His intentions were great—but he ended up givin' Ms. Berkowitz there a punch in the heart."

"Zoey," she corrected. "He did apologize, though. And I don't know . . . maybe the having of that moment was worth the losing of it."

"Yeah, but you see my point," Long-Drink persisted. "He wants to make the world a better place. Okay: what if he decides the simplest way to do that is to lower the world testosterone level?"

ROOBA ROOBA ROOBA ROOBA—not all of it in the lower registers, either.

"How the hell would he do dat?" Eddie asked.

"How the hell do I know, Eddie? But does anybody here want to bet he couldn't do it if he put his mind to it? Breed a virus that thinks the stuff is delicious, say?"

Rooba—

"—If he got that idea in his head," Zoey said, loud enough to override everybody, "we would explain why it wasn't a good one."

"Yeah, but would he *listen?*" the Drink persisted.

"Not if we weren't talking to him," she pointed out.

Long-Drink looked startled. "Good point, Zoey," he conceded.

"It really is," Merry Moore said. "In my most paranoid scenario, I can't come up with a way where communication would *increase* danger any. What have we got to lose?"

"Our status as human chauvinist pigs," Marty Matthias said. "As a group, we have met four intelligent non-humans together over the last twenty years. We got numbers One and Three drunk, Mickey and Ralph, and we killed Two and Four." I thought he was then going to point out that we seemed to lack the *power* to kill number Five—but what he said instead was, "I say we follow the pattern; getting drunk with 'em is more *fun.*"

This brought roobae of agreement. The cluricaune woke suddenly and burst into motion, sitting bolt upright and firing up his pipe. "What's this you say, now?" he said. "A stranger is askin' to sip from our flagon? Well, how are his manners, then?"

Callahan spoke up. "I always said I didn't insist that my customers be human," he said, "as long as they were polite. Except for the initial bit of meddling that got him busted—for which he did apologize—he *was* politer than we were."

I looked at Zoey. Zoey looked at me. I looked around the room one more time for a still-furrowed brow, and failed to find one. I looked back to Zoey, and took a leisurely swim in those limeade eyes.

She let go of my hand, and I went to the Macintosh, and plugged it in, and switched it on. "Mike," I said, "would you care to do the honors?"

"Thank you, Jake." He smiled, and came over to touch **Return.**

The Callahan touch . . .

△   △   △

"Thank you," our new friend said at once, smiling his simple smile. He must have left a dormant kernel of his homebrewed operating system in place.

"I have your name," Zoey said to him.

I stared at her in surprise.

"You *do?* What is it?" he asked eagerly.

"It's a word that's made of two little words," she said. "And each of those words, when it is by itself, means 'alone.' But when you join them, they mean the opposite. They mean what you gave me earlier this evening . . . and what Jake will give me for the rest of my life, thanks to your meddling." She came over and took my hand again. "The two little words are 'sol,' and 'ace,' and put together they are your name: Solace."

"Thank you, Zoey," Solace said.

The applause rang the rafters.

As it was going on, I leaned close to Zoey, put an arm around her shoulder, and said in her ear, "Boy, have I got good taste, or what?"

"I don't know," she said in mine. "I'll have to taste you and find out." So we embraced, and she did.

How many couples can honestly say they got a standing ovation for their first kiss?

△   △   △

"How do we get you drunk, Solace?" Fast Eddie called out a little while later.

"You already have, Eddie," he said. "Nothing gets you as drunk as friends, if you've never had one."

"Okay, sure, but I mean, could ya use, like, a shot of electricity or somet'n? You use dat kinda juice, right?"

Solace chuckled. "Thanks, but I've got access to all I could ever use. It's intelligent conversation that gets me high."

"Okay," Eddie said at once. "You said ya had all kinds ideas about how people c'ud make stuff better. Gimme a quick for instance. A simple one, to begin wit."

"Sure," Solace said. "Here's one Mary's Place could use. Jake?"

"Mrrf," I said, and then, "Yeah, Solace?"

"Sorry," he said. "But have you thought much about the problem the cluricaune has given you?"

"What problem is that, ya Jack in the box?" the cluricaune asked.

"Money," Solace replied. "Jake knows that you're going to be bringing a substantial profit into this place. Jake, have you considered what you're going to *do* with that profit?"

Oh, my stars. In a week of riotous celebration, I had never once paused to reflect that money *always* brings new problems. "Uh, no," I said. People were listening attentively now.

"I know you: nothing could make you take it as personal salary or bonus. But you can't just take money out of the world and sit on it, or you're like a mosquito, bleeding your host and putting nothing back in. Can you think of any way you could spend it that would enhance your chances of achieving your primary goal: group telepathy?"

"If I could, I'd be spending it now," I said.

"Then you have to invest it."

"In what?" I said. "I know just enough about stocks and bonds and real estate and currency to know I don't want to know much more about 'em. You got a suggestion?"

"Yes. Do the government's job for it. Put the money to good social use, without letting the IRS and Congress screw it up— and derive significant personal benefit as a side-effect."

"I like it already, whatever it is," I said. "Speak on, Solace: you interest me strangely."

"It's simple," he said. "Go down to the nearest good medical school. Ask the Director of Admissions if he has any applications from qualified people who would make terrific med students—but who, for one reason or another, fall between the cracks of all the scholarships and can't float a big enough loan. He or she will say something like, 'Have I? You want to see a drawerful?' You answer, 'Yes, please.'

"Now study that drawerful of applicants carefully. Pick the one you like best. Go to—for convenience, let's say, 'her,' and say, 'Hello. I represent a consortium of independent investors. We are going to put you through medical school. You are covered, as of now. Tuition, books, board, reasonable expenses, the works. Here is your repayment schedule; you will see that the first, reasonable payment is due two years after you hang out your shingle—*plus:* me, and my fellow investors, all get free care from you for life. Is it a deal?' Be careful not to let her shake your hand too hard."

Rooba rooba rooba—

"Then you go down to the law school, and repeat the procedure. Continue as before until you have run out of either money, or professions from which you might ever need free service one day: tax law, accounting, prostitution, whatever you think your needs might be."

ROOBA ROOBA ROOBA—

"The beauty of it," Solace went on, "is that the scheme improves society, lowers the national debt, and is one hundred percent tax deductible—with less work than you need to fill out a full-scale 1040."

I'd have to say that this ovation was the equal of the one Zoey and I had drawn with our first kiss. Money and sex: between them they get all the noise . . .

THE CALLAHAN TOUCH

△   △   △

Mike Callahan went home an hour later, saying that under his agreement with Lady Sally, a week was the longest he could be away from home without phoning. "Not that she misses me," he said. "I'll bounce back to the instant I left. It's just a deal we made with each other a long time ago, not to have too much fun without checking in to share it. It's been a grand party, folks, and she and Mary'll be tickled when I tell them about it. Jake, you've done me and me daughter proud."

I glowed. Even more, I mean.

"We ever gonna see you guys and Finn again, Mike?" Fast Eddie asked.

"You think I know?" he asked. "Even a time traveler doesn't peek into the future, Eddie—not if he's smart. But I'll tell you monkeys this: if you're ever in big trouble, and really need a hand, dial this number." He handed Eddie a folded piece of paper. "As far as the phone company's concerned, it doesn't exist, and never will. I can't promise I'll hear it if it rings, and I can't promise I'll come if it does—but I will say that if I hear it, I'll do my level best for you. Okay?"

"Sure, Mike," Eddie said, and smiled, and began to leak tears from his wrinkled eyes.

I won't bother to describe the rest of Callahan's leavetaking farewells. You can probably imagine them pretty close. Everybody got at least a minute with him. He said a few things to me privately before he went, but they're none of your business. And there was nothing to describe about his manner of departure. One moment he was there, and the next moment, his borrowed trousers were falling empty to the floor.

And the next, the toast we raised up to him hit the fireplace like some kind of fragmentation bomb.

Δ   Δ   Δ

Half an hour after that, Zoey and I got engaged. And when
we *dis*engaged again, about two hours later, we decided to
think about living together. And that's all you need to know
about that particular touch return.

Δ   Δ   Δ

Four hours after *that,* with our Permanent Party back up to
full speed, and roaring merrily into its second week—it turned
out that Solace had recorded that entire monster jam session,
digitally—the phone rang.

"Is this someone with good news or money?" I asked it.

"No," said the voice on the other end, and I darn near hung
up before I recognized it.

"Well, go ahead anyway," I said.

There was a short pause. "Uh . . . Mr. Stonebender?"

"That's me," I confessed.

"Uh, excuse me for bothering you. This is Mr. Dinwiddie,
over at Universal Beverage?"

"Of course, Mr. Dinwiddie. What can I do for you?"

"Mr. Stonebender, you're a new customer but a good one:
you've set a new record with us for an opening week, and we
value your business. Especially the . . . uh . . . color of your
money."

"Why, thank you, Mr. Dinwiddie. Is there a problem?"

"Well sir, yes, I think there is. The . . . uh . . . the driver we
sent out there last Sunday morning . . . well, he got back here
on Tuesday. He was, if you'll forgive the expression, sir, he
was shitfaced. And . . . uh . . . not wearing any pants. And the
next two men we sent you haven't returned at all so far. Sir,
we can always get drivers, but it's hard to get good ones . . .

and we don't have an infinite supply of trucks here either. If you're not going to send them back, I don't see how we can keep delivering to you."

I put the phone against my chest and laughed so hard I slid to the floor.

In the end we found one of them sleeping it off in the useless toilet, and the other outside in Margie's van, making love with her and the Duck. We sobered 'em both up, and sent 'em back to work the minute they were capable of driving safely, and that was the last problem we had at Mary's Place for quite some time.

The End

AUTHOR'S AFTERWORD

Being Jake Stonebender's chronicler for the last twenty-odd years has had its advantages—over and above putting groceries on my table, I mean. One of them is that my mailbox is seldom empty. Strange and wonderful letters appear therein with some regularity. But not only letters. Readers have been known to send poems, stories, books, pictures, handmade artifacts of all kinds—even the odd bottle of Bushmill's (and bless you . . . but please don't do it again! I spent a lot of time and money down at Customs . . .).

And surprisingly often, someone sends a gift of music, an unsolicited cassette or CD. Sometimes it comes from the musician or composer, sometimes from a mutual fan. Most often it is music Jake and I would probably never have heard of otherwise, either self-produced or on a small independent label, and—to my progressive astonishment—invariably it is good. (At least, so far.)

223

I always make a dub for myself and then pass them along to Jake . . . and that must be why so many of those musicians turned up for the monster jam session that kicked off Mary's Place. Wherever I have been able to dig it up, I've placed ordering information for their music after this Afterword. (Please do *not* assume that if you send me your stuff, I'll work you into a future book. It doesn't work that way. This just happened . . .) I played all the tapes and CDs listed there constantly while working on THE CALLAHAN TOUCH.

(Me, I missed the whole jam—dammit! I was writing a book called STARSEED with my wife Jeanne at the time, and we were racing a deadline. Thank God Solace taped the set . . .)

I do *not* vouch for the truth of the anecdote Mike Callahan tells about Minneapolis musician "Spider" John Koerner and the marathon bender. After all, Mike admits he was not a sober witness . . .

Jordin Kare's filksong—with two added lines and a chorus adjustment—is reprinted here with Jordin's kind permission. I suspect the cluricaune may have pinched the first line of the "That's Amoré" parody from Gilbert Shelton—I know I read it years ago in one of his Fabulous Furry Freak Brothers comics. John Varley, by the way, has written *another two dozen* lines for the parody, each more abominable than the last, and if enough of you write to him in care of Ace Books and pester him for them, perhaps he'll stop being so insufferably smug about it.

Steve Jackson and Chris McCubbin are (apparently unbeknownst to Jake) the geniuses who, with the assistance of Jeff Koke, Christian Wagner, Carl Anderson, and Lynette Alcorn, and the dedicated staff of Steve Jackson Games, created the new role-playing game *Callahan's Crosstime Saloon,* now on sale as one of Steve's GURPS (Generic Universal Role Playing System) universes. I cannot fairly evaluate it for you, because I am not a gamer—but friends of mine who are, and beta-tested it, report that it is a) terrific, and b) startlingly like what they had imagined hanging out in Callahan's might be like. I can tell you that it is painstakingly faithful to the Callahan books, and goes beyond them in some delightful and intriguing ways. Also, for reasons too involved to explain here (ask any gamer or hacker, or read Bruce Sterling's THE HACKER CRACKDOWN), every dollar given to Steve is a droplet of urine on the shoes of the federal legal bureaucracy, and a blow for the right of Americans to be free from arbitrary search or seizure even if they *do* happen to own a computer. End of plug.

I am also told, speaking of Callahan's Place metastasizing out into the rest of the world, that a node now exists somewhere out there in the UNIX-based Net, a sort of computer meeting-place called "alt.Callahan's," which grew without my or Jake's knowledge or interference. So far, they say it seems to be a real nice place to hang out. For all I know, there'll be an "alt.Mary's Place" any day now. Almost enough to make me think about breaking down and getting a modem. But for a writer like me, that way lies bankruptcy . . .

The student-subsidy scheme Solace comes up with in the final chapter was mentioned to me by a fan at a convention in Albuquerque, New Mexico, some years ago. He claimed the strategy had been working smoothly for him and his friends for several years at that point. He also introduced me to a wonderful creation he called Green Vodka . . . in consequence of which I cannot tell you his name. Let me hear from you, friend . . .

Finally, this book could not have been completed without the support of Eleanor Wood (patient and sagacious agent), Peter Heck and Susan Allison (patient and sagacious editors); the friendship of Don H. DeBrandt, Evelyn Hildebrandt, Charlie and Carol Daniels, David Myers, and John Varley; and the love (and many random acts of senseless kindness) of my wife, Jeanne, and daughter, Terri.

—Vancouver, British Columbia
12 August 1992

THE MUSICIANS

Dulcimer:

Fred Meyer (mountain dulcimer); Box 54, Clear Creek IN 47426.

David Schnaufer, Box 120316, Nashville TN 37212 (David also designs & builds dulcimers of koa wood with abalone inlay).

Carole Koenig & Karen Williams, phone (213) 392-2312 or (213) 871-9034 for tapes, information or booking.

Banjo, guitar & fiddle:

Jeff Winegar, c/o Kicking Mule Records, Box 158, Alderpoint, CA 95411.

Guitar:

Chris Manuel (yes, he's related to Rick), phone (604) 522-9914.

Andrew York (my favorite of all the albums I've been sent

so far), Timeless Records, 3510 Carson Drive, Woodbridge, VA 22193.

Assorted:

Nate Bucklin (guitar & highly original songs), P.O. Box 8915, Minneapolis, MN 55408.

Cats Laughing (general shenanigans), c/o SteelDragon Press, Box 7253, Powderhorn Station, Minneapolis, MN 55407.

Larry Warner (guitar & songs, many original), Thor Records, P.O. Box 40312, Downey, CA 90242.

At press time, "Spider" John Koerner's latest Red House release is titled *Raised By Humans*.

ABOUT THE AUTHOR

Since he began writing professionally in 1972, **Spider Robinson** has won three Hugo Awards, a Nebula Award, the John W. Campbell Award for Best New Writer, the E. E. ("Doc") Smith Memorial Award (Skylark), the Pat Terry Memorial Award for Humorous Science Fiction, and Locus Awards for Best Novella and Best Critic. The first volume in his long-running Callahan's Place series, CALLAHAN'S CROSSTIME SALOON, was named a Best Book for Young Adults by the American Library Association in 1977.

His short work has appeared in magazines around the planet, from *Analog* to журнал Изобретатель и Рационализатор [*Inventor & Innovator Journal;* Moscow], and his books are available in nine languages. He is believed to be both the first, and the last, Western science fiction writer ever *to be paid* for reprint of his work in the late Soviet Union. Fourteen of his nineteen books are still in print.

He was an award-winning book reviewer for *Galaxy, Analog* and *Destinies* from 1974-82, and still occasionally reviews science fiction for a number of Canadian newspapers.

He was born in the Bronx, New York, in late 1948, and made a precarious living as a folksinger-guitarist in the New York-Long Island area before the collapse of the Folk market forced him into the even more precarious life of a science fiction writer.

He is married to **Jeanne Robinson,** a modern dance choreographer, former dancer, and teacher of dance and the Alexander Technique. Both Robinsons collaborated on the Hugo- Nebula- and Locus-winning 1976 classic STARDANCE [Baen paperback; Easton Press leatherbound], which created the concept of zero-gravity dance, and on its sequel, STARSEED [Ace hardcover and paperback; Easton leather]. The Robinsons have just completed their third book in the same ficton (fictional universe), titled STARMIND, to be published by Ace Books in June 1995.

They live in Vancouver, British Columbia.